My heart pounds in my chest as he draws closer. I know the precise moment he sees me. He freezes, stills in the water, sinking low, his lips brushing the waterline.

We stare at each other.

It will happen now. He will call the others. They will swarm on me like hungry predators.

Then he moves, swims closer in an easy glide. A muscle feathers the flesh of his jaw, and something flutters in my belly. He doesn't look hard, as I'd imagined. He doesn't look evil. He looks . . . *curious*.

SOPHIE JORDAN

Firelight

HARPER

An Imprint of HarperCollinsPublishers

Firelight

Copyright © 2010 by Sharie Kohler

All rights reserved. Printed in the United States of America. No part of
this book may be used or reproduced in any manner whatsoever without written permission except in the case of brief quotations embodied
in critical articles and reviews. For information address HarperCollins
Children's Books, a division of HarperCollins Publishers, 195 Broadway,
New York, NY 10007.

www.epicreads.com

Library of Congress Cataloging-in-Publication Data
Jordan, Sophie.
    Firelight / Sophie Jordan. — 1st ed.
        p.   cm.
    Summary: When sixteen-year-old Jacinda, who can change into a
dragon, is forced to move away from her community of shape-shifters
and start a more normal life, she falls in love with a boy who proves to
be her most dangerous enemy.
    ISBN 978-0-06-193509-1
    [1. Dragons—Fiction. 2. Shape-shifting—Fiction. 3. Moving,
Household—Fiction. 4. High schools—Fiction. 5. Schools—Fiction. 6. Hunting—Fiction. 7. Sisters—Fiction. 8. Dating (Social
customs)—Fiction.] I. Title.
PZ7.J76845Fir 2010   2010007033
[Fic]—dc22   CIP
                                                                   AC

Typography by Andrea Vandergrift
15 CG/RRDC 10 9 8 7
❖
First paperback edition, 2011

For my very own Catherine

When once you have tasted flight, you will forever walk the earth with your eyes turned skyward, for there you have been, and there you will always long to return.
—Leonardo da Vinci

Gazing out at the quiet lake, I know the risk is worth it. The water is still and smooth. Polished glass. Not a ripple of wind disturbs the dark surface. Low-rising mist drifts off liquid mountains floating against a purple-bruised sky. An eager breath shudders past my lips. Soon the sun will break.

Azure arrives, winded. She doesn't bother with the kick-stand. Her bike clatters next to mine on the ground. "Didn't you hear me calling? You know I can't pedal as fast as you."

"I didn't want to miss this."

Finally, the sun peeks over the mountains in a thin line of red-gold that edges the dark lake.

Azure sighs beside me, and I know she's doing the same

thing I am—imagining how the early morning light will taste on her skin.

"Jacinda," she says, "we shouldn't do this." But her voice lacks conviction.

I dig my hands into my pockets and rock on the balls of my feet. "You want to be here as badly as I do. Look at that sun."

Before Azure can mutter another complaint, I'm shucking off my clothes. Stashing them behind a bush, I stand at the water's edge, trembling, but not from the cold bite of early morning. Excitement shivers through me.

Azure's clothes hit the ground. "Cassian's not going to like this," she says.

I scowl. As if I care what he thinks. He's not my boyfriend. Even if he did surprise attack me in Evasive Flight Maneuvers yesterday and try to hold my hand. "Don't ruin this. I don't want to think about him right now."

This little rebellion is partly about getting away from him. *Cassian.* Always hovering. Always there. Watching me with his dark eyes. Waiting. Tamra can have him. I spend a lot of my time wishing he wanted her—that the pride would choose her instead of me. Anyone but me. A sigh shudders from my lips. I just hate that they're not giving me a choice.

But it's a long way off before anything has to be settled. I won't think about it now.

"Let's go." I relax my thoughts and absorb everything humming around me. The branches with their gray-green leaves. The birds stirring against the dawn. Clammy mist hugs my calves. I flex my toes on the coarse rasp of ground, mentally counting the number of pebbles beneath the bottoms of my feet. And the familiar pull begins in my chest. My human exterior melts away, fades, replaced with my thicker draki skin.

My face tightens, cheeks sharpening, subtly shifting, stretching. My breath changes as my nose shifts, ridges pushing out from the bridge. My limbs loosen and lengthen. The drag of my bones feels good. I lift my face to the sky. The clouds become more than smudges of gray. I see them as though I'm already gliding through them. Feel cool condensation kiss my body.

It doesn't take long. It's perhaps one of my quickest manifests. With my thoughts unfettered and clear, with no one else around except Azure, it's easier. No Cassian with his brooding looks. No Mom with fear in her eyes. None of the others, watching, judging, sizing me up.

Always sizing me up.

My wings grow, slightly longer than the length of my back. The gossamer width of them pushes free. They unfurl with a soft whisper on the air—a sigh. As if they, too, seek relief. Freedom.

A familiar vibration swells up through my chest. Almost like a purr. Turning, I look at Azure, and see she is ready, beautiful beside me. Iridescent blue. In the growing light, I note the hues of pink and purple buried in the deep blue of her draki skin. Such a small thing I never noticed before.

Only now I see it, in the break of dawn, when we are meant to soar. When the pride forbids it. At night you miss so much.

Looking down, I admire the red-gold luster of my sleek arms. Thoughts drift. I recall a chunk of amber in my family's cache of precious stones and gems. My skin looks like that now. Baltic amber trapped in sunlight. It's deceptive. My skin appears delicate, but it's as tough as armor. It's been a long time since I've seen myself this way. Too long since I've tasted sun on my skin.

Azure purrs softly beside me. We lock eyes—eyes with enlarged irises and dark vertical slits for pupils—and I know she's over her complaints. She stares at me with irises of glowing blue, as happy as I am to be here. Even if we broke every rule in the pride to sneak off protected grounds. We're here. We're free.

On the balls of my feet, I spring into the air. My wings snap, wiry membranes stretching as they lift me up.

With a twirl, I soar.

Azure is there, laughing beside me, the sound low and guttural.

Wind rushes over us and sweet sunlight kisses our flesh. Once we're high enough, she drops, descends through the air in a blurring tailspin, careening toward the lake.

My lip curls. "Show-off!" I call, the rumble of draki speech vibrating deep in my throat as she dives into the lake and remains underwater for several minutes.

As a water draki, whenever she enters water, gills appear on the side of her body, enabling her to survive submerged . . . well, forever, if she chooses. One of the many useful talents our dragon ancestors assumed in order to survive. Not all of us can do this, of course. *I* can't.

I do other things.

Hovering over the lake, I wait for Azure to emerge. Finally, she breaks the surface in a glistening spray of water, her blue body radiant in the air, wings showering droplets.

"Nice," I say.

"Let's see you!"

I shake my head and set out again, diving through the tangle of mountains, ignoring Azure's "c'mon, it's so cool!"

My talent is *not* cool. I would give anything to change it. To be a water draki. Or a phaser. Or a visiocrypter. Or an onyx. Or . . . Really, the list goes on.

Instead, I am this.

I breathe fire. The only fire-breather in the pride in more than four hundred years. It's made me more popular than I want to be. Ever since I manifested at age eleven, I've ceased to be Jacinda. Instead, I'm *fire-breather*. A fact that has the pride deciding my life as if it's theirs to control. They're worse than my mother.

Suddenly I hear something beyond the whistling wind and humming mists of the snow-capped mountains at every side. A faint, distant sound.

My ears perk. I stop, hovering in the dense air.

Azure cocks her head; her dragon eyes blink, staring hard. "What is it? A plane?"

The noise grows, coming fast, a steady beat now. "We should get low."

Nodding, Azure dives. I follow, glancing behind us, seeing only the jagged cropping of mountains. But hearing more. Feeling more.

It keeps coming.

The sound chases us.

"Should we go back to the bikes?" Azure looks back at me, her blue-streaked black hair rippling like a flag in the wind.

I hesitate. I don't want this to end. Who knows when we can sneak out again? The pride watches me so closely, Cassian is always—

"Jacinda!" Azure points one iridescent blue finger through the air.

I turn and look. My heart seizes.

A chopper rounds a low mountain, so small in the distance, but growing larger as it approaches, cutting through the mist.

"Go!" I shout. "Drop!"

I dive, clawing wind, my wings folded flat against my body, legs poised arrow straight, perfectly angled for speed.

But not fast enough.

The chopper blades beat the air in a pounding frenzy. *Hunters.* Wind tears at my eyes as I fly faster than I've ever flown before.

Azure falls behind. I scream for her, glancing back, reading the dark desperation in her liquid gaze. "Az, keep up!"

Water draki aren't built for speed. We both know that. Her voice twists into a sob and I hear just how well she knows it in the broken sound. "I'm trying! Don't leave me! Jacinda! Don't leave me!"

Behind us, the chopper still comes. Bitter fear coats my mouth as two more join it, killing any hope that it was a random helicopter out for aerial photos. It's a squadron, and they are definitely hunting us.

Is this how it happened with Dad? Were his last moments like this? Tossing my head, I shove the thought away. I'm *not* going to die today—my body broken and sold off into bits and pieces.

I nod to the nearing treetops. "There!"

Draki never fly low to the ground, but we don't have a choice.

Azure follows me, weaving in my wake. She pulls close to my side, narrowly missing the flashing trees in her wild fear. I stop and drift in place, chest heaving with savage breath. The choppers whir overhead, their pounding beat deafening, stirring the trees into a frothing green foam.

"We should demanifest," Az says, panting.

As if we could. We're too frightened. Draki can never hold human form in a state of fear. It's a survival mechanism. At our core we're draki; that's where we derive our strength.

I peer up through the latticework of shaking branches shielding us, the scent of pine and forest ripe in my nostrils.

"I can get myself under control," Az insists in our guttural tongue.

I shake my head. "Even if that's true, it's too risky. We have to wait them out. If they see two girls out here . . . after they just spotted two female draki, they might get suspicious." A cold fist squeezes around my heart. I can't let that happen. Not just for me, but for everyone. For draki everywhere. The secret of our ability to appear as humans is our greatest defense.

"If we're not home in the next hour, we're busted!"

I bite my lip to stop from telling her we have more to worry about than the pride discovering we snuck out. I don't want to scare her even more than she already is.

"We have to hide for a little—"

Another sound penetrates the beating blades of a chopper. A low drone on the air. The tiny hairs at my nape tingle. Something else is out there. Below. On the ground. Growing closer.

I look skyward, my long talonlike fingers flexing open and shut, wings vibrating in barely controlled movement. Instinct urges flight, but I know they're up there. Waiting. Circling buzzards. I spy their dark shapes through the treetops. My chest tightens. They aren't going away.

I motion Az to follow me into the thick branches of a towering pine. Folding our wings close to our bodies, we shove amid the itchy needles, fighting the scraping twigs. Holding our breath, we wait.

Then the land comes alive, swarming with an entourage of vehicles: trucks, SUVs, dirt bikes.

"No," I rasp, eyeing the vehicles, the men, armed to the teeth. In a truck bed, two men crouch at the ready, a great net launcher before them. Seasoned hunters. They know what they're doing. They know what they're hunting.

Az trembles so badly the thick branch we're crouched on starts to shake, leaves rustling. I clutch her hand. The dirt bikes lead the way, moving at a dizzying speed. A driver of one SUV motions out the window. "Look to the trees," he shouts, his voice deep, terrifying.

Az fidgets. I clutch her hand harder. A bike is directly below us now. The driver wears a black T-shirt that hugs his young muscled body. My skin tightens almost painfully.

"I can't stay here," Az chokes out beside me. "I've got to go!"

"Az," I growl, my low rumbling tones fervent, desperate. "That's what they want. They're trying to flush us out. Don't panic."

Her words spit past gritted teeth. "I. Can't."

And I know with a sick tightening of my gut that she's not going to last.

Scanning the activity below and the choppers cutting across the sky above, I make up my mind right then.

"All right." I swallow. "Here's the plan. We separate—"

"No—"

"I'll break cover first. Then, once they've gone after me, you head for water. Go under and stay there. However long it takes."

Her dark eyes gleam wetly, the vertical lines of her pupils throbbing.

"Got it?" I demand.

She nods jerkily, the ridges on her nose contracting with a deep breath. "W-what are you going to do?"

I force a smile, the curve of my lips painful on my face. "Fly, of course."

2

When I was twelve, I raced Cassian and won.

It was during group flight. At night, of course. Our only authorized time to fly. Cassian had been arrogant, showing off, and I couldn't help it. We used to be friends, when we were kids. Before either one of us manifested. I couldn't stand seeing what he'd turned into, watching him act like he was God's gift to our pride.

Before I knew it, we were racing across the night sky, Dad's shouts of encouragement ringing in my ears. Cassian was fourteen, an onyx draki. All sleek black muscle and cutting sinew. My father had been an onyx, too. Not only are they the strongest and biggest among the draki, but they are usually the fastest.

Except that night. That night I beat Cassian, the prince of our pride, our future alpha—trained since birth to be the best.

I shouldn't have won, but I did. In the moon's shadow, I revealed myself to be even more than the pride's precious fire-breather. More than the little girl Cassian gave rides to in his go-cart. Cassian changed after that. Suddenly, he wasn't focused on being best, but winning the best. I became the prize.

For years I regretted winning that race, resented the additional attention it brought me, wished I couldn't fly so fast. Only now, as my bare feet scrape over rough bark, preparing to take flight, I'm grateful I can. Grateful I fly as fast as wind.

Az shakes behind me, her teeth clacking. A whimper escapes her lips. I know what I have to do.

And I just . . . go. Dropping from the tree, I surge through the air, wings pulled taut above my back, two great sails of fiery gold.

Shouts fill my ears. Engines rev, accelerating. Loud, indistinct voices overlap. Hard male voices. I whip through trees, the hunters in hot pursuit, crashing through the forest in their earth-eating vehicles. A smile bends my mouth as they fall behind and I pull ahead. I hear myself laugh.

Then fire erupts in my wing. I jerk, tilt, careen wildly. I'm hit.

Fighting hard to keep myself up with one wing, I manage

only a few strokes before I slip through air. The world whirls around me in a dizzy blaze of lush greens and browns. My shoulder swipes a tree, and I hit the ground in a winded, gasping, broken pile, the scent of my blood coppery rich in my nose.

My fingers dig into moist earth, the rich, pungent smell nourishing my skin. Shaking my head side to side, dirt fills my hands, sliding beneath my talons. Shoulder throbbing, I crawl, clawing one hand over the other.

A sound burns the back of my throat, part grunt, part growl. *Not me. Not me,* I think.

I curl my knees beneath me and test my wing, stretching it carefully above my back, biting my lip to stifle a cry at the agony jolting through the wiry membranes, penetrating deep into my back between my shoulder blades. Pine needles scrape my palms as I push and try to stand.

I hear them coming, their shouts. Motors rise and fall as they ascend and descend hills. An image of the truck with its net flashes through my mind.

Just like Dad. It's happening to me now.

Standing, I fold my wings close to my body and run, darting wildly through the crowd of trees as the engines grow louder.

Peering back through the haze of forest, I gasp at the misty glow of headlights. So near. My heart pounds in my ears. I glance up, all around me, trying to find a place to hide. Then I hear something else—the steady song of running water.

I track the sound, feet padding lightly, silently on the forest floor as I sprint. Just in time I stop, grabbing the trunk of a tree to keep from tumbling down a steep incline. Panting, I gaze down. Water burbles steadily from a small fall into a large pond surrounded on all sides with walls of jagged rock.

The air cracks above me. My hair lifts, scalp tight and itchy, and I lunge to the side. Wind whistles as the net hits the ground near me.

"Load another!"

I look over my shoulder—at the truck with two guys in the back readying another net. Bikes bounce over the ground, their angry motors revving as they come at me. The riders stare out through large metallic lenses. They don't even look human. They're monsters. I make out the hard, intent lines of their mouths. Beating chopper blades converge overhead, churning the air into a violent wind that whips my hair all around me.

Sucking air deeply into my lungs, I turn back around. And jump.

Air rushes past me. It's strange. Falling through wind with no intention, no ability to lift up and fly. But that's what I do. Until I hit water.

It's so cold I scream, swallow a mouthful of algae-rich water. How does Az do it? She makes it seem so . . . pleasant. Not this bitter cold agony.

I break the surface, and dog-paddle in a swift circle,

looking, searching. For something. Anything. Then I see a cave. A small ledge really, just inside the rocky wall, but deep enough for me to tuck inside, out of sight. Unless they dive in after me.

I swim for it, heave myself inside. Sliding as deeply as I can into the shelter, I tuck myself into a small ball.

Wet and shivering, I hold my breath and wait. It's not long before hard voices congest the air above me.

"It jumped!" Doors slam, the sound shuddering through me, and I know they're out of their vehicles. I tremble uncontrollably in my shadowed cave, fingers a bloodless clutch on my slick knees.

". . . dived in the water!"

"Maybe it flew." This over the growling of dirt bikes.

"No way! It can't fly. I nailed it in the wing." I shiver at the smug satisfaction in this voice and chafe my arms fiercely against the cold. The fear.

"I don't see it down there."

"Someone has to go after it."

"Ah, hell! Down there? It's freezing—you go!"

"Why not you? What are you, chicken—"

"I'll go." I start at the voice, deep and calm and velvet smooth against the harsh bite of the others.

"You sure you can handle it, Will?"

I hug myself tighter as I wait to hear his reply, wishing I was a visiocrypter so I could make myself disappear.

A body arcs into the pond in a flashing blur. Water hardly

splashes at his clean entrance. *Will.* The one with the velvet voice. I stare out at the glistening surface, holding my breath and waiting for him to emerge. Any moment his head will pop up and he will look around. See the cave. See me.

I moisten my lips, feel the simmering of my blood, the smoke building in my lungs. If it comes down to it, would I do it? Could I use my talent to save myself?

A head breaks the surface, sloshing water with a toss. His hair glistens, a dark helmet against his head. He's young. Not much older than me.

"You okay, Will?" a voice calls down.

"Yeah," he shouts up.

My heart seizes at the sudden nearness of that voice. I push back as far as I can into the rough wall, ignoring the stinging scrape against my wings. Watching him, I pray his vision can't reach as far as me.

He spots the ledge and tenses, his stare fixing straight in my direction. "There's a cave!"

"Is it in there?"

I'm *it.*

I bristle, skin contracting, quivering like the plucked bow of a violin. My wings start to vibrate with hot emotion, shooting lancing pain through the injured membrane and deep into my back. I wince, forcing myself to relax.

He swims closer.

Smoke puffs from my nose. I don't want it to happen. It just . . . *does.* I usually have more power over it, but fear robs me of my control. Draki instincts take over.

My heart pounds in my chest as he draws closer. I know the precise moment he sees me. He freezes, stills in the water, sinking low, his lips brushing the waterline.

We stare at each other.

It will happen now. He will call the others. They will swarm on me like hungry predators. Remembering Dad, I try not to shake. I'm sure he didn't tremble, didn't cower at the end. And I have something, a defense Dad didn't have. *Fire.*

Then he moves, swims closer in an easy glide. A muscle feathers the flesh of his jaw, and something flutters in my belly. He doesn't look hard, as I'd imagined. He doesn't look evil. He looks . . . curious.

He slaps a hand on the ledge and pulls himself inside. With me. No more than a foot separates us. Tight muscles ripple in his arms and biceps as he braces himself in a crouch, fingers lightly grazing the cave floor. Our gazes crawl over each other. Two strange animals inspecting each other for the first time.

I sip air, fight to draw it inside my smoldering lungs. I begin to burn from the inside out.

It's not like I haven't seen humans before. I've seen them lots of times when I shop with Mom and Tamra in town. Most of the time, *I* look human myself, even within the secret boundaries of our pride. But I still stare at him like I've never seen a boy before. And I guess I haven't seen one like him. He's no ordinary guy, after all. He's a hunter.

His black T-shirt is a second skin, plastered to his lean chest. In our shadowed cave, his wet hair looks nearly black. It could be lighter when dry. Medium brown or even a dark blond. But it's his eyes that hold me. Deeply set beneath thick brows, they drill into me with a stark intensity, scanning me, all of me. I imagine myself as he sees me. My wings furled behind my back, peeking up over my shoulders. My supple-sleek limbs that glow like fire even in the gloom of the ledge. My narrow face with its pronounced contours. My ridged nose. My high-arching brows and my dragon eyes— two black vertical slits where the pupils should have been.

He lifts a hand. I don't even flinch as he closes a broad, warm palm over my arm. Feeling, testing. His touch glides downward, and I'm sure he's comparing my skin—draki skin—to human skin. His palm stops, flattens over the back of my hand, rests over my long, talonlike fingers. Heat zings through me at the contact.

He feels it, too. His eyes widen. A lovely hazel. Green with flecks of brown and gold. The colors I love. The colors of the earth. That gaze drifts over the wet snarls of my hair brushing the rock floor. I catch myself wishing he could see the girl within the dragon.

A sound escapes his lips. A word. I hear it, but think, *no*. He didn't say *that*.

"Will!" a voice shouts from above.

We both jerk, and then his face changes. The soft, curious

expression vanishes and he looks angry. Menacing. The way his kind is supposed to look at my kind. His hand flies off mine, all intimacy severed. I rub where he touched me.

"You okay down there? Need me to come—"

"I'm okay!" The deep rumble of his voice bounces off the walls of our small shelter.

"Did you find it?"

It again. I huff. Smoke clouds from my nose. The smolder in my lungs intensifies.

He watches me intently, his eyes hard and merciless. I wait for him to announce my presence, holding his gaze, refusing to look away, determined that this beautiful boy see the face he sentences to death with his next words.

"No."

I suck in a breath as the smolder dies from my lungs. We stare at each other for a lingering moment. He, a hunter. Me, a draki.

Then, he's gone.

And I'm all alone.

3

I wait forever. Long after the sounds of choppers and engines fade. Wet and shaking on my ledge, I huddle, hugging my legs, rubbing the supple stretch of my calves, hands gliding over red-gold skin. My injured wing burns, throbbing as I linger, listening, but there's nothing. Only the whisper of the forest and the gentle sigh of the Cascades around me.

No men. No hunters. No Will.

I frown. For some reason this bothers me. I will never see him again. Never know why he let me go. Never learn if he really whispered what I think he did. *Beautiful.*

In that single moment we connected. Somehow it happened. It's hard to wrap my head around. I thought he was going to rat me out for sure. Hunters aren't big on mercy.

They see us only as prey, a subspecies to be broken and sold to our greatest menace—the enkros. Since the dawn of man, the enkros have been hungry for the gifts of our kind, obsessed with tearing us apart or holding us captive for their use: the magical properties of our blood, our armorlike flesh, our ability to detect gems beneath the earth. We're nothing to them. Nothing with a soul or heart.

So why did Will let me go? His incredible face burns in my mind, imprinted there. The slick-wet hair. The intense eyes peering at me darkly. I should see Cassian's face. Cassian is my destiny. I have accepted it even though I grumble and risk daylight to break free of him.

I wait as long as possible, until I can stand the damp chill of my shelter no more. Wary of a trap, I ease out carefully and glide into the icy water. I scale the wall of jagged rock, my single wing working hard, slapping wind, the membranes taut and aching in their frenzy.

Air saws from my lips as I pull myself to the top. Collapsing, I absorb the thick, loamy aroma of the ground. My palms dig into the moist soil. It sustains me, humming into my body. Buried far below, volcanic rock purrs like a sleeping cat. I can sense this: hear it, feel it, feed from it.

It's always this way—this connection to fertile, arable earth. *This* will heal my wing. No man-made medicine. I draw strength from thriving, life-giving earth.

The smell of rain rides the clinging mist. Rising, I walk into its waiting embrace, start back toward the lake where my bike and clothes wait. Faint sunlight filters through the canopy of branches, battling the mist and turning my chilled skin to a reddish bronze.

I'm convinced Az made it home. I won't let myself consider the alternative. By now the pride will know I'm missing. I start working various explanations in my head.

The pads of my feet fall mutely as I weave through trees, listening for sounds that don't belong, wary of the hunters returning . . . but beneath the wariness lurks a hope.

The hope that one hunter *will* return and satisfy my questions, my curiosity . . . this strange fluttering in my stomach at his whispered word.

Gradually a noise penetrates, ribboning through the air, chasing birds from the trees. My draki skin prickles, flashing from red to gold, gold to red.

Fear shoots through me as the faint growl of engines grows close. At first, I think the hunters have come back for me.

Did the beautiful boy change his mind?

Then I hear my name.

Jacinda! The sound echoes desperately through the labyrinth of towering pines.

Lifting my face, I cup my hands and call, "I'm here!"

In a moment, I'm surrounded. Vehicles brake hard. I blink as doors open and slam.

Several of the elders appear, storming through the evaporating mist with their faces grim. I don't see Az, but Cassian is among them, so like his father with his mouth pressed in an unforgiving line. He usually likes me in draki form, prefers it, but there's no admiration in his eyes right now. He moves close, towering over me. He is always this way. So big, so male . . . so *hovering*. For a moment, I remember the warm strength of his hand when he grabbed mine yesterday in Evasive Flight Maneuvers. It would be so easy to let him in and just do what everyone wants . . . what everyone expects.

I can't meet his gaze, so I study the shine of his ink black hair that falls to his shoulders. He leans down, rustling the hairs near my temple as he growls in his smoky voice, "You scared me, Jacinda. I thought I lost you."

My skin bristles, tingles with defiance at his words. Just because the pride thinks we belong together, doesn't make it so. At least not yet. For probably the hundredth time, I wish I was just an average draki. Not the great fire-breather everyone expects so much from. Life would be so simple then. It would be mine. *My* life.

My mother pushes through the group, brushing Cassian away as if he's just a boy and not a six-foot-plus onyx capable of crushing her. Framed with bouncy curls, her face is beautiful, pleasantly rounded with amber eyes like mine. Since Dad died, several of the males have tried to court her. Even Cassian's father, Severin. Thankfully, she hasn't been interested. In any of them. It's hard enough dealing with Mom. I don't need some macho draki trying to take my father's place.

Right now, in this moment, she looks older. Tight lines edge her mouth. Even the day they told us Dad wouldn't be coming home, she didn't look this way. And I realize this is because of me. A knot forms in my stomach.

"Jacinda! Thank God you're alive!" She folds her arms around me, and I cry out where she crushes my injured wing.

She pulls back. "What happened—"

"Not now." Cassian's father clamps a hand on Mom's shoulder and moves her aside so he can stand before me. At six and a half feet, Severin is as tall as Cassian, and I have to crane my neck to look up at him. Tossing a blanket over my shivering body, he snaps, "Demanifest. At once."

I obey, biting my lip against the pain as I absorb my wings into my body, stretching the wound, ripping it deeper with the bend and pull of my transforming flesh. The injury is still there, only an oozing gash in my shoulder blade now. Blood trickles warmly down my back and I pull the blanket tighter against me.

My bones readjust, shrink down, and my thicker draki skin fades away. The cold hits me harder now, slashes at my human skin, and I start shaking, my bare feet growing numb.

Mom is at my side, sliding a second blanket around me. "What were you thinking?" It's this voice, so critical, so cutting, that I hate. "Tamra and I were worried sick. Do you want to end up like your father?" She shakes her head fiercely, determination hot in her eyes. "I've already lost a husband. I won't lose a daughter, too."

I know an apology is expected, but I would rather swallow nails. It's this I'm running from—a life of disappointing my mother, of stifling my true self. Of rules, rules, and more rules.

"She has broken our most sacred tenet," Severin declares.

I wince. *Fly only under cover of darkness.* I guess nearly getting killed by hunters squashes any argument on the pointlessness of that rule.

"Clearly something needs to be done with her." A look passes between my mother and Severin as murmurs rise in the group. Sounds of assent. My inner draki tingles in warning. I stare wildly around at everyone. A dozen faces I've known all my life. Not a friend in the bunch.

"No. Not that," Mom whispers.

Not what?

Her arm squeezes harder around me, and I lean into her, greedy for the comfort. Suddenly, she's my only ally.

"She's our fire-breather—"

"No. She's *my* daughter," Mom's voice whips. I'm reminded that she's draki, too, even if she has come to resent it. Even if she hasn't manifested in years . . . and likely can't anymore.

"It needs to be done," Severin insists.

I wince as Mom's fingers dig into me through the blankets. "She's just a girl. No."

I find my voice and demand, "What? What are you all talking about?"

No one answers me, but that isn't strange. Infuriating, but not unusual. Everyone—Mom, the elders, Severin—talks around me, about me, at me, but never *to* me.

Mom continues her stare-down with Severin, and I know that although nothing is spoken, words pass between them. All the while Cassian watches me with hungry focus. His purply black gaze would tie most girls up in knots. My sister included; my sister especially.

"We'll discuss this later. Right now I'm taking her home."

Mom walks me swiftly to the car. I glance behind me at Severin and Cassian, father and son, king and prince. Side by side, they watch me go, reprisal gleaming in their eyes. And something else. Something I can't decipher.

A dark shiver licks up my spine.

4

Az is waiting for us at our house, pacing the front porch in tattered jeans and a blue tank top that doesn't come close to competing with the glossy blue streaks in her dark hair. Her face lights up when she sees us.

Mom parks, and Az runs through the perpetual mist that covers our township, courtesy of Nidia. This mist is critical to our survival. No random aircraft passing through our airspace can detect us through it.

Az embraces me in a crushing hug as soon as I step from the car. I whimper. She pulls back in concern. "What, are you hurt? What happened?"

"Nothing," I murmur, sliding a look to Mom. She already knows I'm injured. No point reminding her.

"Are *you* okay?" I ask.

She nods. "Yeah, I did what you said, stayed underwater until I knew they were gone and then flew home for help."

I don't remember telling her to bring help. I wish she hadn't, but I can't blame her for trying to save me.

"Inside, girls." Mom motions us indoors, but she's not looking at us. She's looking over her shoulder, across the road at one of our neighbors. Cassian's aunt Jabel stands on her porch, watching us closely with her arms crossed over her chest. She watches us a lot lately. Mom's convinced she reports everything we do to Severin. With a tight nod, Mom ushers us inside. She and Jabel used to be the best of friends. When I was a kid, before Dad died. Before everything. Now they hardly talk.

When we enter the house, Tamra looks up from where she sits cross-legged on the couch, a bowl of cereal tucked in her lap. An old cartoon blares from the television. She doesn't look "worried sick" like Mom claimed.

Mom stalks over to the TV and turns down the volume. "Do you really have to play it so loud, Tamra?"

Tamra shrugs and digs for the remote in the couch cushions. "Since I couldn't go back to sleep, I decided to try and drown out the alarm."

A sick feeling starts in my gut. "They sounded the alarm?" I ask. The last time they did that was when Dad went missing and they assembled a search party.

"Oh yeah." Az nods, eyes growing large. "Severin freaked."

Tamra finds the remote and punches up the volume. Dropping it back to the couch, she lifts a large dripping spoon to her mouth. "Are you so surprised they rounded up the posse for you?" She slants me a tired look. "Think about it."

The need to defend my actions rises in my chest, but I let it go with a deep breath. I've tried explaining before, but Tamra doesn't get it. She can't understand draki impulse. How can she?

Mom shuts the TV off. Oblivious to any tension, Az spins her hands in the air. "Well? What happened? How did you escape? My God, they were *everywhere*. Did you see those net launchers?" Mom looks ill.

"I thought for sure you wouldn't make it. I mean, I know you're fast . . . and you can breathe fire and everything, but—"

"Like we can ever forget that," Tamra mumbles around a mouthful of cereal and performs an exaggerated eye roll.

Tamra never manifested. It's a growing trend among the draki, alarming to the elders so desperate to preserve our species. For all intents and purposes, my twin sister, only minutes my junior, is an average human. It kills her. And me. Before I manifested, we had been close, together in everything. Now we share nothing more than a face.

I notice Mom then, moving about the living room closing all the wood shutters, dousing the room in shadow.

"Az," Mom says, "say good-bye now."

My friend blinks. "Good-bye?"

"Good-bye," Mom repeats, her voice firmer.

"Oh." Az frowns, then looks at me. "Want to walk to school tomorrow?" Her eyes gleam meaningfully, conveying that I can fill her in on everything then. "I'll get up early."

We live on opposite ends of the township. Our community is shaped like a giant wheel with eight spokes. Each spoke serves as a street. The center, the hub, acts as the heart of our township. The school and meeting hall sit there. I live on First West Street. Az is on Third East. We're about as far apart as you can get. A vine-covered wall surrounds the township, so there's no taking the outer edge to reach each other faster.

"Sure. If you're willing to get up early and trek it over here."

As soon as Az leaves, Mom locks the door. I've never seen her do that before. Facing us, she looks at me and Tamra for a long moment, the only noise the sound of Tam's spoon clinking in her bowl. Mom turns and peeks out between the shutters . . . as if she's worried Az might still be in hearing range. Or someone else.

Turning back around, she announces, "Pack your stuff. We're leaving tonight."

My stomach drops like it does when I dive fast and sudden in the sky. "What?"

Tamra gets up from the couch so quickly her bowl of

milk and cereal tumbles to the floor. Mom doesn't even exclaim over this, doesn't even look at the mess, and that's when I know everything has changed—or is about to. She's serious.

"Are you for real?" Tamra's eyes are feverishly bright. She looks alive for the first time in . . . well, since I first manifested and it became clear she wasn't going to. "Please. Tell me you're not joking."

"I wouldn't joke about this. Start packing. Bring as many clothes as you can—and anything else you think is important." Mom's eyes settle on me. "We're not coming back."

I don't move. I can't. Somehow the burn in my shoulder intensifies, like a knife is there, twisting, burying itself deeper.

With an excited squeal, Tamra races into her room. I hear the sound of her closet door flinging open and hitting the wall.

"What are you doing?" I ask Mom.

"Something we should have done a long time ago. After your father died." She glances away, blinking fiercely before looking back to me. "I guess I always held out hope that he would one day walk through the door, and we needed to be here for him." She sighs. "But he's never coming back, Jacinda. And I need to do what's best for you and Tamra."

"You mean what's best for *you* and Tamra."

Leaving the pride is no big deal for Mom and Tamra. I know that at once. Mom deliberately killed her draki years ago, let it wither away from inactivity once it became obvious

Tamra would never manifest. I guess she did it so my sister wouldn't feel so alone. An act of solidarity.

I'm the only one who feels connected to the pride. The one who will suffer if we leave.

"Don't you see how much easier, how much *safer* it will be if you just let your draki go?"

I jerk as if slapped. "You want me to deny my draki? Become like you?" A dormant draki passing for human? I toss my head side to side. "I don't care where you take me, I won't do that. I won't forget who I am."

She places a hand on my shoulder and gives me a little squeeze. For encouragement, I guess. "We'll see. You might change your mind after a few months."

"But why? Why do we have to go?"

"You know why."

I suppose a part of me does but refuses to admit it. Suddenly I want to pretend everything is right with our life here. I want to forget about my unease with Severin's dictatorship of the pride. I want to forget Cassian's possessive gaze. Forget my sister's sense of isolation in a community that treats her like a leper and forget the guilt I've always felt about that.

Mom continues, "Someday you'll understand. Someday you'll thank me for saving you from this life."

"From the pride?" I demand. "They *are* my life! My family." A crappy alpha didn't change that. Severin wouldn't be in charge forever.

"And Cassian?" Her lip curls. "Are you prepared for him?"

I step back, not liking the emotional quiver in her voice. From the corner of my eye, I see Tamra stiffen in the doorway of her bedroom. "Cassian and I are friends," I say. Sort of. At least we used to be.

"Right."

"What do you mean?"

"You're not eight years old anymore, and he's not ten. A part of you must know what I've been protecting you from. *Who* I've been protecting you from. Ever since you manifested, the pride has marked you as its own. Is it so wrong to want to claim my daughter from them? Your father tried, fought constantly with Severin. Why do you think he flew out alone that night? He was looking for a way . . ." She stops, her voice choking.

I listen, transfixed.

She never talks about that night. About Dad. I'm afraid she'll stop. Afraid she won't.

Her gaze settles on me again. Cool and resolved. And that frightens me.

Familiar heat builds inside me, burns and tightens my throat. "You make the pride sound like some fiendish cult—"

Her eyes flash. She waves an arm wildly. "They are! When are you going to understand that? When they demand I give my sixteen-year-old daughter to their precious prince so they can begin mating, they *are* fiends! They want you to be their broodmare, Jacinda! To populate the pride with little fire-breathers!" She's close now. Yelling near my face. I wonder if Jabel or any of the other neighbors can hear. Wonder if Mom cares anymore.

She steps back and takes a deep breath. "We leave tonight. Start packing."

I rush into my room and slam the door. Dramatic, but it makes me feel better. Pacing my room, I breathe in and out. Steam wafts from my nose in angry little spurts. I drag a palm down the side of my face and neck, over my warm skin.

Falling back on the bed, I release a puff of breath and stare straight ahead, seeing nothing, feeling only the heat bubbling at my core. Gradually the fire inside me cools and my eyes begin trailing over the glittery stars hanging from the ceiling on strings. Dad helped me hang them after we painted the ceiling blue. He told me it would be like sleeping in the sky.

A bitter sob scalds the back of my throat. I won't sleep in this sky ever again, and if Mom has anything to do with it, I won't fly either.

Hours later, while the township sleeps, we creep through Nidia's fog. The very thing that protects us, hides us from the outside world that would harm us, aids in our escape.

Once we turn off our street and move onto Main, Mom

sets the car in neutral. Tamra and I push as she guides the vehicle through the town center. The school and meeting hall sit silently, watching us with darkened windows for eyes. Tires crunch over loose gravel. My calves burn as we push.

Holding my breath, I wait, listening for the alarm as we approach the green arched entrance of our township. Nidia's little ivy-covered cottage looms ahead, a guardhouse nestled at one side of the opening. A dull light glows from the large mullioned window of her living room. Surely she will detect us. It's her job to let nothing in—or out.

Every pride has at least one shader—a draki who shrouds the village with fog, as well as the mind of any human who should stumble within. Nidia's fog could make a person forget his own name. Her talent surpasses my own. The pride lives in fear of her death . . . the day our grounds will become exposed, visible to passing aircraft and anyone who travels deep enough into the mountains.

I hear nothing from her house. Not a sound. Not even when I let the soles of my shoes slide and grind against the gravel a little too loudly, earning a glare from Tamra.

I shrug. So maybe I want Nidia to catch us. Once we clear the arch, Mom starts the old station wagon. Before I climb in, I take a final look behind me. In the soft glow of Nidia's living room window, a shadow stands.

The pulse at my throat skitters wildly. I inhale sharply, certain she will sound the alarm now.

The shadow moves. My eyes ache from staring so hard.

Suddenly the light vanishes from the window. I blink and shake my head, bewildered. "No," I whisper. Why doesn't she stop us?

"Jacinda, get in," Tamra hisses before ducking inside the car.

Tearing my gaze away from where Nidia once stood, I think about refusing to go. I could do that. Here. Now. Dig in my heels and refuse. They couldn't overpower me. They wouldn't even try.

But in the end, I'm just not that selfish. Or brave. Unsure which, I follow.

Soon we're whisking down the mountain, rushing into the unknown. I press my palm against the window's cool glass, hating the thought of never seeing Az again. A sob wells up in my throat. I didn't even get to tell her good-bye.

Mom clenches the steering wheel, staring intently out the windshield at the little-traveled road. She's nodding. Nodding as if every bob of her head increases her determination to do this.

"A fresh start. Just us girls," she proclaims in an overly cheerful voice. "Long overdue, right?"

"Right," Tamra agrees from the back.

I glance over my shoulder at her. As twins, we've always shared a connection, a sense of the other's thoughts and feelings. But right now I can't read past my own fear.

Tamra smiles, staring out the window as if she sees

something in all that black night. At least she's finally getting her wish. Wherever we're going, she'll be the normal one. And I'll be the one struggling to fit in a world not made for me.

I belong with the pride. Maybe I even belong with Cassian. Even if it breaks Tamra's heart, maybe it's right. He's right. I don't know. I only know that I can't live without flight. Without sky and moist, breathing earth. I could never willingly surrender my ability to manifest. I'm not my mother.

How can I fit in among humans? I'll become like Tamra, a defunct draki. Only worse. Because I would remember what being a draki felt like.

I once saw a show about an amputee who lost his leg and still feels it. He actually wakes up at night to scratch his leg as if it's still there, attached to him. They call it a phantom limb.

I would be like that. A phantom draki, tormented with the memory of what I once was.

5

Air struggles up my throat and past my lips as Mom talks with our new landlady. Even with the air conditioner working at full blast, the air is thin, dry, and empty. I imagine this is how it feels for someone with asthma, this constant fight for breath. As if you can't ever fill your lungs with enough air. I glare at Mom. Of all the places in the world to relocate, she had to choose a desert. I'm certain she's a sadist.

We follow the waddling Mrs. Hennessey out the back door of her house, instantly plunging back into the arid heat. It sucks at my skin, pulls the moisture from my body like a great vacuum, and makes me feel weak. Only two days in Chaparral, and the desert is taking its toll. Just like Mom knew it would.

"A pool!" Tamra exclaims.

"It's not for your use," Mrs. Hennessey injects.

Tamra's frown is only momentary. Nothing can dent her optimism. A new town, new world. A new life within her grasp.

I fall behind Mom and Tamra. Each lift of my foot requires enormous energy.

Mrs. Hennessey stops at the pool's curled lip. She motions behind us toward the fence. "You can come and go through the back gate."

Mom nods, bouncing against her leg the rolled-up newspaper where she'd found the ad for this rental.

The keys jingle in Mrs. Hennessey's hand. She unlocks the door to the pool house and hands the keys to Mom. "Next month's rent is due on the first." Her rheumy gaze skitters over me and Tamra. "I like it quiet," she says.

I leave Mom to give assurances and enter the house. Tamra follows. I stare at the dismal living room that smells faintly of mold and chlorine. If possible my heart sinks even lower.

"Not bad," Tamra announces.

I give her a look. "You'd say that no matter what."

"Well, it's only temporary." She shrugs. "We'll have our own house soon."

In her dreams. Shaking my head, I check out the other rooms, wondering how she thinks that's going to happen. Mom counted change to pay for dinner last night.

The front door shuts. I dig my hands into my pockets, rubbing the lint in the corners between my fingers as I move back into the living room. Mom props her hands on her hips and surveys the house—us—with what seems like genuine satisfaction. Only I can't believe that. How can she be so happy when I'm so . . . *not*?

"Well, girls. Welcome home."

Home. The word echoes hollowly through me.

It's evening. I sit at the edge of the pool, dipping my feet in. Even the water is warm. I tilt my face, hoping for wind, missing the mist, the mountains, cool, wet air.

The door behind me opens and shuts. Mom lowers down beside me and stares ahead. I follow her stare. The only thing to see is the backside of Mrs. Hennessey's house.

"Maybe we can get her to change her mind about the pool after we've been here awhile," Mom says. "It would be nice to swim this summer."

I guess this is her way of trying to cheer me up, but the only words I hear are *after we've been here awhile.*

"Why?" I snap, swishing my legs faster. "You could have chosen a thousand other locations. Why this place?"

She could have picked anywhere to live. A small town nestled in cool misty hills or mountains. But no, she chose Chaparral, a sprawling city smack in the middle of a desert, ninety miles outside Vegas. No cooling condensation to nourish my body. No mists or fogs for cover. No easily accessible hills or mountains. No arable earth. No escape. It's just cruel.

She inhales. "I thought it might make it easier for you—"

I snort. "Nothing is easy about this."

"Well, it will make the choice for you." She reaches out and brushes the hair off my shoulder. "Nothing like a barren environment to kill off a draki quickly. I should know."

I cut her a glance. "What do you mean?"

She sucks in a deep breath. "I lived here during my tour."

I pull back and stare at her. Lots of draki take a tour to gain exposure to the outside world. For a short time anyway. A year, maybe two. But never to someplace hot and dry. Never in a desert. A draki needs to know how to fake being human for survival. Occasionally, rarely, a draki chooses to remain in the human world.

"I thought you went to Oregon. You and Jabel took your tours together and shared an apartment there."

Mom nods. "I started my tour with Jabel, but after a few months I decided . . ." Here she pauses for breath. "I decided I didn't want to go back to the pride."

I straighten. "How come I never knew this?"

Her lips twist. "Clearly, I came back. I didn't need everyone to know that it took a bit of arm-twisting."

Then I get it. I understand who did the arm-twisting. "Dad," I say.

Her smile softens. "He never toured, you know. There wasn't any point. He never wanted to be anything but draki." Her lips wobble and she touches my cheek. "You're a lot like him." Sighing, she drops her hand. "Anyway, he visited me once a month in Oregon . . . and every time he tried to per-suade me to come home with him." Her smile grows bleak. "He made it very difficult."

She looks me squarely in the face. "I wanted to get away from the pride, Jacinda. Even then. It was never for me, but your dad didn't make it easy. So I ran. I came here."

"Here?"

"I figured your dad wouldn't find me here."

I rub one of my arms. My skin already feels dry and chalky. "I should think not."

"Almost at once my draki began to wither. Even when I broke down and risked flight a few times, it wasn't easy to manifest. It was working. I was on my way to becoming human."

"But you went back."

"I finally faced reality. I wanted to give up the pride, but I missed your father. He couldn't live without being a draki, and I couldn't live without him."

I stare out at the water's surface, still and dead without the faintest ripple of wind, and try to imagine loving someone that much. So much that you would give up all you ever wanted for yourself. Mom did that.

Couldn't I make a sacrifice for those I loved? For Mom and Tamra? I'd already lost Dad. Did I really want to lose them, too?

The hunter, Will, flashes in my mind just then. I don't know why. Maybe it was because he let me go. He didn't even know me, but he let me go . . . even though he was trained to do the opposite. He fought what doubtlessly came naturally to him. Hunting and destroying my kind. If he could break from his world, then I could break from mine. I could be that strong.

Mom's voice rolls over me. "I know it's hard to accept right now. That's why I chose this town. The desert will take care of things for you. Eventually."

Eventually. I only have to wait until my draki is dead. Will I be glad then? Will I thank Mom one day like she seems to think?

She squeezes my knee. "Come inside. I want to go over some things with you and your sister before we enroll you in school."

My chest clenches at this, but I stand, thinking about all Mom has given up for me, all she's lost. And Tamra. She's never had anything of her own. Maybe it's finally time. Time for both of them.

"Jacinda Jones, come up here to the front and introduce yourself."

My stomach twists at these words. It's third period, which means it's the third time I've had to do this.

I slide out from my desk, stepping over backpacks as I move to the front of the room to stand beside Mrs. Schulz. Thirty pairs of eyes fasten on me.

Mom enrolled us last Friday. She insisted it was time.

That attending high school is the first step to assimilating. The first step to normal. Tamra is thrilled, unafraid, ready for this.

All last night, awake in my bed, sick to my stomach, I thought about today. I thought about the pride and all I was giving up. So what if daylight flight was forbidden? At least I could fly. The rules I chafed against with the pride suddenly pale beside this new reality. I'm not even sure why I resisted Cassian so much anymore. Was it only for Tamra? Or was there something within me other than loyalty to my sister that opposed being with him?

Teenagers surround me. *Human* teenagers. Hundreds of them. Their voices ring out, loud and nonstop. The air is full of false, cloying scents. A draki's worst hell.

It's not that I never expected to live in the outside world. Among humans. I would probably have taken a tour. But no one tours during adolescence. Only as an adult, as a draki strong and fully developed, and never in a desert like this. All for good reason.

I resist the urge to scratch my arm. It's only spring, but the heat and dryness make my skin itch. Beneath the buzzing fluorescent glare, a sick, wilting sensation coils through me.

Clearing my throat, I speak in rusty tones. "Hi, I'm Jacinda Jones."

A girl near the front twirls a strand of her hair. "Yeah. We already know that." She smiles, her lips obscenely glossy.

Mrs. Schulz saves me. "Where are you from?"

Mom drilled these answers into me. "Colorado."

An encouraging smile. "Lovely, lovely. Do you ski?"

I blink. "No."

"Where did you go to school?"

Mom covered this, too. "I was homeschooled." It was the easiest explanation to get us enrolled. We can't exactly ask the pride to forward my school transcripts.

Several kids laugh outright. The girl twirling her hair rolls her eyes. "Fuh-reak."

"Enough, Brooklyn." Mrs. Schulz looks at me again, her expression less welcoming now. More resigned. Like I just confessed to reading at a first-grade level. "I'm sure that has been an interesting experience."

Nodding, I start for my desk, but her voice stops me, holds me hostage.

"And you have a twin sister, right?"

I pause, wishing the interrogation would end. "Yes."

A boy with a patchy red face and small ferret eyes mumbles, "Double the pleasure."

Other kids laugh. Boys mostly.

Mrs. Schulz doesn't hear, or pretends not to. Just as well. I want this over so I can slink back to my seat and work at being invisible.

"Thank you, Jacinda. I'm sure you'll fit right in."

Sure.

I return to my desk. Mrs. Schulz dives into a one-sided discussion on *Antigone*. I read the play two years ago. In its original Greek.

My gaze swings to the window and the view of the parking

lot. Above the gleaming cars' hoods, far in the distance, mountains break the sky, calling to me.

I've decided to try to fly. Mom did it when she lived here. It's not impossible. Right now it's hard to sneak away. Mom sticks so close. She's determined to pick us up and drop us off from school like we're seven-year-olds. I'm not sure if it's because she's afraid the pride will track me down at school or if she's worried I'll run. I like to think she trusts me enough to know I wouldn't do that.

Sneaking away to stretch my wings for a little while isn't stopping Mom and Tamra from having the life they want so badly.

I shift in my seat, the crinkle of the city map in my pocket my only hope right now. I've pored over it several times already, memorizing every park in the area. Just because I live here doesn't mean I'm willing to wither away. The thought of flying again is the only thing keeping me going. Risky or not, I'll taste the wind again.

The bell rings, and I'm on my feet with everyone else.

Ferret Eyes turns to me and introduces himself. "Hey." He nods slowly, giving me a full appraisal. "I'm Ken."

"Hi," I manage, wondering if he somehow thought his "double the pleasure" remark won me over.

"Need help finding your next class?"

"No. I'm good. Thanks." Stepping past him, I hurry to my locker, head down.

Tamra's waiting for me. "How's it going?" she asks brightly.

"Fine."

Her smile slips. "You have to be open to it, Jace. Only you can decide to be happy."

I work the combination, mess up, and try again. "Enough with the psychology please."

She shrugs and fingers her iron-flat hair. It took her an hour in the bathroom to accomplish the feat, but she saw it in a magazine and wanted to match the picture. My own red-gold hair trails down my back in a frizzy, crackling mess. Wild with static. Like the rest of me, it misses the mist.

I survey her, so chic in her snug red top, dark jeans, and knee-high boots she bought over the weekend at a thrift store. Several guys walk past and do a double take. She's at home in this world, not suffering any of my unease, not even pining for Cassian anymore. And I'm happy for her. Really. If only her happiness wasn't my misery.

"I'll try," I promise, meaning it. It's not like I want to ruin this for her.

"Oh. I almost forgot." She digs in her satchel. "Look. They're having tryouts for next year's cheerleading squad."

I glance down at the bright orange flyer in her hand and wince at the cartoons of tiny pom-poms and somersaulting, short-skirted girls.

She waggles the paper. "We should try out together."

I finally get my locker open and swap out textbooks. "Nah. You go ahead."

"But you're so"—her amber gaze sweeps over me meaningfully—"athletic." She might as well have said draki.

I shake my head and open my mouth to stress my unwillingness, then stop. My flesh shivers. The tiny hairs at my nape prickle in alert. A textbook slips from my fingers, but I don't move to pick it up.

Tamra lowers the flyer. "What? What is it?"

I stare over her shoulder, down the crowded hall. A warning bell peals, and everyone's movements become frenzied. Lockers slam and the soles of shoes squeal against the tiled floor.

I remain still.

"Jace, *what*?"

I shake my head, unable to speak as my gaze darts over every face. Then I find him. See him. The one I sought before I even realized it, before I even understood. . . . The beautiful boy.

My skin snaps tight.

"Jacinda, what is it? We're going to be late to class."

I don't care. I don't move. It can't be him. He can't be here. Why would he be here?

But it is him.

Will.

He leans against the lockers, taller than everyone around him. Twirly-hair Brooklyn plays with the hem of his shirt, shamelessly leaning into him, glossy lips moving nonstop. He smiles, nods, listens as she chatters, but I sense that he doesn't really care, that he's somewhere else . . . or wants to be. Just like me.

I can't look away.

Honey brown hair falls over his brow carelessly, and I remember it darkly wet and slicked back from his face. I remember the two of us alone in a cave, his hand on mine and that spark that passed between us before his face became so stark and angry. Before he vanished.

Tamra sighs beside me and twists around to see. "Ah," she murmurs knowingly. "Yummy. Too bad though. It looks like he's got a girlfriend. You'll have to set your sights on someone else—" Facing me, she gasps. "Jace! You're glowing!"

That jerks my attention back. I glance down at my arms. My skin blurs in and out, shimmering faintly, like I've been dusted with gold.

The draki in me stirs, tingling, yearning to come out.

"God, get a grip, jeez!" Tamra hisses, leaning closer. "You see a hot guy and start to manifest? Have some control."

But I can't. That's what Tamra never understood. When emotions run high, the draki surfaces. In times of fear, excitement, arousal . . . the draki comes out. It's the way we are.

I look back at Will and pleasure whips through me. And beneath it, fear at what his being here means.

49

My sister grabs my arm and squeezes almost cruelly. "Jacinda, stop it! Stop it now!"

Will's head lifts with the suddenness of a predator scenting its prey and I wonder if hunters are really human at all. If maybe they aren't just as otherworldly as the draki. He looks around, searching the hall as I struggle to get myself under control. Before he sees me. Before he knows.

My lungs start to smolder, the familiar burn catching the exact moment his hazel eyes lock on mine.

The slam of my locker jars me and I tear my gaze off him. To Tamra. Her hand presses flat my locker, her fingertips white where they dig hard into the metal.

The last bell sounds.

With a quick dip, she grabs my books off the floor and drags me toward the bathroom. I glance over my shoulder as bodies empty the hall in a rush of unnatural scents. Perfumes, colognes, lotions, hair sprays, gels . . . they clog my senses. Here, nothing feels real. Except the boy staring after me. He watches. His gleaming gaze following, stalking me like the predator I sense in him. He moves away from the lockers in a loping, catlike motion.

My draki continues to stir, awake and alive at the hungry way he watches me. My skin quivers, the flesh of my back tingling, itchy where my wings push. I keep them buried. Buried, but not dormant.

Tamra's hand tugs harder, pulling me. And I lose sight of him. He's swallowed up in the flurry of humankind around me, like so many moths bumping and dancing around a light, congesting the hallway.

But I still feel him. Yearn for him. Know he's there even when I no longer see him.

My nostrils flare against the harsh bite of astringent. Instantly, my draki withers at the unnatural odor. I press a hand to my mouth and nose. The hint of fire in my lungs dies. My back stops tingling.

Tamra's gaze slides over me, and she exhales, clearly satisfied to see it's me again. The *me* she approves of, the only me she wants around. Especially here in this new world she hopes to conquer for her own.

"You've stopped glowing. Thank God! Are you trying to blow it for us?"

I stare toward the bathroom door. Almost like I expect him to follow. "Did he see?"

"I don't think so." She shrugs one shoulder. "He wouldn't know what he saw anyway."

That's true, I suppose. Even hunters don't know draki manifest into human form. It's been our most carefully guarded secret. Our greatest defense. And it's not like I was unfurling my wings in the hallway. Not quite, anyway.

I hug my arms as the invigorating hum fades from my core. This is my chance, I realize. I can tell her about Will . . . confess just how much I risked that day in the cave with him . . . confess how much I risk right now. I can declare everything as I stand in this putrid bathroom. Tamra squints at my face. "Are you going to be okay? Should I call Mom?"

I consider this. And more. Like what Mom would say if I tell her everything. What would she do? And instantly I know. She'd yank us out of school. But she wouldn't take us back to the pride. Oh no. She would just plant us in some other town. Some other school in another desert. In a week, I would be redoing this wretched first day all over again, suffering the heat and climate somewhere else without a beautiful, exciting boy around. A boy whose mere presence has revitalized my draki—the very part of me that hasn't felt alive since we left the mountains. How can I walk away from that? From him?

Tamra shakes her beautiful mane of hair off her shoulders as she surveys me. "I think we're okay." She wags a finger at me. "But stay away from him, Jacinda. Don't even look at him. At least not until you've gotten yourself under better control. Mom says it shouldn't take long before . . ."

She must see something in my face. She looks away. "Sorry," she mutters. Because she's my sister and she loves me, she says this. Not because she's really sorry. She wants my draki dead as much as Mom does. Wants me normal. Like her. So we can lead normal lives together and do stuff like cheerleading.

My stomach cramps. I take my books from her. "We're late."

"They'll cut us some slack. We're new."

I nod, plucking at the severely dog-eared corner of my geometry book. "See you at lunch?"

Tamra moves to the mirror to check her hair. "Remember what I said."

I pause, staring at her beautiful reflection. Hard to believe I'm a twin to such a polished creature.

She drapes a perfect strand of her red-gold hair over her shoulder. The end curves slightly inward. "Stay away from that guy."

"Yeah," I agree, but even as I walk out into the deserted hallway I stop and scan to the left and right of me, looking, searching. Hoping. Dreading.

But he's not there.

6

I hide during lunch. Cowardly, I know, but when I faced
the double doors leading to the cafeteria, the volume
alone made me feel sick. I couldn't bear the thought of
going in.

Instead, I walk the halls, ignoring my hungry stomach and the guilt I feel at not being there for Tamra. But
somehow, I know she'll be fine. At least I convince myself
of this. She's been waiting for this day since we were kids.
Ever since I manifested and she didn't. When Cassian
began to ignore her and became a dream forever beyond
her reach.

I find the library. Immediately, I inhale musty books and
savor the silence. I slide into a table near the windows that

faces the quad and rest my head on the cool Formica until the bell rings.

I float through the rest of the day. Relief seizes me when I make it to the last class of the day. Almost done.

My seventh-period study hall is packed with people who either opt out of athletics or lack the requisite GPA to play sports. This I learn from Nathan, my shadow ever since fifth period.

He slides in beside me. His fleshy lips spit out each word with a faint spray of saliva. "So, Jacinda. What are you?"

I blink, inching back, before I understand. Of course. He couldn't mean *that*. "Uh, I don't know."

"Me?" He juts a thumb to his swelled chest. "I can't pass English. Which is too bad, because our football team might actually win a game if I was on the line. What about you?" His gaze travels my long legs. "What are you doing in study hall? You look like you could play basketball. We got a good girls team."

I tuck a wild strand of hair behind my ear. It springs loose again and falls back in my face. "I didn't want to join any teams midsemester." Or ever.

The room is comprised of several black-topped tables. Mr. Henke, the physics teacher, stands behind a larger version of our table at the front of the room. He stares out at the class with a dazed, bleak expression, as if unclear where the overachievers from the previous period went. "Find something to do. No talking. Study or read quietly, please." He brandishes an orange pad. "Anyone need a pass to go some-where? Library?"

Nathan laughs as half the class lines up for passes. The bell hasn't even sounded, but it looks like most of the kids will be gone before it does.

"And there goes the herd." Nathan looks at me, leans in conspiratorially. "Want to get out of here? There's a Häagen-Dazs not far."

"No. My mom is picking me and my sister up after school."

"Too bad." Nathan crowds me. I scoot closer to the edge of the table. His gaze flits over me.

My elbow knocks over one of my books, and I grate-fully hop off the stool to pick it up. Squatting there on the grimy tiles, my hands reaching for a book, the tiny hairs at my nape start to vibrate. My breath goes faster. I press my lips together, trying to quiet the sound. My flesh pulls and tightens with awareness, and I know it's him before he enters the room.

I know it. And I *want* it to be him, even with Tamra's warning ringing in my head. Wiping a sweaty palm on my jeans, I peer at the door from beneath the table. Recognition burns deep in my chest, but I remain where I am, huddled close to the floor, watching as he steps inside.

I hold myself still, waiting. Maybe he'll get a pass, too. Disappear with the others.

But he doesn't get in line. He moves into the room, a

single notebook clutched loosely in his hand. Then, he stops, angling his head strangely. Like he hears a sound. Or smells something unusual. The same way he looked in the hall today. Right before he saw me.

I toy with my book, letting the pointy corners bite into the sensitive pads of my fingers.

"Hey, you okay?" Nathan's voice booms above me.

Wincing, I force myself to stand, crawl back onto my stool. "Yeah." I can't hide forever. We're in the same school. Apparently the same study hall.

I stare straight ahead, at the chalkboard. Anywhere but at him. But it's impossible. Like forcing my eyes to remain wide-open when biology demands I blink. So I look.

His gaze finds me. He walks toward our table. I hold my breath, wait for him to pass. Only he doesn't. He stops, the sliding scrape of his shoes on the floor a long scratch down my spine.

This close, I stare into eyes that can't decide on a color. Green, brown, gold—if I look too hard I get lost, dizzy. I remember the ledge—the two of us, enclosed in that damp, tight space. His hand on my draki skin. The word that I think he said.

Shivering, I break free of his gaze and stare down at the table, concentrate on inhaling slow even breaths. I look back up at the sound of his voice, ensnared in the velvet-smooth rumble.

"Mind if I sit here?" he asks Nathan while looking at me.

"Guess not." Nathan shrugs, shoots an uncertain look at me as he grabs his backpack. "I was heading to the library anyway. See you later, Jacinda."

Will waits a moment, stares at the vacant stool before sitting. As though he expects me to say something. Stop him? Invite him? I don't know.

He turns slightly on his stool and smiles. Just a small smile, but lovely. Sexy.

A dangerous warmth begins to build inside me. Unwanted right now. My skin pulls tight, eager to fade into draki skin. The familiar vibration swells up through my chest. A purr grows from the back of my throat. Instinct takes over and I'm almost afraid that if I do say something, it will be in the rumbling cadence of draki-speak.

Funny. In this desert, I worried my draki would shrivel, die as Mom wants. But around this boy I've never felt so alive, so volatile. I chafe a hand over my arm, willing my skin to cool down. For my draki to fade. At least for right now.

In silence, we sit. And it's the strangest thing. He knows about me. Well, not me. He couldn't possibly know that this me is *that* me. He knows about us though—my kind. He saw me. He knows we exist. *He saved me.* I want to know everything about him. And yet I can't speak, can't say *anything*. Not a single word. I'm too busy focusing my thoughts, on keeping the core of me cool, relaxed. *Keeping the draki away.* I want to know him better, but without breathing, without speaking, I can't see how.

The only thing I need to know about him is that his family hunts. I must not forget that. Ever. They kill my kind or sell us to the enkros. In their foul hands, we're either enslaved or butchered. My skin shrinks, and I remind myself he is part of that dark world. Even if he helped me escape, I should avoid him. And not because Tamra told me to. I should gather up my stuff and move to another table.

Instead, I stay where I am, balancing so carefully on my stool, making certain our bodies don't brush.

"So," he says, like we're in the middle of a conversation. Like we know each other so well. A nerve ticks, jumps near my eye at the sound of his voice. "You're new."

I summon the strength to strangle something out. "Yeah."

"I saw you earlier."

I nod and say, "Earlier in the hall. Yeah. I saw you, too."

His eyes warm, slide over me. "Right. And in PE."

I frown. I don't remember seeing him during fourth period, don't remember *feeling* him.

"You were running around the track," he explained. "We were up in the natatorium. I saw you through the windows."

"Oh." I don't know why, but it thrills me to know he was watching me.

"You looked pretty fast."

I smile. He smiles back, the grooves along his cheek deepening. My heart squeezes tighter.

"I like to run." When I run really fast, the wind hits my face and I can almost pretend I'm flying.

"Sometimes," he continues, "the guys and girls run together during PE. Although I'm not sure I could keep up with you." His voice is low, flirty. Heat licks through me, curls low in my belly.

I imagine this scenario, imagine running side by side with him. Is that what he's saying he wants to do? Air shivers past my lips. Of course, I'd love running with him. But I shouldn't. I can't. That wouldn't be a good idea.

Two guys drag in late as the final bell rings. They look our way. At Will, not at me. I'm beneath their notice.

One with raven-dark hair shaved close to his head walks ahead of the other. His face is elegant, narrow, and beautiful with dark, liquid eyes. Apprehension curls through me. His eyes are dead cold, calculating.

His bulky friend swaggers behind him—his hair so red it makes me squint.

"Hey." The dark one nods at Will, stopping at our table. I shrink, feeling oddly threatened.

Will leans back on his stool. "What's up, Xander?"

Xander looks almost . . . confused. Arching his brow, his attention drifts to me. And then I get it. He doesn't understand why Will is sitting here. *With me.*

I don't understand either. Maybe on some level, Will remembers, recognizes me. Sweat dampens my palms. I squeeze my thighs under the table.

Red gets to the point. "You're not sitting with us?"

Will shrugs one shoulder. "Nah."

"You pissed or something?" This from Red.

Xander doesn't speak. He continues to watch me. That ink black gaze makes me queasy. One word fills my head. *Evil.* A bizarre thought. Melodramatic. But I'm draki. I know evil exists. It hunts us.

I shift uneasily on my stool. Clearly Xander understands what his friend hasn't grasped. For whatever reason, Will *wants* to sit with me. I consider moving to another table, but that would just draw more attention to me.

Natural. Just act natural, Jacinda.

"I'm Xander," he says to me.

"Jacinda," I offer, feeling Will's stare on the side of my face.

Xander smiles at me. Darkly beguiling, I'm sure it works on most girls. "Nice to meet you."

I manage a brittle smile. "You too."

"I think you're in my health class." His voice is smooth, silky.

"You must mean my sister, Tamra."

"Ah. Twins?"

He says "twins" like it's something rich and decadent, chocolate in his mouth. I can only nod.

"Cool." His gaze lingers on my face in a way that makes me feel exposed. Finally, he looks away, claps a hand on Red's back. "This is my brother, Angus."

I blink. They are nothing alike. Except in the menace they emit.

He continues, "And I guess you've already met Will."

I nod, even though we haven't actually met.

"We're cousins."

Cousins. Hunters. Only not like Will.

My lungs expand with smoldering heat. I hold my breath. Suppress the surge of heat at my core, the rumbling vibration inside me. Strangely though, I feel no surprise. Prickly hot alarm has been there since the pair walked into the room. They are different from the other humans surrounding me. They are a threat. Instinct tells me this.

Xander and Angus would never let me escape. They would relish the chance to kill me. I don't know where to look. Awareness of them, these cruel hunters, crushes down on me. I worry they will see the truth in my eyes. My gaze darts around, looking for a safe place to rest.

"Really," I say with a muted voice, unable to stop myself from looking at them again. "Cousins. Cool."

Angus's lip curls, lifts over his teeth, and I know I sound stupid. A vapid girl.

With a smirk at Will, he shrugs and walks to the back of the room, dismissing me. Relief washes over me, but only a fraction. Xander lingers. With his cunning eyes he is the greater threat. The smarter of the two.

He looks back and forth from me to Will. "Are you coming tonight?" Xander asks.

"I don't know."

Xander's demon-dark eyes flash with annoyance. "Why not?"

"I have homework."

"Homework." Xander drops the word like it's something foreign he never heard before. For a moment, he looks on the verge of laughter. Then, he's all business, his voice a hard bite as he says, "We've got stuff to do. Our dads expect you there."

Will's hand curls into a fist on the table. "We'll see."

His cousin glares at him. "Yes. We will." Then, he looks at me. His inky eyes soften. "See you around, Jacinda." With an idle tap on our table, he strolls away.

Once he's gone, I breathe easier. "So," I say to Will, "your cousins seem . . . nice."

He smiles a moment but his eyes are grave. "You should stay away from them." Will's voice is low, a stroke of warm air that reaches across the distance to my skin.

I already plan on doing that, but I ask anyway. Anything to better pick him apart. "Why?"

"They're not the kind of guys a nice girl should hang out with." The tendons on his forearm flex as he opens and shuts his hand. "They're jerks. Most anyone will tell you that."

I try for a flirty tone to lighten the dark mood. "And what will most anyone tell me about you? Are you a good guy?"

He turns and faces me. Those changeable eyes pull me in, remind me of the lush greens and browns of the home I left behind. His face isn't soft. The angles are hard, chiseled.

"No. I'm not." He swings his face forward again.

Mr. Henke ignores the class, tapping a staccato rhythm at his computer.

My chest feels tight and prickly. Smoldering warm. "Why are you sitting with me?"

The silence stretches so long I begin to wonder if he's going to answer when he finally admits, "I don't know. Still trying to figure that out."

I don't know what I expected him to say. That on some level he knows me? Neither of us cracks a book. I barely breathe, too afraid that the heat mounting inside me might find a way out through my lips or nose. I take small sips of air and wait for the bell.

Conversation buzzes at a steady drone throughout the room. Mr. Henke's typing stops. I watch his eyes drift shut and his head bob to his nonexistent neck. His glasses slip on his nose.

I jump at a burst of shrill laughter behind me. I look over my shoulder and see a girl in the back, her chair squeezed between Will's cousins. Angus tickles her side and she jumps, her long blond hair flying like streamers in the air. She clings to Xander's arm as if he might save her from the delightful torture.

Xander wears a lazy smile—looks bored. As if he senses me watching, his gaze cuts to me, the smile vanishing from his face. His dark eyes seize hold of me.

"Turn around."

My pulse jackknifes against my throat at the deep voice. I look back at Will.

His lips barely move as he speaks. "Trust me. You don't want to be one of the girls Xander notices. It never goes well for them."

"I've hardly spoken to him. I don't think he—"

"*I* noticed you."

A dark thrill races through me. I wipe damp palms on my jeans.

He laughs then. Low and soft. An unhappy sound. "So, yeah. He noticed you." His lips twist. "Sorry about that."

The bell rings, its unnatural peal jarring me as it has all day.

And he's gone. Out the door before I can even grab my things or say good-bye.

7

I'm fighting with my locker again, the steel lock a cold kiss on my fingers. Bodies bump and rush past me. Strangely, my eyes burn. Tears want to spill. Which is stupid. Just because I can't get my locker open is no reason to wimp out.

But it's more than this. I know that. It's everything. I scan to the left, hoping Tamra will get here soon, so we can get out of this wretched place.

"Will Rutledge. Impressive." At the droll voice, I turn and recognize a girl from fourth-period PE. She was faster than most of the other girls. I remember lapping her only once around the track today. Her sleek brown hair reminds me a little of Az, but her eyes are large and blue-green, staring widely from beneath a choppy fringe of bangs. The bangs are a little too long, slightly uneven as though she takes scissors to them herself.

"Excuse me?" I say.

"Will and his cousins. They're the show around here." Her voice is low, guttural, dragging each word.

"Really," I murmur.

"Rich, hot, and they've got that bad-boy edge going for them." She nods. "Xander and Angus are users. Been through half the girls in this school. Not Will though. He's . . ."

I lean forward, eager for anything she will impart about him.

"Well. Will . . ." A wistful smile curves her mouth. "He's elusive. None of the girls here interest him." She rolls her magnificent eyes and sighs dramatically. "Course that just makes us want him harder."

Stupid delight flutters inside my chest.

"I'm Catherine," she announces.

"Hi, I'm—"

"Jacinda. I know."

"How do—"

"Everyone knows your name. And your sister's. Trust me. It's not *that* big of a school." She steps forward and brushes my hands off my lock. "What's the number?"

I toss out the six digits, vaguely wondering if I should be giving out my combination to a stranger and how I'm ever going to learn to open the thing myself. Catherine's fingers fly. She lifts the handle and frees the door.

"Thanks."

"No problem." She leans a shoulder against the lockers, looking content and natural. Like we do this every day. "Word of advice. You might want to stay away from him."

"Will Rutledge?" I ask, getting a thrill from just saying his name.

She nods. For a moment, I feel like I'm talking to Tamra again. Frustration seeps through me. My whole life I've been given advice that I'm expected to follow.

I hold on to my chemistry book and slide my lit book down from its shelf. "Why is that?"

"Because Brooklyn Davis will pulverize you or any girl who goes after him."

I thought maybe she had been warning me off Will because he's trouble. Like he told me himself. This, I could believe. This, I already know. I'm reminded of it every time he's near in the tightening of my flesh.

"Oh." I nod, remembering the girl from my English class. Then, I shrug. After running for my life from hunters, a girl with too much lip gloss doesn't register on my fear radar. I've dealt with girls who didn't like me before. Miram, Cassian's younger sister, leaps to mind. That girl hated me. She couldn't stand the amount of attention her family gave me—her father, Cassian. Even her aunt doted on me in a way that always creeped me out. Like she thought she was my mother or something. But because Catherine is looking at me like I should say something more, I add, "I'm not going after him."

"Good. Since you're the new girl, Brooklyn can make your life hell." She winces and readjusts the strap of her backpack on her shoulder. "Well, really if you're *any* girl, she can make your life hell. Take it from me. I've been there."

I shut my locker. The sound bleeds in with all the other slams ricocheting down the hallway. "Then it doesn't really matter either way, does it?"

"Just a warning. She's probably already heard that he sat with you and is plotting your slow demise as we speak."

"So he sat with me." I shrug. "We hardly spoke."

"This is Will Rutledge we're talking about," she reminds me, as if that means something. And of course, it does. But not in the same way it does for other girls.

With Will, I feel connected, drawn. Every fiber of my being remembers those moments in the cave, prey and predator finding communion in each other. But because the last thing I want to do is reveal that Will is anything special to me, I say, "So."

"So?" She stresses the word. "He doesn't date high school girls. He hardly talks to any of us. No one knows that more than Brooklyn. Just watch your back around her."

"So if Brooklyn can't have him no one can?"

"Pretty much," she replies.

Incredible. I've only been here a day and I already have an enemy? "Why are you telling me this?"

"Call me a Good Samaritan."

I smile and decide that I might like Catherine. Maybe I could find a friend in this place, after all. I'm not opposed to friends. I miss Az like crazy. Not that Catherine could ever replace her, but she might make being here more bearable. "Thanks."

"Sit with me in study hall tomorrow."

Instead of Will. As if Will might want to sit with me again. "Sure."

"Great." She shoves off the lockers and tosses her choppy bangs back from her eyes. "Can't miss my bus. See you tomorrow." As she disappears into the throng of students, I spot Tamra walking between a guy and a girl. She hasn't spotted me yet. She's smiling. No, beaming. Happier than I've seen her since Dad died. Even further back than that. Since it became clear she wouldn't manifest.

I can't help feeling sad. Sad and lonely as I stand in a crowded hall.

Mom's one of the first at the curb when we step outside. Heat blurs the air. It tastes like steam in my mouth and nose. My skin itches, roasting in the hot, drying atmosphere. I press my lips tight and hurry toward the car.

Our blue and rust-stained hatchback noses to the head of a long, coiling serpent of vehicles.

Tamra groans next to me. "We need our own car."

I don't bother asking how we might pull that off. When

Mom traded in the wagon several towns ago for the hatchback, she still had to toss in some cash. And there is the small matter of survival . . . keeping a roof over our heads, food in our bellies. We barely scratched enough together to cover rent and a deposit on a place to live. Thankfully, she starts work tonight.

Tamra slides me a look. "Not that you would be allowed behind the wheel. I'll have to drive us."

I roll my eyes. It's a running joke in the family. I can fly, but I can't drive to save my life. No matter how many times Mom has tried to teach me, I'm hopeless behind the wheel.

Tamra takes the front seat. I climb in the back.

"Well?" Mom asks, all loud and peppy. Too bad she can't try out for cheerleading with Tamra. She has the enthusiasm down pat.

"Great," Tamra offers. As if to prove her point, she waves out the window to the kids I saw her walking with in the hall. They wave back.

I feel sick. Lean to the side and let my face rest against the warm, sunbaked glass.

Mom looks over her shoulder. "What about you, Jacinda? Did you meet some nice kids?"

Will's face floats in my mind.

"A couple."

"Fantastic. See, girls? I told you this move would be great for us." Like we collectively decided to make a fresh start and didn't abscond in the middle of the night. Like I had been given a choice.

Apparently Mom can't hear the misery in my flat voice. Or she chooses to ignore it. The latter, I suspect. It's easier for parents to ignore, to pretend that everything's great and then do whatever they want while convinced it's something you want, too.

Thankfully the car moves forward, turning into the busy parking lot. We jerk to a stop several times as students reverse from spaces with reckless abandon, cutting in front of our car. All except the kids who linger, loitering in groups around their cars.

Then, I spot it. A vehicle I've seen before. With the memory comes fear . . . filling my mouth, as metallic and coppery as blood. My skin tightens, eager to fade out. I fight the manifest, shake off my fear. The draki instinct intended to protect me works against me now.

The gleaming black Land Rover with a light bar on top is parked backward in its slot like it might need a quick escape. This vehicle serves a function. It's more than a status symbol.

It's a machine designed to bring me down.

Old springs groan beneath me as I lean forward. "Can we get out of here?"

Mom motions to the cars before us. "What do you suggest? I just plow through the line?"

I can't help myself. I glance at the Land Rover again.

A group of girls loiter near the front bumper, close to Xander and Angus, who lean against the hood. Brooklyn is there. She talks with her whole body, tossing her shampoo-commercial hair, hands hopping on the air.

I sink down in the backseat, wondering why *he* is not among them, both glad and disappointed he isn't.

And almost as if I've summoned him, I feel him arrive. My skin shivers, and the tiny hairs at my nape stand on end. Like in the hall today before I even saw him, but knew he was near.

Given the pattern, I sit higher and search the parking lot. He emerges between two vehicles, striding with the ease and confidence of a jungle cat. The sun hits his hair, gilding it.

Seeing Will again makes my chest tighten and lungs burn. I breathe air deeply through my nose, trying to cool the heat rising inside me.

I must have made a sound, a gasp maybe. I don't know, but Tamra looks back at me. Maybe it's just the twin thing. It reminds me of when we were still connected. She gives me a funny look, and then peers out the window. I can't help it. I look, too. I can't *not* look.

Will stops, lifts his face. Like he's scented me on the air, which is impossible, of course. He can't sense me the way I sense him. But then he finds me.

For a moment, our gazes lock. Then his mouth curves into a smile that makes my stomach flip. He resumes walking. Brooklyn skips toward him. He doesn't break stride for her and she falls behind him, struggling to keep up.

Tamra mutters something beneath her breath.

"What?" I ask, defensive.

"You're not manifesting, I hope."

"What?" Mom demands in her old voice. The high-pitched anxious tone that I'm so used to hearing. No more pep.

"Jacinda nearly manifested at school today," Tamra tattles in that singsong voice of whiny kids everywhere. It reminds me of when I would take her dolls and give them haircuts.

Mom's eyes find me in the rearview mirror. "Jacinda?" she demands. "What happened?"

I shrug and look back out the window.

Tamra is nice enough to answer for me. "She started to manifest when she saw this cute guy—"

Mom asks, "What guy?"

Tamra points. "That one over—"

"Don't point," I snap, fresh heat washing over my face.

Too late, Mom looks. "You just . . . *saw* him?"

"Yes," I admit, sliding lower in my seat.

"And started to manifest?"

I rub my forehead, feeling the beginnings of a headache. "Look, I didn't *try* to do anything. It just happened."

Through the grimy window, I watch as Will gets behind the wheel. His cousins hop inside, too. For not liking them much, he definitely spends a lot of time with them. It's a needed reminder. He belongs with them.

Brooklyn watches him, too, next to her friends, arms

crossed tightly across her chest.

"Jacinda." Mom says my name softly, with such disappointment that I want to throw something. Yell. It hurts that I'm such a frustration for her. It makes me feel like she can't love me as I am.

Dad loved me—had been so proud when I first manifested. And beyond proud when it became obvious I was a fire-breather. The first in generations.

Not Mom. Never Mom. With Mom there had only ever been wariness . . . as if I were some dangerous being she gave birth to. Someone she had to love, but wouldn't have chosen.

Our car moves at last. I resist staring after the Land Rover as it pushes through the throng of cars.

Tight lines edge the sides of Mom's mouth as she pulls out of the school. She nods her head, as if the motion is convincing her of something.

"It's okay," she says. "As long as you don't actually manifest . . . which shouldn't be easy to do here." She tosses me a stern look. "It's like a muscle. It will lose strength if you don't exercise it."

Like with her. I have only vague memories of Mom manifesting. It's been years. Even when she could, she rarely did, preferring to stay home with Tamra and me while Dad flew. She gave it up altogether when Tamra failed to manifest. "I know."

Only I'm not like her. As stifled as I felt with the pride,

uncertain of myself around Cassian . . . living in this desert, deliberately killing my draki, is worse.

"Just to be safe, keep your distance from that boy."

It's my turn to nod now. "Sure," I say, even as I think no. Even as I think I might hate my mother just a little bit. Because even though I know I should stay away from Will, I'm tired of her making all my decisions. Could what the pride had in store for me have been so bad that we needed to come here to be *safe*? Is Cassian really that bad? It's not that I didn't like him. I just didn't like him being chosen for me. Especially since my sister had wanted him from the age of three. He always gave Tamra piggyback rides even though Mom would shout at him to put her down. Me, I just tried to keep up. And then I didn't have to anymore. Cassian manifested and forgot us both. He didn't notice me again until I manifested. And Tamra . . . well, never manifesting sealed her fate. Cassian forgot her completely.

Safe. Safe. Safe.

That word comes up a lot with Mom. Safety. It's everything. It's led me to this. Leaving the pride, killing my draki, avoiding the boy who saved my life, the boy who awakened my draki in the midst of this scorched sea—the boy I want very much to know.

Can't she understand? What good is safety if you're dead inside?

8

Mrs. Hennessey stares at us through her blinds. She must have been waiting for us to come home. We enter quietly through the back gate, careful not to let it clang after us.

And yet, as quiet as we are, she is ready, peering at us from the security of her house. She's done that a lot since we moved in. As if she's not sure she didn't rent her pool house to a family of convicts.

Apparently I'm not the only one who notices. "She's watching us," Tamra hisses. "Again."

"Don't stare," Mom commands. "And keep your voice down."

Tamra obeys, whispering, "Isn't it kind of creepy living in some old lady's backyard?"

"It's a lovely neighborhood."

"And all we could afford," I remind Tamra.

We skirt the pool, walking one after the other. Mom leads, balancing a small bag of groceries on her hip. I'm last. I look down into the cerulean blue pool to see a shuddering reflection of myself. The chemical odor stings my nostrils.

Still, the water looks refreshing in this dry, skin-shriveling heat that makes my thirsting pores contract. We don't even have a tub. Just a shower stall. Maybe I can sneak a swim later. I've never been good at following rules.

Tamra grumbles, "I just hope she doesn't go through our stuff while we're gone."

What stuff? It's not like we smuggled out much in our haste. Clothes and a few personal belongings. I doubt she could find our gems. *I* haven't even been able to find them. And I looked when Mom left us to job hunt, hungry for the sight of them. Just a touch. A revitalizing brush against my skin.

Mom unlocks the door. Tamra follows her inside. I pause and take another look over my shoulder—find Mrs. Hennessey still watching. When she sees me looking, the blinds snap shut. Turning, I walk inside the moldy-smelling pool house, wondering what time she goes to bed.

That water is calling my name. And for now, it's closer than the sky.

As Tamra and I wash dishes, Mom changes for work. The smell of rich butter and cheese lingers in the tiny kitchen.

Mom's five-cheese macaroni with her unique blend of herbs is my favorite. Not that she's not a fantastic cook in general. She's a verda draki—*was*, I mean.

Verda draki know everything there is to know about herbs, specifically how to optimize them into food and medicines. She can bring the blandest dish to life. In the same vein, she can also concoct a poultice that gets rid of a pimple overnight or draws poison from a wound.

Tonight's dinner was for me.

She's trying to be good to me—feels sorry for me, I guess. It's me Mom worries about. Me she wants to be happy here. With Tamra, it's a given—she wanted to leave the pride years ago.

Dinner tasted good, delicious. Like home. My stomach is pleasantly full from too much food.

Mom emerges from her room, dressed in black slacks and a purple sequined halter top. Her bare shoulders gleam like pale marble. Maybe she'll get a tan here. I frown. Maybe we all will.

"You sure you girls will be all right?" She looks at me as she asks this.

"We'll be fine," Tamra replies cheerfully. "Now go out there and earn those tips."

Mom's smile is shaky. "I'll try, but I do hate leaving you girls alone."

I know it's terrible and selfish of me, but I'm glad she got hired on for nights. It's too hard to be around her right now. And this way I only have to worry about Tamra if I sneak out. *When* I sneak out. Once I decide on the safest place for me to manifest. It can't be far. I'll have to walk to get there after all.

Laughter bubbles like acid inside my chest. Because no place is safe to manifest here. It's a desert. Without mists and mountains for cover, I'd never be fully cloaked.

"Don't stay up too late," Mom instructs. "And do your homework."

It's her first night working at the local casino. The night shift pays best. She'll be gone from ten at night until five in the morning. This way, she can see us off to school, get a nap and then head back for a few hours during the day, clocking out in time to pick us up from school and spend the early evening with us. Ideal as long as she can keep functioning on five hours of daytime sleep.

"Remember, Mrs. Hennessey is just next door."

I snort. "Like we're going to bother her."

"Just be careful." Her gaze swings meaningfully between me and Tamra, and I wonder what's really worrying her. That the pride might show up to drag us back? Or that I'll take off and return to them all on my own?

"You know," Tamra points out. "You could just sell a few rubies, an emerald or diamond." She shrugs. "Then you wouldn't have to leave us alone. You wouldn't have to work so much." My sister glances around the small, wood-paneled living room. "We could rent a nice condo."

Mom picks up her purse. "You know we can't do that."

Because the pride would know instantly if any of the jewels that had been in our family for generations started circulating. They would be looking for that very thing. That's what they would expect us to do to survive.

If not for that, I know Mom would sell off every gem we possessed. It's not as though she places any sentimental value on them. The stones are our draki family legacy, after all—and she wants to kill all ties to that.

Jewel salvaging's part of our ancestry. This, in part, is why we are hunted. Money. Greed. Besides the greed for our blood, skin, and bones—which are said to hold healing properties for humans—we're tracked down for our troves.

But for us, it's not about money. It's about life.

Arable earth sustains us, but gems offer something more. They're the icing on the cake, the earth's purest energy. They fortify us. As with our dragon forefathers, we can detect gemstones beneath the ground. We're attuned to their energy. Without proximity to either arable earth or gems, it's akin to starving.

Tamra props her hands on her hips. "C'mon. Just sell one. I need some new clothes."

Mom shakes her head. "I get paid on Friday. We'll see what we can spare then."

"Would it be such a big deal to sell one little stone?" I say lightly, pretending I'm not fully aware of the potential danger. Not to mention the pain of losing one of my family's gems. Selling one would be like selling a piece of me.

But maybe worth it. Because nothing will be left of me if I have to stay here. This way the pride would find us and take us back.

Mom's gaze swings to me, all glittery and hard. She sees through my words, knows my game. "That would be a bad idea, Jacinda."

It's a warning. Her threatening tone rings final.

"Fine," I reply, setting the last plate into the dish rack and marching through the living area to the room I share with Tamra.

"Jacinda," she calls as I drop onto the bed. Mom follows, stops in the doorway, her expression soft. "Don't be angry."

I punch a limp pillow. "What about any of this is sup-posed to make me happy?"

"I know it's hard."

I shake my head—roll onto my side. Can't even look at her. She does understand. She's been there. That's what makes me the maddest. "You *chose* to let your draki die. And now you're choosing for me."

"It's not easy for me either."

I glare at her over my shoulder. "*You're* the one who decided we had to do this."

She shakes her head, sadly, and for a moment I think that maybe I can convince her this is a mistake. Maybe she'll realize I don't belong here and never will.

"I know it was my decision. I didn't give you an option," she agrees. "But I want you safe."

A sinking sensation fills me. Safety again. How can I argue against that?

She continues, "And staying with the pride isn't safe anymore. I'm your mother. You're going to have to trust me on this. Moving here was the right thing to do." Something lurks in her tone . . . something that makes me think she still isn't telling me everything. That there's even more danger with the pride than she wants me to know about.

I look away again, stare at the plaid curtains. Inhale the chemical pool-house smell, burning my nostrils. It's stronger in this room. Even beats out the aroma of mold. "Aren't you going to be late for work?"

Her soft sigh floats over the air. "Good night, baby. I'll see you in the morning."

Then she's gone.

She and Tamra say something to each other. Too softly for me to decipher, so I know they're talking about me.

I hear the front door open and shut, sealing me in my prison.

I haven't shared a room with Tamra since we were seven years old. I'm not sure how I'll endure her optimism in the midst of my misery, but I'm trying. No sense raining on her parade.

"What are you wearing tomorrow?" She stares into our closet. Hard. For several moments. As if something will magically appear that wasn't there a minute ago.

Mom gave us the bigger room with the bigger closet. Still, it's not very full. The size of the closet only emphasizes the scarcity of our wardrobe.

I shrug. "Jeans."

"You wore jeans today."

"It won't matter if I wear jeans again. I'll switch tops."

She plops down on her bed.

I sit Indian-style on mine, rubbing lotion into my legs. Again. I'm almost halfway through the bottle, but my flesh is still dry and thirsty, hungering for more.

"You don't miss anything back home?" I ask, hoping that maybe there's something. Something that might encourage her to consider returning.

"Nope."

"Not even Cassian?" I dare to ask.

Instantly, her mood changes. Her expression clouds over as she tosses out, "He's not mine to miss, is he?" And it's there. The old wound.

"That didn't stop you from wanting him all these years."

"Cassian can't be with a defunct draki. His father would never allow it. Right away, I understood that."

Did she? Then why did I sense anger? Hurt? Why did her gaze follow him everywhere all those years if she understood?

"You two used to be close friends," I remind her.

"All three of us were. So?"

"I wasn't as close to him as you were."

She sighs. "That was a long time ago. We were kids then, Jace." Shaking her head, she looks at me. "Where are you going with this? You think you can get me to believe that I have a shot at Cassian? That I'll go back for him? Wow, you're really desperate to go back if you think I'm stupid enough to fall for that."

Embarrassing heat washes up my neck. Am I that transparent? "I just find it hard to believe you've totally forgotten him."

Her eyes spark and her voice trembles with feeling. "Would you rather I keep deluding myself? I don't have a chance with him. The pride won't let it happen. *Cassian* won't let it happen. I'm starting over here." Her eyes harden, chill me. "I have my dignity, Jacinda. I won't let some stupid crush stop me from finally having a life, so can we just drop the subject?"

Ignoring the request, I ask something I haven't brought up in a long time, haven't dared, reluctant to give my sister false hope. "What if you haven't given it enough time . . ."

Her eyes flash furiously. "Don't go there. If I was going to manifest, I already would have."

I shrug. "Maybe you're just a late bloomer? Nidia manifested late—"

"A thirteen-year-old is a late bloomer, not me. Now, please, can we drop it already? I don't want to talk about the pride anymore!"

"Okay, okay," I say, returning my attention back to my legs. Dry again.

I shake my head fiercely, furiously. My hand works harder, pressing the lotion deep into my skin. Scent-free lotion because I've had enough with the odors, the smells that constantly suffocate me in the human world.

Already, I feel different. It's working. Mom's getting her way. My draki is withering. Dying in this desert.

Except around Will.

My fingers slow, still on my skin. Hope flutters inside my chest. *Except around Will.* Around him my draki lives. *Will.* Of course there's risk in that, too. But these days, risk is like air to me. Everywhere. My life is a far cry from safe—no matter how hard Mom clings to the notion.

9

I follow the throng of girls heading to the gym, trying to keep a healthy distance from the press of bodies. It's all so overwhelming. The foreign smells, the grating sounds, the lack of open space and fresh air. Dribbling balls beat the stale air, echoing off the wood floor, growing louder as we near the gym's double doors.

"Looks like we're working out with the guys today," Catherine says as we step through the doors into sour, sweat-saturated air.

That feeling comes over me again, and immediately I know he's here. I spot Will across the gym, watch as he shoots a three-pointer, bouncing lightly on the balls of his feet. Even before the ball clears the net, he's looking at me.

Familiar heat creeps up my chest to warm my face.

"Boys this side, girls this side!" A coach blows a whistle and gestures to separate sides of the court.

"Ugh, the dreaded basketball unit," Catherine mutters in her slow drawl. "I'd rather run the track."

We file into line to shoot free throws. At half-court, the end of the boys' line collides with the end of the girls'. It's a little chaotic here, where the lines converge and the sexes mingle to abuse each other good-naturedly.

From the corner of my eye, I spot Will getting out of line and dropping back to where Catherine and I stand at the end of our line.

"Hi," he greets me.

"Hi."

Catherine looks back and forth between us. "Hey," she volunteers dryly.

Will and I both look at her.

"Yeah," she says slowly, shaking the bangs from her eyes and moving in front of me, giving us her back.

"So," Will begins, "do you play ball as well as you run?"

I laugh a little. I can't help it. He's sweet and disarming and my nerves are racing. "Not even close."

The conversation goes no further as we move up in our lines. Catherine looks over her shoulder at me, her wide sea eyes assessing. Like she can't quite figure me out. My smile fades and I look away. She can never figure me out. I can never let her. Never let anyone here.

She faces me with her arms crossed. "You make friends fast. Since freshman year, I've spoken to like . . ." She pauses and looks upward as though mentally counting. "Three, no—four people. And you're number four."

I shrug. "He's just a guy."

Catherine squares up at the free-throw line, dribbles a few times, and shoots. The ball swishes cleanly through the net. She catches it and tosses it back to me.

I try copying her moves, but my ball flies low, glides beneath the backboard. I head to the end of the line again.

Will's already waiting at half-court, letting others go before him. My face warms at his obvious stall.

"You weren't kidding," he teases over the thunder of basketballs.

"Did *you* make it?" I ask, wishing I had looked while he shot.

"Yeah."

"Of course," I mock.

He lets another kid go before him. I do the same. Catherine is several ahead of me now.

His gaze scans me, sweeping over my face and hair with deep intensity, like he's memorizing my features. "Yeah, well. I can't run like you."

I move up in line, but when I sneak a look behind me, he's looking back, too.

"Wow," Catherine murmurs in her smoky low voice as

she falls into line beside me. "I never knew it happened like that."

I snap my gaze to her. "What?"

"You know. Romeo and Juliet stuff. Love at first sight and all that."

"It's not like that," I say quickly.

"You could have fooled me." We're up again. Catherine takes her shot. It swishes cleanly through the hoop.

When I shoot, the ball bounces hard off the backboard and flies wildly through the air, knocking the coach in the head. I slap a hand over my mouth. The coach barely catches herself from falling. Several students laugh. She glares at me and readjusts her cap.

With a small wave of apology, I head back to the end of the line.

Will's there, fighting laughter. "Nice," he says. "Glad I'm downcourt of you."

I cross my arms and resist smiling, resist letting myself feel good around him. But he makes it hard. I want to smile. I want to like him, to be around him, to know him. "Happy to amuse you."

His smile slips then, and he's looking at me with that strange intensity again. Only I understand. I know why. He must remember . . . must recognize me on some level even though he can't understand it.

"You want to go out?" he asks suddenly.

I blink. "As in a date?"

"Yes. That's what a guy usually means when he asks that question."

Whistles blow. The guys and girls head in opposite directions.

"Half-court scrimmage," Will mutters, looking unhappy as he watches the coaches toss out jerseys. "We'll talk later in study hall. Okay?"

I nod, my chest uncomfortably tight, breath hard to catch. Seventh period. A few hours to decide whether to date a hunter. The choice should be easy, obvious, but already my head aches. I doubt anything will ever be easy for me again.

Catherine saves me a seat at lunch. I slide in across from her and her friend. Apparently one of the other three people she's spoken to thus far in high school.

She introduces us. Brendan is all gangly limbs and bobbing Adam's apple. He hunkers over his packed lunch, nibbling on a peanut butter sandwich clutched between his two large hands as if someone might snatch it from him.

"Hey," he says quietly, almost inaudible. His darting brown eyes never looking too long at my face. At anything or anyone really, except Catherine.

"Hi," I return, then search for my sister, ignoring the faces staring back at me. Like I have tried to ignore them all day.

I spot her across the crowded lunchroom. Holding her

tray, she stands with another girl. She looks so confident. So self-assured. I've never seen her this way.

I fidget in my chair. Push a frizzy, coarse lock back behind my ear. Watching her, I scratch a bit desperately at my arm, at my suffocating skin, and wince when it starts to sting. I glance down at the splotchy, irritated flesh. I've been this way all day. Uncomfortable, slightly ill. The butterflies in my stomach definitely not the good variety. Except during gym today. I'd felt good then . . . around Will.

Tamra sees me, registers that I'm sitting with people, and looks relieved. Permission granted to sit wherever she wants. She nods to me as she joins a table crowded with beautiful, well-dressed teenagers. Clearly the cream of Chaparral High. Brooklyn is among them, of course.

My dose of her in third period supported everything Catherine told me. Apparently she heard about Will sitting with me yesterday and took exception. Every time Mrs. Schulz turned to the blackboard, Brooklyn would swivel in her seat and level me with a killing glare. I wonder if she knows he talked to me during PE.

I suppose a glare like that would send most girls whimpering into themselves. I didn't care. I have bigger problems.

I haven't seen Will since PE. As I haven't decided whether to go out with him, it's a relief. Yes, being around him feeds my draki, and it's all about that right now. About me doing whatever I can to keep that part of myself alive. But he's everything I should avoid.

For a draki, he's death. Ironic, huh? To keep that part of me alive, I have to be close to that which kills it.

I scan the lunchroom but don't spot him. He must have another lunch period. Regret stabs my heart. And then I'm angry for that. Confused. My fingers fumble with a packet of ketchup.

At least I haven't seen his cousins. There's no confusion when it comes to them. They should be avoided at all costs. Xander with his sly eyes and Angus with his curling lip. I don't know how I would have handled Tamra sitting at a table with them. Brooklyn is one thing. But them?

"Your sister fits right in," Catherine comments.

"Yeah," I murmur, popping open my soda can, fighting hard to look okay with that. Because I am.

I am.

It makes sense. She should fit in around them. She's practically human herself. She always loved the trips into town—anywhere we ventured in the outside world, away from the pride. "She's good at that," I murmur.

"What?"

"Fitting in," I reply, sipping my orange soda. The kind of junk drink Mom never lets us have. The citrus burn-tickles my throat. The tangy aroma fills my nose.

"Why aren't you over there with the beautiful people?"

I shrug.

"You could be," Brendan quietly interjects, picking at the crust of his sandwich, a shy, half-smile bending his lips. "You're as pretty as she is."

"Well, duh." Catherine playfully nudges him in the side. "They're twins."

My lips twist into a smile. I pause with a potato chip halfway to my mouth. "Is that all it takes? You just have to be attractive to hang out with that crowd? You're pretty. It must involve more than that." Biting into my chip, I open my hamburger and examine the questionable patty. Wrinkling my nose, I place the bun back on the burger.

"Anyway, your sister should be careful."

Brendan-of-few-words adds, "They'll make her one of them."

Like they're vampires. Still, his portentous words send a small chill through me.

Then I shake it off. Tamra and I are sisters. We love each other. We would never hurt each other. Nothing will change that. Maybe it's finally her turn to belong somewhere.

Catherine nods, tossing her too-long bangs out of her seawater eyes. "He's right. You don't want her to become one of them."

I don't want a lot of things. I don't want to be here. I don't want to lose myself in this new life-sucking world. My sister hanging out with populars? Should I now add that to the list? Even if it makes her happy?

Catherine waves her burger with one hand. "I'm telling you, those girls over there are a pack of wolves."

Because I don't want to worry about this, because I just

want to get through the day and figure out what to do about Will, I joke, "You're really upbeat, aren't you? Don't tell me. I bet you're a cheerleader."

Brendan snorts.

Catherine's mouth sags—the picture of horror. Color burns her cheeks. She shrugs. "So maybe I have an ax to grind with Brooklyn."

"Really?" I mock.

"They used to be best friends," Brendan volunteers. "In junior high."

"I told you never to mention that," Catherine rebukes.

"Really?" I ask again, this time minus the mockery.

"Yeah, well. That ended the first week of freshman year when the gods of popularity—"

"Seniors," Brendan supplies.

"—chose Brooklyn as their little protégé. Since then, I'm just a bad memory."

And I can't help thinking of Cassian, of *me* and all the other draki blessed with talents the pride deems invaluable. We were the lucky ones. There, I had been admired, prized. While Tamra became invisible. She and the others who never manifested.

Funny. Here, I am insignificant. Expendable in the eyes of my peers. A strange girl uncomfortable in her skin—well, her human skin. Uncomfortable in her surroundings. Who doesn't know how to talk, act, or dress.

It makes me want to go home all the more. Home to the

pride. Even if the pride does try to control me. At least there, I'm me.

A slow certainty steals over me. I need to keep my draki alive long enough to get back. The thought of it dying terrifies me, makes me desperate. Desperate enough to do something I shouldn't.

Desperate enough to tell Will yes.

"You're probably wondering what you did in a past life to get stuck with us." Catherine says this as she drowns a fry in ketchup, her many rings glinting as she works her fingers.

"Gee, thanks," Brendan murmurs.

She gives him a look. "Don't be so sensitive. You know I adore you."

I lower my mostly uneaten burger. "Of course not. Just glad for anyone who wants to be my friend."

"Hey, Jacinda!" Nathan calls from his table, half rising. He waves and jerks his head, beckoning me over.

Catherine's smile slips. She reaches for another fry, avoiding my gaze. "You've got plenty of people willing to be your friend. Go on. Sit with Nathan. He's a decent guy—unfortunate pink shirt and all. No hard feelings."

I send Nathan an easy wave but remain in my seat. "I'm good where I am." Good at least in this. In hanging out with Catherine and the quiet Brendan. They're undemanding. Uncomplicated. Easy to be with when everything else is so hard right now. I need that. "Unless you want me to go."

"No." Catherine flashes a grin. "Stay."

Nodding, I eat another chip. My gaze drifts across the room, to my sister. Her hair falls smoothly past her shoulders, gleaming like flaming silk.

The same boy who walked with her in the hall yesterday sits beside her. Across from her, another one vies for her attention. Cute guys. My heart expands a little. For her. Who knew she could flirt? Cassian wasn't the only one who rejected her, after all. Showed her his back when she came around. The boys in the pride rarely spoke to her. They couldn't. Their families too afraid of letting them get involved with a defunct draki. They wouldn't risk contamination of their gene pool.

I look away, stare down at my tray. Sorry that I can't share in her pleasure. Sorry that I have to do everything in my power to simply abide this life that gives her such happiness.

Sorry that maybe, in the end, I will lose the battle and have to leave her behind.

10

The day stretches on, endless. It feels like seventh period will never arrive. The hands on the round-faced wall clocks crawl, skipping over each minute in nervous twitches. By the time I reach study hall, the pulse at my neck jumps in time with that bouncing minute hand.

I hover in the doorway for a moment, scanning the near-empty classroom. Now, finally. I will see him again.

Heart pounding, I sit at the same table as yesterday and hope he arrives before Catherine does, so I don't have to explain to her that I *want* to sit with him. And I do, I realize—I accept. I want to sit with him, talk to him, see him, go out with him . . . everything. As long as I'm here, anyway. And not just for the sake of my draki. I would have liked Will Rutledge no matter what I was.

With a quick smile at me, Nathan veers to another table. At least I don't have to worry about him trying to sit with me again. The warning bell peals overhead. My breath comes faster. I watch the door. Any second now.

Catherine rushes in, long bangs flying. I try to hide my disappointment as she, not Will, drops next to me. The final bell rings. Still, I wait, look for Will.

Mr. Henke's voice drones at the front of the room, reciting the same speech as yesterday. Still, I look at the door.

"He's not here."

I start at Catherine's voice. "Who?"

"Will. I saw him and his cousins leave during fifth period."

I shrug like I don't care. Like I hadn't decided to go out with him. Like he hadn't asked. Like every fiber of my being isn't weeping in need for him.

"It's okay. After the vibes you two were giving off yesterday and today in PE, I figure you were looking for him."

I don't respond. My hands are shaking. I tuck them under the table. I had counted on seeing him. On feeling my draki again. On him bringing me to life, making me remember . . . *me*. I needed that, and now that I can't have it my chest feels crushed. The weight of my disappointment presses down on me.

Catherine digs in her backpack. Desperation feeds my heart enough to ask, "So. Where is he?" As if I expect her to know.

"Here." She slides a note across the table to me. "He

gave me this to give to you."

I stare at the folded square piece of paper for a long moment, my heart hammering. Finally, I take it. The paper is cool and crisp beneath my trembling fingers as I unfold it, taking my time to smooth out the creases and study his handwriting.

Jacinda,
Sorry, but I had to leave town for a family thing. Try not to knock any other teachers unconscious while I'm gone.
See you soon (but not soon enough),
Will

A sigh rattles loose from my lips. I shake my spinning head. This is crazy. Me pining for a hunter. A hunter pining for me. I should know better, even if he can't. Especially if he can't.

"He and his cousins miss a lot of school," Catherine continues.

I can believe that. They would have been north of here a little over a week ago. Hunting me in the Cascades. I doubt they limited their activities to weekend hunts. They would have had to miss school.

"Really." My fingers tap my lips now. They feel chapped. Dry like the rest of me.

"Uh-huh." Catherine takes out her chemistry book, opens to the periodic table, and begins filling out a worksheet. "And get this . . . you know why they miss so much?"

I shake my head even though I do know. Better than her. My heart clenches like a fist in my chest, squeezing . . . squeezing . . .

"Their family is big into fly-fishing. Nice, huh? Ditching school to fish." She drums the end of her pencil on the table as she studies the chart. The sound echoes the stutter of my heart. I slide off my stool, clutching the edge of the table.

Fly-fishing. It was almost amusing. If it didn't make my chest hurt so much.

Catherine continues, "They take these trips about every . . . Jacinda, are you okay?"

Will has gone . . . *hunting* again. Probably back where they nearly captured me. Hunting my pride.

Will's not my savior. He's a killer.

It's the wake-up call I need. I'm a fool to think a hunter is going to save me. Protect me. Keep me alive. I'll find another way. My fist clenches around his note, crumpling it into a ball in my hand. I'll forget about Will. Sever whatever bond I feel with him. Only the decision doesn't make me feel any better. My chest hurts even more.

Over the next few nights, I manage to sneak away to the neighborhood golf course twice to fly. Each time ends with me violently ill. The manifests are painful and difficult, but I'm no less determined. I have no choice. I have to keep trying. I have to fly. Even if Will was here, I would need to do this, need to learn to keep my draki alive all on my own.

I also work on Mom. Nag and plead every chance I get.

Until she gazes at me dully, quietly, beyond arguing but still firm on us staying in Chaparral. Tonight, however, it's Tamra hassling her.

Mom turns from the stove, a marinara-coated spoon in her hand. She asks again in that incredulous tone, "How much?"

Steam from a pot of pasta rises on the air behind her. I try not to stare at the billowing cloud that reminds me of the mists back home. My skin starts to ache.

I force my gaze back to Mom. She looks tired. Closer to her actual age of fifty-six. Draki age differently, more slowly. Our average life span runs about three hundred years. Once we reach puberty, the aging process slows. Right now, I look close to my age, but I'll look like a teenager for several years to come. Even when I'm thirty.

Time is catching up with Mom though. The consequences for relinquishing her draki. She's human now, and she finally looks it. In the creases on her forehead. In the tiny lines edging her eyes. Those lines are perpetual. Not just when she's worried anymore.

I stand at the table with three dinner plates in my hands, watching as Tamra waves her flyer, deftly avoiding Mom's question. "Come on, Mom. It looks great on college applications."

I lower my head. Center a plate on the placemat. Hide rolling my eyes.

This is what Tamra wants. I should try to support her.

Try not to choke on the image of Tamra hanging out with Brooklyn and her sisters of cheer.

"It's a lot of money, Tamra."

"Money we don't have," I can't resist adding. Because I see how hard Mom works. Stale cigarette smoke from the casino clings to her, even after she showers and washes her hair. It's there. Deep in her pores.

Tamra glares at me. I stare back, undaunted. Doesn't she see the shadows under Mom's eyes? Doesn't she hear her come in at five in the morning?

"I can get a part-time job. Please, Mom. Just sign the form. We don't even know if I'll make the team. We only have to pay if I do." The desperation in Tamra's voice is something new. Before, with the pride, I had only ever seen it in her eyes. Never heard it in her voice. Back home she wanted a lot of things, but she was resigned to life the way it was. I wonder why she wants this so badly?

I blurt the question out without thinking.

Tamra looks at me, her eyes hard chips of amber. "It's something I never even hoped for—and now it's possible."

And I get it. She can have it now. *Normal. Acceptance.* For however long we last in Chaparral. I feel the burden of that. I know it's largely up to me whether things work out here.

This is a piece of her fantasy. The fantasy of being a normal girl with a normal life. For Tamra, cheerleading is the piece of ordinary she wants.

Mom stares at the permission form, the grooves around

her mouth deepening. If she signs, Tamra can try out, and if she makes the squad, we'll have to come up with the money for uniforms and supplies.

I have no doubt Tamra will make the squad. I watch, curious to see what Mom will do, if she will surrender to at least one daughter. I know this is different, but I can't help thinking, *Why doesn't she care what I want?*

Mom nods, the motion weary, defeated. "Okay."

And in that moment, I feel defeated, too.

My life has fallen into a quiet pattern since Will left. School, dinner with Mom, homework, listening to music and watching TV with Tamra.

I walk the halls like a coldly functioning robot. My draki continues its slow descent. Suffering in silence, that part of me fades into dark. Like a healing wound, it throbs less, hurts less, feels less. Wildly, I want to tear it open, rip wide the jagged edges . . . make it bleed. Make it remember.

By Friday I wonder if something hasn't happened to Will. Almost every moment I wonder where he is, where he hunts. My pride isn't the only one out there, but we don't interact with others so I don't know where they are—where Will might be.

It's wrong of me, but I hope his family is hunting another pride. Just not mine. I want those I left behind safe—Az, Nidia . . . even Cassian.

When it comes to Will, my feelings are terrible and

confusing. To want him safely back one moment, but pray that whatever draki he hunts is safe and free in the next. The two wishes conflict.

I convince myself my pride is safe. We aren't a weak species. We have our talents. Our strengths. When innocent hikers stumble past Nidia's mists, she shades their memories and guides them back out. But hunters?

I cringe. It's one of those things never discussed, but always understood. The pride must be protected. Even if Nidia shaded a hunter's memory, he could return to hunt our kind. He would forever be a predator.

A predator that needed destroying.

Before now, I never thought anything wrong with the practice. Especially after Dad. But now . . .

I see only Will's face. At the thought of him dead, my throat aches. For the boy who spared me. The boy whose beauty seems an impossible dream, unreal to me now, so many days since I've had my last glimpse of him.

"Hey, Jacinda."

I look up, startled. The face is familiar. I think she's in my English class.

"Hi." I nod at her. Don't remember her name.

I try to wake up as I move down the hall. Switch off the autopilot. I've become like the desert that surrounds me on every side. Dry and barren. Accustomed to living in a state of nothing.

It is *this*. The quiet pattern that worries me. The lulling tide of acceptance threatening to pull me under. Mom's right. Nothing like a barren environment to kill off one's draki.

I can't stay like this. I can't remain here. I have to find a way out. I have to fly—have to keep trying.

Before I enter study hall, I take a deep breath. We didn't see the boys in PE today. They worked in the weight room while we scrimmaged in the gym. I don't know if Will's back, but I tell myself it shouldn't matter either way. I can't go out with him, can't let myself rely on him. I *won't*.

Big words. I feel like such a fake. Because despite my vow to forget him, I haven't. I remember everything about him. I feel his absence. Like the loss of shaded skies, mists, and pulsing earth.

He cannot possibly be all that I remember, all that I crave to see again. Even as I know it's wrong. Even as I know that I must avoid him.

Walking into study hall, my steps falter when I spot Xander and Angus in the back of the room. Cold prickles down my neck.

They're back.

11

Immediately, I search for Will. See him nowhere.

My treacherous heart sinks. Xander watches me, his tar black eyes impenetrable. He sends me a hello nod. Angus talks to the girls at the table beside them, his big crushing hands moving the air. He doesn't notice me.

Only one desperate thought echoes through my mind. *No Will. No Will.*

I sink onto my stool. Face forward. Catherine hasn't made it to study hall yet. She has a long trek from the art building.

I rub my hands over my jeans. Everyone begins lining up at the front of the room, eager for a pass, looking for escape. I feel Xander's stare on my back and consider joining them in line.

He's just returned from the hunt. Does draki blood, purple

and iridescent, stain his hands? Does he, like a bloodhound, have a nose for prey? For draki? For *me*? That would explain the avid way he watches me.

The warning bell rings its ear-bleeding screech. I've grown accustomed to the sound. Hardly jerk where I sit. Bleakness swirls through me. I blink once, hard, squeezing my eyes tight. I don't want to get used to any of this.

"Hey, Jacinda. Want to go to the library with me and Mike?" Nathan pauses near my table, an easy grin on his boyish, rounded features.

"Thanks, but no. I'm going to study here with Catherine."

Shrugging, Nathan and his friend step into the pass line, and I wonder if I shouldn't have joined them. If I still should.

Then my thoughts of escape grind to a stop. That much-missed vibration ignites in my chest, spreads to my core. My skin snaps alive. My head turns, eyes searching, honing in on Will as he walks into the room.

Everything about him is brighter than I remember.

The gold streaks in his brown hair. The gleam of his hazel eyes. His height. The breadth of his shoulders. He makes every other boy look small. Young and silly.

Suddenly, the days without a glimpse of him feel like forever. I have waited too long for this moment. To see him again. For my lungs to tighten. For my heart to pound and swell against my rib cage.

To feel my draki stir.

His gaze lands on me, the hazel eyes bright and hungry in

a way that makes my skin flare hotly. But his eyes aren't the only ones I feel. Behind me, Xander's stare sinks deep.

Will approaches my table, and I forget about everyone else. I forget that I'm supposed to stay away from him. This near to Will, I even forget whatever vague fear Xander feeds in me. I only want Will to stop, to say something, work his magic on my withering soul. I need that. He's almost to my table now. My lungs expand, smolder. Steam wells up in my throat. It feels wonderful. It feels like life.

My tightening skin heats, flashes a brief shimmer of red-gold. I clasp my arm, my fingers tight and hurtful. As if the press of my hand can stop me from manifesting in a room full of humans.

He's so close now I can see the shards of green, gold, and brown in his eyes. One more stride and he's even with my table.

I hold my hot breath. Search him for some sign . . .

He looks away from me then, over my head to where his cousins sit. Something passes over his face, a ripple that washes clean the rapt intensity. With a bored expression, he walks past me where I tremble on my stool.

His cold rejection steals my breath. The heat leaves me in a slow sizzle of air out my nose. The blaze in my lungs dies, fades to embers.

Nothing. Not a word?

I think of the last time I saw him—his warm attention. I think of the note he left me. It doesn't make sense. My hands shake. I press them together, squeeze them tightly. I shouldn't feel so shattered. I'd decided to avoid him after all. To end it before it ever really began.

The bell rings just as Catherine slides in next to me, those bright eyes of hers luminous beneath the room's harsh fluorescent glare.

"Hey," she says, breathless from her long hike from the art building. "What's up?" She glances over her shoulder and continues mildly, "I see that they're back. Oh . . . and here he comes."

I watch from the corner of my eye as Will passes our table, subtly dropping a note next to Catherine's elbow.

Her lips twist into a smile. "I'm guessing that's for you."

I glare at the paper, resist seizing it. "I don't want it. Tear it up."

She looks at me in surprise. "Are you serious?"

I snatch up the note, tear it into small pieces as Will collects his pass from Mr. Henke. When he turns to leave the room, our eyes meet for the barest moment. His gaze slides over the tiny pile of shredded paper. A shutter falls over his eyes, like clouds descending on a forest, and my chest tightens.

"Ooookay." Catherine looks from the torn pile of paper to me. "That was dramatic. Want to tell me what's going on?"

Unable to speak, I shake my head, crack open my chemistry book, and stare blindly at the page, telling myself that I'm glad he ignored me. I needed this to remember the vow I made to myself to stay away from him. I'm even glad I ripped up his note. Glad he saw the shredded little pile.

Tonight. Now more than ever, I have to fly, have to give it another try. I have only myself to rely on, and I'm enough. I have to believe that. It's always been true before.

Later that night, I slide out from beneath the covers and locate my shoes at the foot of the bed. I was careful to mark where I left them, not wanting to fumble in the dark and risk waking Tamra.

This late, the room is dark. No outside light slips through the blinds. Tamra's side of the room is tomb black. Hopefully, the night outside is just as dark. With clouds. Clouds and dark night. The perfect cover.

Hooking my fingers inside the heels of my shoes, I ease out of the bedroom, wincing when the floor creaks beneath my weight. I hold my breath and speed tiptoe through the house, not even exhaling until I'm safely outside.

Mrs. Hennessey's lights are off—luckily her yappy little dog doesn't break into barking at the gate's soft clink.

At the street, I squat on the curb and slip my socks and shoes on, looking to the sky as I tie my laces. Full moon and cloudless. Unfortunate, that. But not enough for me to change my mind.

On my feet, I set out, walking toward the golf course I'd visited before, telling myself that tonight would be different. I'd manifest easily, lift high, swim on the air like I used to do . . . like I'm born to do. I cover the five miles in good time. The course lifts up like a shock of green undulating sea ahead, an abrupt change from the desert and rock everywhere else.

With a stealthy look around, I cross into a world of pulsing, verdant green. The closest thing I've seen to vegetation since I left the mountains. Except for the heat, the dryness that makes my hair crackle and skin itch, I could almost pretend that the desert has vanished.

Slipping off my shoes and socks, I step onto the green, enjoying the cushion of grass under my feet. I pass a sand trap. A strategically placed set of boulders. Ahead, a pond shines like glass. My pace lengthens as I stride to a small copse of trees. I shed my clothes, and dry heat hugs my body.

Sighing, I lift my face and inhale the thin, baked air, bringing it inside me, letting it fill my lungs. I stretch out my arms, willing the manifest. . . .

I close my eyes, focus and concentrate like never before.

No! It's even harder than the other times.

The bones of my face pull, hone to sharply cut lines and angles. My breathing quickens as my nose shifts, ridges pushing forth with a slight crackling of bone and cartilage. It hurts a little. Like my body doesn't like it. Fights it. Doesn't want it to happen.

Gradually, my limbs loosen, lengthen. My human skin melts away, replaced with thicker skin—tight, contracting draki flesh.

A hot tear slides down my cheek. A moan spits from my

lips, pushing me over the edge.

My flesh blurs, glimmers gold and red. Deep, purring vibrations well up from my chest.

At last, my wings push free, unfurl, the gossamer width of each one snapping open behind me, circulating the loose air. I push off immediately and want to weep at the struggle of it, the impossibility of it all.

My muscles burn, scream in protest. Behind me, my wings work, snapping savagely to lift me up on air. Air with no density. No substance. My wings fight for purchase, for something to grasp, struggling to climb higher. *So. Hard. So hard!*

I lift up, breathless from the effort. Frustrated tears prick my eyes, blur my vision. Moisture I don't need to lose.

Green swells far beneath me. I blink, scan wide, focus on the red-tiled rooftops stretching into the horizon. In the far distance, the lights of cars on a highway look small. Farther still, mountains spill like a splash of liquid against the night.

I hover, suspended in ink, the smack of my wings on the air jarring slaps.

My body doesn't feel right. Even my lungs feel oddly . . . *small*. Powerless and ordinary. The coldly functioning human Jacinda feels more natural than this. And that makes me want to scream. Grieve.

Still, I force it, fly over the green course, struggle to gain speed, too wary to fly beyond in case I can't hold the manifest. I drink air, forcing it down my throat in gulps. Only it doesn't help. Doesn't fill me. Doesn't expand my shriveling lungs.

I persist, exerting myself until my ragged breath is the only sound ripping through my head. At last I give up, stop, descend in an unwinding circle. Like the fluttering of a dying moth.

With a sobbing breath, I touch down, return to the copse of trees. Demanifest. There, I bow at the waist, clutch my stomach, my body punishing me for what it's no longer willing to do. Spasms rack me as I dry-heave. The wretching sounds are ugly. The agony endless.

I grab a tree with one hand, dig my fingers into the bark. Feel a nail split from the pressure.

At last, it ends. With shaking hands, I dress myself, and then fall weakly onto my back, arms wide at my sides, palms open. Limp. The beat of my heart fades to a dull fearful thud perceptible only at the wrists.

The ground beneath me is quiet. I sense no gems. No energy. Below the carpet of grass there is only hard, dead earth.

I knot my hand into a fist and beat the ground once. Hard. It doesn't give. Beneath the thin cushion of grass, the earth sleeps without a heart.

I stare up at the black night through the latticework of branches. For a moment, I can kid myself. Pretend that my body does not hurt. Pretend that I'm home again, staring up at the night through a thick growth of pine branches. That nurturing forest presses around me. Shielding and covering with a loving hand.

Az is near me. Together we stare up at the sky, talking, laughing, unworried for tomorrow. I delude myself awhile longer. Smile like a fool in the dark as I enjoy this game of pretend, remembering when everything was simple and I had only Cassian's dark-eyed stare to endure.

In hindsight, it seems such a small nuisance. Before this hell.

12

*E*ventually, I rise and head for home. *Home.* The word lacks any comfort.

It's slow going. My body aches, feels beaten and heavy with every stride. The night is still. No cars drive through the quiet neighborhood at this late hour. My soles scrape the pavement. I follow the meandering sidewalk, watching my shoes fall one after the other on sun-bleached concrete. I turn the corner of my street.

Close now to Mrs. Hennessey's, I look up.

Headlights round the opposite corner, growing larger. I edge the sidewalk, distancing myself from the street. The vehicle is nearly even with Mrs. Hennessey's house, its engine a heavy purr.

It slows. So do I.

I don't need anyone spotting me out this late. Don't need a friend of Mrs. Hennessey or another neighbor mentioning it to my mother.

By now, I can tell it's not a car. A truck? The windshield glints like a mirror as it rolls closer to the curb. My skin shivers and my pulse jackknifes against the flesh at my neck. I've seen enough crime television to feel instant apprehension. And I know enough to trust my instincts.

I brace myself, slowing down so that I'm barely walking. I wait, watch, assess with a quick darting of my eyes. I grab hold of my apprehension before it explodes into full-scale fear and I manifest . . . assuming I can.

Then I see it. There's a light bar on top, unlit. Like it's in stealth mode. I see that and I understand.

They're here. Where I live. Stalking me. Somehow they figured it out. Figured out the truth about me. Maybe Will recognized me at last and is here to revoke his act of mercy from that day in the mountains.

They see me then. The Land Rover guns forward, straight for me.

Turning, I run.

Adrenaline pumps through me and overrides my sick weariness of moments ago. I'm being hunted all over again. Except this time I'm in a strange city. In a body I no longer know.

Before, this afraid, I would have instantly manifested. It's an instinct a draki is powerless to resist. That I'm still clinging to my human form can only mean I'm dying, weakening.

My sneakers pound against the sidewalk, the loud slaps filling my head, mingling with the rush of blood in my ears . . . the accelerating roar of the Land Rover's engine behind me. Like a great monster come to life.

The street stretches ahead of me. Nowhere to hide, nowhere to lose myself as long as I follow its open path.

I risk it, launch across the street and cut a hard right into a yard. Tires screech, burn on asphalt. I move, not looking back as I attack a fence, the soles of my shoes stomping upward, shuddering over the wood. I grab the top. The pointy tips of the pickets cut into my palms.

I haul myself over the fence and through a yard of rock and cacti. Scale another fence and find myself in someone's front yard.

My flesh tightens, ripples with heat. The bridge of my nose pushes out, ridges rising. My lungs start to burn and smolder, chest vibrating. My draki at last. I suppose I should take comfort in this. Joy that I can feel myself responding. That I'm *not* completely dead inside.

A screech of brakes attacks my ears. Headlights swing wildly in the night. I turn and hit a fence again.

"Jacinda! Stop! Wait!"

I can't help it. The voice instantly reaches me, pulls me back like an invisible hand. Dangling from the fence, I look over my shoulder.

He stands beneath a streetlight, his brown hair gleaming

gold where the light strikes. His eyes seem gold, too. Glittery and burning as they stare at me, the Land Rover purring only a few feet from him. He holds out a hand, as if to pacify some wild creature he intends to tame.

"Will." The name escapes me, too soft for him to hear.

I blink long and hard, let the fear fade . . . and with it my draki. Opening my eyes, I drop down from the fence.

My gaze scans the street, looking for others. Unless someone's hiding in the car, he's alone. I release a shaky breath.

That hand still stretches toward me.

"What are you doing out here this late?" A frown pulls at his mouth. "It's one in the morning."

"Me?" I walk across the lawn slowly, still not fully trusting. "What are *you* doing here?" And no, I don't believe he had just been driving by. "Are you stalking me?" *Hunting me?* I want to add.

He blinks. Some of the tension carving his face loosens then. Replaced with something else. He rubs at the back of his neck. The move is self-conscious. Innately human. *Embarrassed.*

"I—"

"You *are*," I pronounce, an unbidden smile coming to my mouth.

"Look," he grumbles, his eyes angry. Defensive. "I just wanted to see where you live."

I stop before him. "Why?"

He rubs the back of his neck again, this time the motion is savage, annoyed. With me or himself, I'm not sure. To our left, a porch light flares on. I jerk, squint against the flood of unfriendly yellow light.

"C'mon!" Will urges at the sound of a front door lock clicking free.

Panicked, I run—don't even hesitate as Will yanks open the passenger door for me. I jump inside, instantly assailed by the smell of leather upholstery. The door thuds shut behind me.

For a moment, I'm alone. I glance around at all the shiny gadgets and knobs in the vast dash. I peer at the back. It's huge and could comfortably hold several bodies. I shudder at the thought of who those bodies usually are.

Will climbs in beside me before I can rethink where I'm sitting and pulls away from the curb just as a man in a bath-robe emerges from his house.

Slowly, it dawns on me. I'm with a draki hunter. At one in the morning. We're all alone.

And no one knows where I am.

That this could be the stupidest thing I've ever done crosses my mind. When Will drives in the *opposite* direction of my house, I'm convinced it is.

"You do know where I live, right?" I ask.

"Yes."

"So why aren't you taking me there?"

"I thought we could talk."

"Okay," I say slowly, squeeze my thighs with both hands. When he doesn't say anything, I ask, "How did you know where I live?"

"It's not hard to find out. Your address is on file in the school office."

"You broke into the school office?"

"No. I know one of the office aides. She got me your address that first day."

My first day. He's had my address all this time. Why? I cross my arms. Cool air blasts from the vents, I shiver a little. Only not from the cold.

He adjusts a dial. "Cold?"

"Why did you need my address?"

"Just in case I wanted to find you. See you."

Evidently, he did.

"That's funny considering you ignored me in class today."

"You ripped up my note," he accuses. A muscle feathers the flesh of his jaw.

"It doesn't matter." I shrug and roll a shoulder, rotating the joint.

"Yes. It does. You should have read it."

I resist asking what the note said, refusing to be sucked in. I decided to stay away from him. I can't care, can't let him get to me. "Were you planning on ringing my doorbell at one in the morning?"

"Of course not—"

"Then why—"

"I don't sleep well. I figured I could at least see where you live."

He didn't sleep well? That makes two of us. But what keeps him awake? Guilt? The blood of my kind that stains his hands? Or could it have to do with me?

He asked me out and then changed his mind—treated me like a leper in study hall. Why? I want to know, but don't dare ask. That's only inviting trouble. Opening a door I had vowed to forever seal.

Quiet surrounds us. So thick I can taste it. He sends me a sidelong glance, the gold of his hazel eyes sparking warmth in my chest, igniting a burn I thought was dying.

With a single look, the embers stir. Leaves rattling, waking from a sudden wind. He does that to me. No matter how I try to believe I don't need him to wake my draki, he proves me wrong every time. Maybe there's no separating need from want.

13

He drives for a while, aimlessly. Turning down street after street. They all look alike. Middle-class homes in varying shades of white and beige stucco line the sidewalks. Tiled roofs undulate like a red sea.

My heart races, excited at his nearness. Alive as it hasn't felt in the days that stretch like years behind me.

I'm aware of the promise I made to myself. The promise to avoid him. I feel its echo in my head. In my bones.

But I recall the other promise I made to myself when I first came here. A promise to keep my draki alive whatever the cost. And around him, my draki can hardly contain itself. It *definitely* lives.

I gently grip my thighs and slide my hands over my skin,

chafing my goose-bumped flesh. Until I persuade Mom to take us back, getting close to him might be the only way. And letting him get close to me . . . My heart trips at the thought of this.

His low voice breaks the stillness. "You didn't say what you were doing out this late."

"I couldn't sleep either," I reply. Not a lie.

His mouth curves. "So we're perfect for each other. A pair of insomniacs."

Perfect for each other.

I grin a mad, stupid smile.

Even when his smile fades, I can't stop grinning—can't play down the dumb happiness tripping through me.

"You're bleeding," he announces, quickly veering to the side of the street and setting the car in park.

I follow his gaze down, to the streak of blood on the top of my thigh. Panic squeezes my heart. Flipping my hand over, I see the small tear in the plump ridge of my palm oozing blood. *Please, please, please.* Don't let him notice.

In full light, it's easy enough to detect the purple shimmer of my blood. In this gloom, it's surely too subtle for him to note. At least I tell myself this as I draw in a deep breath.

"It's nothing. I cut myself on the fence." Will pulls his shirt over his head. My breath locks in my throat. His chest is broad, smooth. Muscles and sinew cut his body, ripple beneath his skin. He wads up the fabric of his shirt and presses it into my palm. Like I've suffered a mortal wound.

"N-no, really," I sputter, fingers flexing, itching to touch his chest, to feel him. "You'll ruin your shirt."

"It was my fault you were on that fence. Let me do this, okay."

Mutely, I nod. I can't resist anyway. The press of his fingers on my hand feels like points of heat on my skin. I close my eyes in a slow blink. His gallantry reminds me of the first time we touched. Together in that small cave. The closeness. The way his eyes devoured me.

This close to him, I inhale, drink in his smell. The salty warmth of his skin. Lush forest. Wet wind. I know where he's been. Where he hunted. Instantly, I'm home.

I open my eyes and study his face, the rapid pulse jumping against his throat. His nostrils flare, like he's scenting me back.

His gaze drops to the smooth stretch of my thigh and to the streak of plum-colored blood. My flesh gleams golden from the light of a nearby streetlight. At least I think it's because of that. *Please, don't let me be manifesting, too.*

He lowers his hand. It shakes on the way down. His head bends close to mine. Our breaths merge, mingle. I quiver, tense as his hand touches my trembling thigh. Air hisses between my teeth.

His gaze flicks to my face for a moment. Questioning. The centers of his eyes are so dark, the surrounding hazel irises luminous and glowing. He looks back down, his face stark, intent on my thigh, on the smudge of blood marring my skin.

Again, I'm reminded that he's a predator. In that hungry look on his face, I see him for what he is. A hunter.

His thumb grazes the thin streak of blood, smearing it. I gasp, singed from the caress.

"Your skin." His thumb strokes again.

My belly tightens, almost hurting.

He frowns. "It's so hot."

And I am, I realize, feeling the deep fume building inside. Steam expands my lungs. I need to stop him. Pull away from his touch. The familiar shaking vibration starts at my core, and I know what's coming if I don't break away.

So many things about this—about *him*—should fill me with fear. Should make me want to run. But I only want more. More Will.

My stomach clenches at the sensation of his hand on my thigh. His thumb brushes me, wipes the blood clean, then lifts away. I inhale through my nose.

He lifts his shirt from my hand and examines my injury. "It's not bad," he announces.

I nod, my heart racing too fast for me to speak.

He continues, "Do you have antiseptic at home?"

I still can't speak. Is he really talking about first aid? My leg tingles, throbs where he touched me. His gentle grip on my hand has the same effect.

At my silence, he looks up. Traps me in those hazel eyes,

the pupils dilated, large and tar black. Strange but beautiful. I wonder then if he's on some kind of drug. Something inside me denies this though. Either because I can't sense it in him, or I simply don't want it to be true.

"You're different," I whisper, staring, forgetting about his question. My palms prickle, tickling at the centers, yearning to feel him . . . to touch his face, the broad expanse of his chest.

He stares back, consuming me with his eyes.

You're different from your cousins, I think. Different from anything I ever heard about hunters. Different from the draki boys I've known. Cassian's watchful eyes never made me breathless. Never brought my draki to life, made me pulse with awareness.

I wet my lips and take a deep, shuddering breath. "Where are your cousins? Don't you pretty much do everything together?"

Because I need to remember this. Always. Because even if I don't think he's a threat to me, they are.

A shutter falls over his eyes. He pulls back, releases my hand. "Someone's been educating you on me and my family, I see."

"You're the one who told me to stay away from them. Naturally you provoked my curiosity. People talked, I listened." Well, Catherine at least.

He nods slowly. "Yeah. I said that. And you should." Sighing, he drags a hand through his hair. "And while you're at it, I guess you should stay away from me, too. That's what I *should* be telling you." He drops his head back on the head-rest and closes his eyes, his expression suffering and intense. Again, I want to touch him, to stroke a hand down the plane of his cheek and ease whatever it is that gnaws at him.

His words echo inside me. *You should stay away from me.* Something I already know, but sitting in the front seat of his car, I'm not quite succeeding at that. I wish I could. Wish I didn't feel this pull, this constant tug toward him. Wish my draki didn't revive around him. I slide my left hand beneath my thigh, trapping it there.

"You're the one who chased me down," I remind him, then wince. I slip my hand free to rub my thigh, where the burn of his touch still pulses.

"You're right." Opening his eyes, he puts the Land Rover in drive and rolls away from the curb. After a few turns, I realize he's driving me home. Desperation spikes inside me, makes me ask quickly, "Why did you come to my house tonight?" *In the middle of the night?*

His knuckles whiten where they clutch the steering wheel. "I didn't expect to see you outside, but . . ."

"Yes?" I prompt.

He slams the vehicle to a stop in front of my house. Kills the lights. Twists in his seat to face me. Leaning close, he stretches one arm along the back of my seat, nearly touching my shoulder.

His expression is inscrutable. His eyes look strange with

their pulsing pupils. "You're not like other girls. You're special."

Intoxicating warmth crawls over my cheeks. I'm glad at this confession. Glad that I'm as unique to him as he is to me. Back home, I only ever felt safe, protected, and revered. Even with Cassian, I never felt like he liked me for *me*, but rather for what I brought the pride.

Every moment with Will, I feel at risk, exposed. Danger hangs close, as tangible as the heavy mists I've left behind. And I can't get enough of it. Of him. I crave his nearness still. Like a drug needed to survive, to get by each day. An addiction. A powerful, consuming thing.

"I've tried to deny it," he continues, "but it's there, staring me in the face every time I see you. If you were like other girls . . ." He laughs hoarsely. "If you were like other girls I wouldn't even be here."

Suddenly self-conscious, I fidget, flex my fingers around my knees. He wouldn't be here if he knew the truth. Who I am, *what* I am.

I wet my lips. "I'm not what you think . . ."

It's close. Too close. As close as I can ever get to admitting the truth to him.

"I thought maybe—" He stops, shakes his head.

"What?" I barely recognize my voice it's so strained, so tight. The beat of my heart fills my ears. A hope I can't understand, never felt before, flutters inside my belly.

"Never mind. It's stupid." His voice drops, hoarse and

nearly inaudible. "Just forget I came to see you." He mutters something so low I can't make it out, but I think it's a curse. "This can't work. Not with my family. They're . . . different."

"What's wrong with your family?" I ask even though I already know. Well, I know what's wrong with them according to me. Will's reasons may differ.

His lips twist, make him look almost cruel. Like the hunter I don't want him to be. "Let's just say we don't get along."

I try for an innocent look. "Your father—"

"He's not exactly the toss-a-football-in-the-backyard type. As soon as I graduate, I'm gone."

Relief runs through me. This confirms that he's not like them. Not a hunter, not a killer. I try not to look too happy. To keep what I'm feeling on the inside from surfacing.

Wetting my lips, I ask, "And in the meantime, you can't have any friends?"

He drags a hand through his hair. The gold-brown locks feather, then fall back into place. "It's a bit complicated, but yeah, I don't want to get close to anyone . . . bring anyone around my family." His gaze locks with mine. Grim. Resolute. "They're poison, Jacinda. I can't expose you to them. I wouldn't expose anyone I care about to them." He shakes his head. "I didn't mean to lead you on. I'm sorry I asked you out, sorry that I can't . . ." His fingers flex on the steering wheel until he regains his voice. "I'm just *sorry*."

130

My chest aches. Because he feels it, too. This thing, the connection between us. He feels it, and he would kill it, deny it. Whatever impulse brought him here, he won't act on it.

I suppose that's a good thing, but I can't muster up much gratitude.

He motions to Mrs. Hennessey's house. "You better go inside."

Angry heat tightens my skin. "Never took you for a coward," I blurt.

His head snaps in my direction. "What do you mean by that?"

"You came here tonight for a reason. Why don't you own up to it?" Before I can think about it, I lean across the center console and stare him directly in the face. "Do you always run from what you want?"

Maybe I'm going out on a limb to imply he wants *me*, but the pulse throbbing at his neck tells me it's so. And he is here, after all.

His gaze drops to my mouth. "I can't think of the last time I had anything I truly wanted," he says huskily, so low I could hardly hear him. It's more like I felt him.

His words echo through me, striking a chord so deep that I'm sure there's a reason for all this. A reason we've found each other, first in the mountains and now here. A reason. Something more. Something bigger than coincidence. "Me too."

He leans across the console. Sliding a hand behind my neck, he tugs my face closer. I move like fluid, melting toward him. "Maybe it's time to change that then."

At the first brush of his mouth, stinging heat surges through me, shocking me motionless. My veins and skin pop and pulse.

I rise on my knees, clutch his shoulders with clawing fingers, trying to get closer. My hands drift, rounding over his smooth shoulders, skimming down a rock-hard chest. His heart beats like a drum beneath my fingers. My blood burns, lungs expand and smolder. I can't draw enough air through my nose . . . or at least not enough to chill my steaming lungs.

His hands slide over my cheeks, holding my face. His skin feels like ice to my blistering flesh, and I kiss him harder.

"Your skin," he whispers against my mouth, "it's so . . ."

I drink him in, his words, his touch, moaning at his taste, at the sudden burning pull of my skin. The delicious tugging in my back.

He kisses me deeper with cool, dry lips. Moves his hands down my face, along my jaw to my neck. His fingertips graze beneath my ear, and I shiver. "Your skin is so soft, so warm . . ."

And then I grasp what exactly the tingling itch in my back means. My wings are awake. Ready and eager in a way I haven't felt since arriving in Chaparral. They push at my back, on the verge of bursting free.

I break away with a cry and reach for the handle. With a pained gasp, I fling open the door and stumble out, land hard on my knees on the lawn.

I get to my feet and don't bother shutting the door . . . just rush away.

His desperate shout follows me. "Jacinda!"

Several feet away, a safe enough distance that he won't be able to detect any of the subtle differences in my appearance, I stop and look back, my chest rising and falling with deep, overheated breaths.

He leans across the console, practically in the passenger seat. Something passes over his face. An emotion I can't read. Can't understand. "I'll see you at school," he calls with such decisiveness, it's like there's no question of this.

Without answering him, without agreeing, I turn and storm up the driveway as fast as my legs can carry me. Right.

"Jacinda!" he bellows my name, and I wince, hoping he doesn't wake Mrs. Hennessey or the neighbors.

I didn't say it, but my answer was there, in my face, in my stumbling haste to get away from him. He heard it loud and clear, and apparently he didn't like it. Apparently, our kiss only convinced him that we needed to pursue this thing between us.

Except, our kiss told me the opposite. Kissing him told me what I already knew, but had been denying. I can't risk being with him. Even if he got over his hang-ups about being around me, I still have plenty of my own. It's one thing to draw strength from him . . . another thing entirely to become so swept up that I manifest in his presence. I know that now. Know what I have to do.

At school, I won't talk to him, won't look at him . . . and I certainly won't ever *touch* him again.

If it kills me, I'll ignore him and forever keep my distance.

As I hurry down the path, my fingers curl inward and brush my injured palm, lightly, idly tracing the torn flesh, stroking the dampness there. *Blood.* My blood. Evidence of what I am.

Panic claws my heart, squeezes tightly in my chest.

I jerk to a stop and whirl around like I still might find Will at the curb, but he's gone. The shirt . . . is gone. Gone and headed into the den of my enemies.

Closing my eyes, I shake my head, dread clawing up my throat. He's gone. He left with a shirt covered in my blood. My purple-hued draki blood.

When he sees it he'll figure it out. He'll know exactly what I am.

The house is silent when I slip inside, moving like a shadow through rooms that feel like they're closing in on me. Now more than ever. Tamra is a motionless shape beneath the covers as I quietly kick off my shoes.

The bed dips from my weight. I exhale as I pull the covers to my chin, fold my hands over my chest, and strive for a calm I don't feel, all my thoughts tangled up in the shirt bearing my blood that's now in Will's possession.

"If you ruin this for me, I'll never forgive you."

Strangely, my sister's disembodied voice stretching across the dark doesn't startle me. Not with my head spinning with rapid schemes to reclaim the evidence that I'm not human.

She doesn't ask for an explanation, and I don't offer one. It's enough that I snuck out, and she knows it. As far as she's concerned, I can't be up to anything good.

Her bed squeaks as she rolls onto her side. I can think of nothing to say. Nothing to reassure her. Nothing to make me feel less guilty, less selfish.

My lips hum from the memory of Will's kiss. I almost lost it back there. Almost exposed myself. Almost ruined us all.

And that still might happen if I don't get my hands on Will's shirt.

I have to get it back. At any cost.

14

The following day sweat traces my spine as I run the last mile to Will's house, the hard smack of my shoes on asphalt strangely fortifying.

I promised Mom I would be back before dinner. She likes to eat early on Saturday evenings. There's enough tension in the house that I don't want to upset her.

If I'm lucky, Will uses a hamper like Tamra and I do. I picture the shirt wadded up inside it, my blood, purple and iridescent and gleaming even when free of my body, unnoticeable. Hopefully. He of all people would recognize the purple stains for what they are. Discovering I'm draki exposes us all. Puts every draki at risk, even Mom and Tamra. Just by relation to me their lives would be forfeit.

I slow as I approach his house, spotting the Spanish-tiled roof between the trees. I memorized the directions Catherine gave me over the phone. I knew I liked her for a reason. Other than a meaningful *hmmm*, she didn't pry and ask why I wanted to know where Will lived.

The gate is open, so I run down the drive, hesitating only a moment before the sweeping portico when I notice the Land Rover parked outside the detached garage. I jerk in place for a moment, debating my next move.

In a perfect world, the house would be vacant with a window left open or unlocked. I would slip inside, find the shirt, and be out in five minutes. But my world has never been perfect.

I don't have a choice. I can't risk another day. I just have to play it out. With an ugly mutter, I push on.

Before I can reconsider, I'm up the front steps and knocking on the large double doors. The sound echoes, like a great cavern or abyss stretches out on the other side. I wait, wishing I had worn something other than my striped running shorts and tank top. I'd scraped my hair back into a ponytail that hangs like a horse's tail down my back. Not my best look.

When the door starts to swing open, that feeling sweeps over me again and I know Will's on the other side before I see him.

He doesn't even try to look happy to see me. Given how fast I fled his car yesterday, it's no wonder he looks surprised.

"Jacinda. What are you doing here?"

I toss back his explanation from the night before. "I thought I would check out where you live. You know. Just in case."

He doesn't laugh, doesn't even smile at my joke—the reversal of his words last night. Instead, he looks uneasily over his shoulder. At least he's not shouting out an alarm that a draki is on his doorstep. Clearly he hasn't examined his shirt closely.

"Aren't you going to invite me in?"

"Will? Who's here?" The door pulls wider. A man with Will's hazel eyes steps up beside him. The similarity ends with the eyes. Not as tall as Will, he's wiry, like he spends a lot of time in the gym, honing his body.

"Oh, hello." Unlike Will, he smiles easily, but it's empty. Like he does it all the time without meaning.

"Dad, this is Jacinda. From school."

"Jacinda," he says warmly, reaching for my hand. And I offer it to him. Shake hands with the devil himself, see in his eyes, feel in his touch, that he's nothing like Will. This hunter would never let a draki escape.

"Mr. Rutledge," I manage to say in a normal voice. "Nice to meet you."

His hand surrounds my crawling flesh. "Likewise. Will doesn't bring many of his friends around."

"Dad," Will says tightly.

He releases my hand and claps Will on the back. "Okay,

I'll stop embarrassing you." He looks at me again, his expression avid as he surveys me with obvious approval. "Jacinda, join us. We're grilling on the back deck."

"Dad, I don't think—"

"I would love that," I lie. Eating with Will's dad ranks right up there with having my teeth drilled, but I have to get inside. It's not just about me. Tamra, Mom, the pride, draki everywhere . . . leaving *that* shirt in *this* house puts us all in peril.

Mr. Rutledge waves me inside. I sweep past Will into the frigidly chill house.

"Do you like brisket, Jacinda? It's been smoking since this morning. It should be ready soon."

Will falls in beside me as we follow his dad through the vast entrance hall. Our steps echo over the tiled floor. The house is coolly perfect. Lifeless art hangs on the walls and solid white fans whir down at us from the double-high ceiling as we file down a wide corridor.

Will's voice is a rasp near my ear. "What are you doing here?"

And with that question, I'm struck with being *here*. In *his* home, my enemy's lair. Is this where they bring captive draki? Before selling them to the enkros? My skin ripples, fear dangerously close. I suck in a breath and chafe a hand over my arm, reining in my imagination.

"Are you so disappointed to see me?" I ask, finding courage. His dad rounds a corner ahead of us. "You wanted to see me last night." I nearly choke on the reminder. Last night I almost thought he would chase me into my house.

He grabs my arm and pulls me to a stop. Those changeable eyes of his rove my face, searching. I sense his confusion, his inability to understand me . . . or why I'm here. "I want to see you, I haven't thought of anything else. . . ." He pauses, looking uncomfortable. "Just not here."

"Will? Jacinda? Come on!"

He flinches at his father's voice. His gaze flickers beyond me, over my shoulder. "We can see each other somewhere else. I told you how I felt about my family. You shouldn't be here," he says quietly.

"Well, I *am* here, and I'm not leaving." I pull my arm free and walk ahead, calling over my shoulder, "Just in time, too. I'm hungry."

"Jacinda," he pleads, his voice tinged with a desperation I just don't get. I'm certain his determination to keep me out of his home, away from his family, is tangled up in the fact that he's a draki hunter. But what does that have to do with me? He doesn't know what I am. His family shouldn't suspect anything just because he has a girl over to his house.

Will catches up with me in a kitchen of gleaming surfaces and state-of-the-art appliances. I sense his anxiety as we step through the French doors onto the deck. Several faces turn to stare. No one speaks.

Mr. Rutledge motions at me as he opens the lid to the smoker. "Everyone, this is—"

"Jacinda," Xander supplies, rising from a wrought-iron chair, a sweating bottle of soda in his hand. "Will, I didn't know you were bringing a date."

Angus munches from a large bag of potato chips, not bothering to stand or speak, just watching with his thuggish stare.

"Must have slipped my mind." Will guides me to one of the patio tables and introduces me to the others: Xander's parents, a set of uncles and aunts, several more cousins. Hunters all, I realize. At least those over thirteen. I don't imagine the toddler sucking a juice box or the swinging seven-year-old hunts. Yet.

They all welcome me, assessing me with the same avidity I'd endured from Will's father. As we eat, I'm subjected to a battery of questions. *Where do you live? Where did you move from? What do your parents do? Do you have siblings? Do you play sports?* Like I'm being interviewed. Mr. Rutledge seems most interested that I run . . . that I ran the seven miles to their house.

"She's fast, too," Will volunteers, almost grudgingly, like he knows small talk is expected but doesn't wish to contribute.

"Really." Mr. Rutledge arches his brows. "Long-distance running requires great stamina. I've always been impressed with those capable of such endurance."

Throughout our dialogue, Xander studies me across the table, quietly intent. Will at my side gives me some comfort.

That and the gentle misters spraying cooling vapor over the patio. My skin drinks it in.

When the meal winds down, Will's aunts rise to fetch dessert from the kitchen. I see my chance and jump up to help. In the kitchen, I break free, excusing myself to use the restroom.

I take the stairs off the main entry. My sneakers race silently over a red runner as I open doors and stick my head inside room after room until I find Will's.

Even if I didn't sense his long-imbued presence, I would have known the wood-paneled room belonged to him. It lacks the cold precision of the rest of the house. The bed is made, but otherwise it feels lived in. Books and magazines litter a bedside table. His literature book lies open on the desk, a half-written essay beside it. A framed photo of a woman with Will's gold-brown hair sits there also, and I know it's his mother, see him in her smiling face.

Tearing my gaze away, I open his closet and spot the hamper below his hanging clothes. Digging through the garments, I pull out the bloodied shirt with a gasp of relief. Clutching it in my shaking hands, I close the closet door, my pulse a feverish throb at my neck. What am I going to do with it now?

As I carefully peer out into the hall, an idea forms to hide the shirt somewhere outside, maybe in the front bushes where I can collect it later, after I've managed to extricate myself. The plan burns through my mind as I hurry down the hall, pleased with myself but still wary. Locating the shirt had almost been too easy.

Gradually, a sound penetrates—thudding footsteps ascending the stairs.

Panic flares hotly in my chest. I dive into the nearest room, closing the door with a soft click behind me. I grip the door latch, ears straining to hear the slightest movement on the other side. I stave off the fiery grip of fear with sharp sips of breath and focus on cooling my lungs. Manifesting now would be the worst possible scenario.

My gaze drills into the door, almost as if I can see through it to the other side. Releasing the latch, I ease back a step, then another. My eyes fasten, unblinking on that door as I strangle the shirt in my hands. As if I might somehow kill it, cease its existence. If I could manifest and burn it to cinders without setting off any smoke alarms I would.

As the moments pass, and no one comes, the tension ebbs from my shoulders. Breathing easier, I turn my attention to the room in which I find myself.

Horror strikes me full force. Cripples me motionless. My gaze flies, taking it all in with dizzying speed.

Draki skin stares back at me . . . everywhere.

The desk, the lamp shades, the furniture. All are covered in the flesh of my brethren. Bile climbs up my throat.

My knees give out and I stagger, reach to a chair for support then snatch my hand away with a pained hiss. I drop the shirt, gazing in horror at the gleaming black upholstery I touched, onyx flesh, shockingly familiar with its iridescent winks of purple. My father flashes across my mind. *Could it be . . .*

No! Sick fury seizes me. I slap both hands over my mouth, stifling a scream, fingers digging into my cheeks. My eyes sting and I realize I'm weeping. Tears tumble over my hands.

Still, I look around, rotate in a small circle, choke back a sob at the pillows on the sofa covered in the deep bronze of an earth draki—the second-most common type of my kind, marked for its hyper-ability to find gems, edible vegetation, underground water . . . anything relating to soil. To see their remains here, in this house, in this desert, so far from the earth they love, is devastating.

I look away, too sick to look at the vile evidence of my race's murder.

My gaze lands on a giant map of North America stretched out on one wall. Black, green, and red flags scatter widely across it, grouped predominantly in mountainous areas ideal for draki existence. My stomach tightens as the significance sinks in. I lower my hands from my face and inch closer, my eyes devouring the sight of all those black flags. So many. I tremble at what they might represent.

Only two red flags jut out from the map, but they're larger than the others. Isolated, no black or green flags surround them. One is in Canada. The other in Washington. *Kill zones? Dead zones?*

My eyes feverishly scan the map, honing in on the Cascade Mountains, the small corner where I'd lived my entire life. And there, I see two other flags. One green. One black. I twist my hands until I can't feel my fingers anymore.

The green flag sits in the general area of my home, and beside it, the single black flag casts its shadow. *A single black flag.* Automatically, I think of Dad. He's the only draki in our pride to have met an unnatural end in two generations. I stare at that single black flag until my eyes ache. A dark, terrible knowing drags across my flesh. It's a kill flag.

A horrible suspicion sinks into me, coiling around me like a serpent. *Will might be part of the group that killed my father.*

We're only a few hundred miles south of our pride. . . . It should have occurred to me sooner. And maybe it had, maybe it's been there all along; I just refused to face it. Staring at the map, I can't avoid it anymore. Clearly, they hunt in our area. I've always known that.

My eyes start to sting and I blink rapidly. It's horrible to believe. A bitter pill going down, sticking in my throat.

Dad understood me. Understood that I needed to fly. Because he felt the same way. He would never have expected me to suppress my draki. I don't want to believe Will is responsible for taking the only member of my family who loved me for me.

I shake my head hard. He was probably too young to hunt then. In my gut, I believe this. He's different. Will let me escape. He couldn't have killed my father.

But his family could have. And they're just downstairs.

Bending, I snatch the shirt back up, urging myself to go, run, escape this house before it's too late. Before I can't leave.

But I can't tear my eyes from that wall. Like a horrible car crash, it's all I can see.

The sound of a door clicking shut behind me jerks me from my horrified trance.

15

I try to keep it together as I turn to face Xander, pushing the fear down with a desperate swipe, struggling not
to think about where he's found me . . . about the horror
of standing in a room buried in the severed skin of my
race.

"What are you doing here?" he demands.

"I was looking for a bathroom." Blinking my eyes dry, I
breathe air thinly through my nose, concentrating on chilling the expanding heat of my windpipe.

"There's one off the kitchen." He cocks his head, studies
me with glinting-dark eyes. "Why did you come upstairs?"
His gaze moves around the room, flicking to the map before
coming back to rest on me with piercing intent. "Why are

you snooping around in here?"

"I'm not," I deny, swallowing down my throat's rising scald.

He motions to Will's shirt. "What do you have there?"

I clench the wadded fabric. "Nothing. Just a shirt."

"Will's? Why do you have it?" His gaze narrows, his lids heavy and suspicious over dark eyes. "Don't tell me you're one of those girls who sleeps with her boyfriend's lock of hair. You didn't strike me as that pathetic."

Our eyes lock. I hold silent, as still as stone. He reaches for the shirt, and I jerk back a step. I know my reaction is extreme—especially over an alleged *nothing*—but I can't help it. No way can I hand this shirt over to *him*.

He follows, crowding me. "What are you up to? Why are you really here?"

I edge back. "Will. I like Will, that's all. Why else would I be here?" I shove at his encroaching chest once with the base of my palm, my anger surpassing my panic so that I'm actually willing to touch him. "Back *off*."

He ignores me, keeps coming. "I think he likes you, too. And that's a first." His gaze rakes over me insolently, nothing spared. "What's so special about you, huh?"

I bump into the desk. My hand reaches out to grasp the edge. I gasp at the touch, remembering. Appalled, I jerk my hand away, lifting my body off the onyx-skinned desk.

He smiles darkly, not missing my reaction. "Beautiful,

isn't it?" His arm brushes mine as he reaches out and strokes the desktop.

My stomach twists violently. Afraid I'm about to be ill, I surge past him before I say or do something horrible, something I can never take back.

He grabs me as I pass, forcing me to face him again. Revolted from his touch, my skin flashes red-gold for a fraction of a second. "I can't remember the last time Will liked a girl. He doesn't *let* himself like girls. Not since he got sick . . . which leads me to believe you're something more. I confess, I'm curious."

Sick? When did Will get sick? I want to ask, but don't dare stand here another moment in this terrible room, holding a shirt bearing my blood, suffering Xander's touch and probing questions about why I'm so different.

I wrench my arm free and drive a hard line past him, air turning to wind on my face.

I don't get very far before he swings me around again. That's when the very real dread that I may never leave this room takes hold of me. His face pushes so close that I can almost see myself in the dark reflection of his eyes. "I want to know what you're doing here."

My chest rises with rapid breath, steam building, whisking to fire inside me.

"Let her go."

The voice rolls over me, a cool tide of relief. Will fills the threshold, his hands opening and flexing at his sides.

Still, Xander doesn't release me. "I caught her snooping around."

Will advances, his expression as cold as marble. "Let her go."

Xander squares off, positioning me to the side of him, still holding my arm. "Start using your brain. I caught her in *here*."

"You're making something out of nothing." Will strides forward and pulls me free. I stumble. Xander snatches the shirt from my hand.

"No," I gasp, diving back for it.

It's too late. Xander steps out of range, tossing the shirt in his hand, examining it with feigned boredom. "What's so special about this?"

He doesn't care about the shirt. Only that I seem to want it . . . and taking it upsets me.

My eyes fasten on the purple blood stains because that's all that really matters right now. My breath eats up my chest in a cloud of fire.

I know the moment Xander realizes what he's looking at, watch him closely as incredulity passes over his face, as bright and vivid as a burst of lightning.

Will recognizes it, too, and we all stand there for a stricken moment, a frozen tableau, waiting for someone to move, speak.

Will is first. He grabs the shirt from his cousin.

Xander lets it go without a fight. I can't move, don't know

what to say, do. The various scenarios I created in my mind never played out like this.

"Is that your . . . ," Xander says to Will. I think he wants to say blood. I hear it in that pause. Xander swings his gaze to me, dark eyes flashing.

I tremble, bewildered, unsure what's going on inside his head.

He turns to Will then. "What do we know about your little girlfriend here? Have you been talking out of turn? Sharing family secrets? What do *you* even know about her?"

"Don't be stupid. Let it go," Will hisses, one of his hands sliding down my arm to seize my hand. A gesture of support? Restraint? "You're wrong—and you're the one talking without thinking so *shut up.*"

Wrong about what? What does Xander suspect? I look wildly between the cousins, lost. Why isn't Xander freaking out at the draki blood on Will's shirt? Why isn't he demanding an explanation?

Will glances down. His eyes glass over as he looks at the shirt in his hand . . . sees my blood. His thumb traces a smudged purple stain, the gesture almost reverent.

"Are you going out alone now? Is that it?" Xander demands. And I get it. Xander is accusing Will of hunting draki alone. "Does your ol' man know about the risks you're taking? Damn you, Will. You think you're hot shit. . . ."

The rest of his words are lost.

Will grabs Xander by the shirtfront. "Shut *up!*"

Xander looks over Will's shoulder at me, darkly assessing. He doesn't appear concerned that he may have revealed too much. And why should he? As far as he's concerned I either already know or can't possibly guess the truth. It's too incredible.

Will flings Xander away as if he can't stand the touch of him. "If you're finished being a neurotic nut, I'd like to go downstairs for some of your mom's brownies. What about you, Jacinda? Want some brownies?" The absurdly normal question is asked roughly, like I don't have a choice at all. Will's putting an end to this interrogation.

I nod dumbly, thinking only that this is far from done. Xander saw the blood. *My* blood. Even if he doesn't realize it. And Will saw it, too. A shiver chases down my back because *he* must know.

Xander mutters something, turns to leave, but stops, an ominous glint to his eyes as he stares at me. I barely check myself from running, bolting, my draki instinct kicking in.

Will edges close to me. His nearness injects me with courage, a calm I so desperately need right now. "Go on, Xander. We'll be down in a sec."

Xander exits the room with angry strides.

Facing me, Will cuts straight to the point. "Who are you?"

I remember us in the mountains, the tenderness on his

face as he looked at me as a draki. It's on the tip of my tongue to tell him the truth, but I swallow the words back, not that foolish. It's not my place to make such a confession. Nor is *this* the place to do it. There's more to consider than myself.

"I don't know what you mean."

He stares at me for a long moment before looking away, his gaze flitting over the room with distaste. His eyes darken to the color of a shaded forest, and I know he's seeing it all for what it is. Like I do. Dead draki everywhere.

Then, his gaze drops to the shirt in his hand. "I wore this shirt when you cut your hand. This is *your* blood." He holds the shirt in the air between us, silent evidence I can't refute.

I say nothing. . . . What kind of defense can I muster?

"There's only one way a human can have blood this color," he adds.

I struggle to hide my shock. *A human can have draki blood? How is that possible?*

"*Are* you an enkros?" he demands. "How else can you . . . ." His voice fades and he gives his head a slow, dragging shake, looks a little sick.

I moisten my lips. "What's an enkros?" Is it just me or did my voice warble a bit, strangle on the question whose answer I already know?

He stares at me, waiting. As if I might make a confession now. His drilling gaze tells me he doesn't buy it. He knows I'm hiding something. He's got the shirt to prove it. He's close now, an unrelenting presence, staring at me so expectantly, determined to have his answers. "C'mon, Jacinda. You can't have blood like that and *not* know." The pupils of his eyes darken, looking as still and black as dead water at night. "Tell me. What *are* you?"

I try to step around him. "We should go—"

He says my name sharply, blocking me. There's no way of getting around him, no way of avoiding this. Cornered like a rabbit, my pulse skitters at my throat as if it might burst from my burning skin.

I can't explain it away. He knows too much, understands too much . . . I can't come up with a reasonable explanation.

So I do the only thing I can to stop his questions.

I grab his face with both hands and pull his head down to mine. He's still for the barest moment when my lips touch his. His skin feels like warm, sunbaked rock beneath my palms. And then he's kissing me back.

With a ragged breath, he pulls me flush against him. His hands flatten over my back. I fit against him, settling my softness into all his hard lines and angles. Like we're two pieces of a puzzle that just click together.

I fight the rising heat, the swelling vibrations from deep in my center. Then I hear it, the purr in the back of my throat, the sound inherently draki. Definitely not human.

I risk a little more of him, steal a few moments more, forgetting why I initiated this kiss, forgetting everything but the sensation of his mouth on mine, the taste of him, as sweet as a misty wind on my lips. The hard press of his palms at my back push me against him as if he wants to weld us together, fuse us permanently.

Then I can risk no more.

Not when I'm like this, lungs fully expanded with steam, the flesh of my face pulling and tingling even in this room of death.

I break away, gasping.

He's shaking, too. His hands grope the air, reaching for me. His expression is a bit dazed, hazel eyes so dark it's nearly impossible to detect the green. I hold my breath, convinced he means to haul me back to him, and hoping he will. Hoping he'll take the choice from me. Then his hand drops to his side. He looks at me starkly, like I'm something lost to him, stolen.

"Let's go have dessert," I say breathlessly, my lips tingly, all of me itchy hot, alive like last night in the front seat of his car, exhilarated like when I dive through air and mist, wind rushing over my face.

I hurry from the room before I break down and kiss him again . . . or before he thinks to resume his interrogation. He still holds the shirt, but I figure the damage is done now.

As we descend the stairs, I can't shake off the words, *There's only one way a human can have blood this color.*

How? How can draki blood run through a human? I've never heard of such a thing. Does it have something to do with the enkros and their terrible practices? It seems the only possibility, but I just don't know.

It dawns on me that as much as Will's in the dark about my species, I know even less of his world . . . and I'm hungry to know more. Everything. The knowledge could mean my life.

16

Monday I walk down an empty hall, bathroom pass in hand, glad for any moment free of the boisterous crowd. Posters flutter along the walls, like moths with their wings pinned, unable to escape. The air conditioner purrs like a sleeping beast in the belly of the school. Muted sounds spill from the classrooms as my footsteps echo flatly on aged tile.

It's a nice break. Ferret Eyes Ken talks to me in English despite Mrs. Schulz's threats for him to face the front. She never follows through and everyone knows it. The class is a zoo.

Back home, we never dared disrespect our teachers. Not when your science teacher is one of the oldest onyx in the pride. Or your music teacher is a lark draki that can break glass with the power of her voice.

I stop at the water fountain and drink deep, loving the salving coolness running over my lips and tongue, down my throat. At the end of the hall a locker slams and I jump. Straightening, I catch the water dribbling down my chin with the back of my hand, watching as a girl walks away from her locker with textbook in hand.

I sigh shakily. I've been on edge all day, all weekend really—ever since Will's house. It's almost like I expect a troop of hunters to descend on me at any moment.

Natural, I guess. I was caught in *that* room . . . holding *that* shirt . . . and miraculously avoided giving any real explanation to Xander or Will.

Xander's suspicious, but nowhere close to figuring out the truth. At least that's what I've convinced myself. If he thought I was draki—or even *could* be—I would never have left that house alive.

Will is another story. He can connect the shirt directly to me. If he ever considers the possibility that draki can alter themselves, he'll have the truth.

I pause at the door to the girls' bathroom, at the sound of soft, hurried voices and muffled laughter. A girl stumbles out, face flushed, eyes glassy bright as she tries to smooth out her mussed hair.

"Oh," she chirps, seeing me. She dabs at her mouth like she's afraid her lipstick is smeared. Only she's not wearing lipstick. At least not anymore.

One step behind her, familiar dark eyes settle on me. Apprehension seizes my gut.

I quickly step aside, eager for them to pass.

The girl clings to Xander's hand, tugging him along like it's no big deal that she was in the girls' bathroom with a boy. "C'mon, Xander." She giggles. "Let's get back to class."

"Hey, Jacinda." He moves past me, slowly. Brushes against me. Air hisses between my teeth.

My throat tightens, my mind leaping to the memory of a shirt stained with my blood in Xander's hands. He held the proof of what I am and doesn't even know it.

My nod hello is hard to manage. Fear and panic war inside me. The fear I fight off even as my fingers curl at my sides, ready to defend. Smoke rises in my lungs, eats up my throat, widening my windpipe.

"Come on, Xander." The girl tugs harder on his hand, turning a savage glare on me, clearly not appreciating losing his attention.

"See you in study hall, Jacinda." He says my name like he's tasting it. "You going to sit with us today?"

I shake my head. "I'll sit with Catherine."

He laughs. "You too scared to sit with us?"

The girl laughs, too, but I can tell she's confused, feels left out of the joke.

"I'm not scared of anything," I snap, the brave words only marginally true.

"No?" He leans close. I resist stepping back, resist the rising burn in the back of my throat, the urge to manifest.

Wouldn't that be just perfect? "Maybe you should be."

Draping an arm over the girl's shoulder, he turns and leaves me standing outside the bathroom.

Dull dread eddies through me as I watch him saunter arrogantly down the hall. The memory of my desperate flight through snow-capped mountains flashes through my mind. My muscles burn as I recall the wild, hopeless run through the woods—the stinging panic.

For a moment, I'm there again, hunters in fast pursuit. Wet cold hugs my body. Agony lances my wing, tearing the membrane. It took days for that to heal, for the pain to fade. I drag that memory close, hold it tight, determined to remember. Xander is part of that memory. But then, so is Will.

Maybe that's something I've let myself forget.

I shouldn't have. I can't. Even with the taste of him still lingering sweetly on my lips, I vow never to forget again.

In seventh period, I perch on my stool and wait for them to enter the room, bracing myself. Catherine is beside me, talking about a band coming to town next weekend that she and Brendan are going to see and would I like to go with them. I think of the crowds, the overwhelming odors and sounds, and murmur an excuse. After that, I don't say anything else because I feel Will's arrival.

He enters the room, sees me. My heart flutters treacherously as he walks straight for my table.

He looks at Catherine, asks kindly, "Mind if I sit with Jacinda?"

"Yes. She does," I volunteer before Catherine can agree. "We need to study."

I can read nothing in his eyes. The dark centers are flat, a motionless black as he gazes at me. Then his voice rolls across the air, anything but flat. The rough rumble puckers my skin to gooseflesh. "We'll talk later," he says, a promise. *A threat.*

I smile innocently and hold my breath until he walks away, grateful that I've avoided him and any more unanswerable questions. For now anyway.

"What's up with that?" Catherine's drawl comforts as she leans sideways into me. Her shoulder brushes mine.

I open a book. "Nothing."

Lowering my gaze, I pretend to read. Pretend not to care that he wants to talk to me, that we sat together in his car last Friday and kissed so intensely that I began to manifest. That he touched my leg, cared for my wound. That he protected me from his cousin in that nightmarish room where I kissed him again.

I can forget him. Turn off everything I'm feeling. I can. I *will.* He's too dangerous for me to be around. I can do this. For Mom and Tamra, I can.

After dinner, I find Mom in her room, kneeling beside her bed, a steel lockbox before her. A car chase blasts on the television in the living room.

From outside the doorway, I watch her unlock the box and open it. Even from where I stand, I *feel* it. *Them.* The contents of that box rush over me. My blood pumps with a surge of life. The air changes. A subtle shift. A lilting whisper. To my ears, it seems like countless tiny voices saying my name over and over again. *Jacinda. Jacinda. Jacinda.*

Unable to stop, I step closer, lean forward, drawn to the beguiling voices, the soft, crooning melody of my name.

To anyone else, gems are cold, lifeless. Noiseless. Only draki can hear their voices, feel their energy. They are our fuel. Our life force.

I've searched Mom's room for the gems since we moved in. With no luck. Eager for anything other than Will that might fortify me and keep my draki going.

Apparently, she hid the lockbox well. Mom lifts a stone in her hand. A piece of amber that barely fits in the pocket of her palm. She brushes her fingers over it. The gesture is almost loving, which seems odd. Wrong coming from her because she shouldn't be affected.

A glow radiates from the box. Colors the air in shades of red, gold, and green. Calling my draki. These gems are connected to me, to my blood, the blood of all my draki family, as far back as my dragon forefathers.

I sigh, air tremoring from my lips. Mom hears me and looks over her shoulder, snapping the lid shut at the same time.

No sense hiding anymore. I step inside the room. "What are you doing?"

With a tight expression, she locks the box. Slips the key in her pocket. I watch as she rises to her feet and slides open the door to her closet. My heart thumps with need. I stare after the box hungrily as she puts it on the top shelf of her closet, glancing back slyly. And I know instantly. It won't be there when I look later.

"Nothing," she replies, removing her work clothes from the closet. "Just getting ready for work."

She's going to sell a stone.

My throat tightens, aches with this certainty. Even though I suggested she sell a gem before—as a way for the pride to track us down—I can't bear the thought now.

"You can't do it," I say, watching as she removes her shirt and lifts her sequined halter top off the hanger.

She doesn't even bother with denial. "We need the money, Jacinda."

"Those gems are a part of us."

Her lips pull tight as she dresses. "Not anymore."

I try a different approach, one that will affect her. "The pride will find us. Track us down. They'll know the minute—"

"I'm not going to sell them here."

"Where then?"

She turns to her dresser mirror. Applies lipstick that looks raw and bleeding against her pale face. "I'm going to ask for a few days off. I'll sell them someplace else. Far from here. We'll be safe."

Mom always has the answers, only never the ones I want.

I knot my hands together, trying to still their shaking. "You. Can't."

She looks at me then. Faces me with disappointment in her eyes. "Can't you understand, Jacinda? This is the right thing to do."

Her steady calm is exasperating . . . makes me feel even more alone. Sad. *Wrong.* Like I should be a better daughter. One who understands she's only trying to help me.

But I'm not. I don't. I can't ever be that daughter no matter how hard I try. Not as long as she's trying to kill a part of my soul.

17

The next evening, Mom doesn't bring up selling a gem again, and neither do I. Silly, but I feel like maybe not mentioning it will help her forget that she wants to sell one of them.

While she and Tamra wait on our pizza at Chubby's, reputedly the best pizzeria in Chaparral, I walk three doors down to pick out a movie for the night. Preferably a comedy. Anything to distract me.

It happens on the way back.

Movie in hand, I'm crossing the mouth of the alley right before Chubby's when I'm yanked off my feet and dragged inside the narrow enclosure, hauled between twin walls of concrete, the odor of the nearby Dumpster ripe in my nostrils.

I fight, hissing and spitting steam, fire eating up my windpipe. Twisting my head, I try to spin around and face my attacker, turn him into a crackling pile of bones and ash.

"Stop!"

I recognize the smoky voice instantly and feel no real surprise. In the back of my mind, I knew if the pride ever tracked me down, found me . . . he would be the one leading the charge.

He gives me a little shake. "Are you done? I'm not going to turn you around until you promise not to incinerate me."

I laugh brokenly. "Not sure I can promise you that."

After a long moment, the large hands on my shoulders relax. I stagger free and spin around.

"Hello, Jacinda," he says like our meeting here is the most natural thing in the world.

My eyes are slower to process, to accept, what I already know. I stare up at him. The immensity of him, a looming wall. Well over six feet. I forgot about his size. His sheer presence. Somehow, with time and distance, here in the human world, he had shrunk in my mind. Now I get all over again why he's the leading onyx of my pride. Second only to his father.

"How'd you find us, Cassian?"

He cocks his head. Purply black strands stroke his shoulders. "Did you think I wouldn't?" he asks.

"I don't know why you had to try."

"Don't you?"

"Why couldn't you just forget—"

"I can't do that."

"Because your daddy said so," I hiss, thinking of his father.

Charcoal black flashes beneath the olive hue of Cassian's skin, his draki flesh ready to burst free. "I'm not here for my father *or* the pride."

As his purple-black eyes bore into me, I feel this truth. Know what he's really saying. *He's here for himself.*

I cock my head. "News flash, Cassian. I'm not looking to go home." At least not like this. Not with him dragging me back.

He responds to this in typical male draki fashion. His face tightens into stark lines, his nose broadening with several sharp ridges, his skin flashing, blurring in and out. Black dragon skin one moment, human flesh the next.

I brace myself, flex my toes inside my shoes. Steam puffs from my nose like warm breath on a wintry day. "Your macho display doesn't intimidate me." A lie. "I'll fight you," I warn.

He may be stronger, but I'm not defenseless. He knows that, of course. That's why he's here. He wants me for what I can do after all.

He studies me, considering.

"Are you up for that?" I challenge.

"Are you?" he counters.

Am I ready to incinerate him with a single breath? For all his glowering looks, he's a part of my past, one of my kind, the legacy Mom would pack away and sell like old baby clothes.

After a moment, he answers. "You can't fight the entire pride."

I arch a brow with a mildness I don't feel. "Oh, you're bringing the pride into this? I thought you were here on your own behalf."

"I am, but they were going to send someone after you. I volunteered, but if I go back empty-handed, they'll just send someone else. Probably Corbin."

I try not to shiver. Corbin. Jabel's son and Cassian's cousin. He and Cassian never got along. They didn't even bother trying.

"Come home with me, Jacinda. It's inevitable."

My hands curl into a fist, nails slicing into my palms. "Is that what you want? For me to go with you and hate you for the rest of my days because you gave me no choice?"

"You'll get over—"

"No, I won't."

He looks surprised for a moment, then a little sad. His eyes narrow as though seeing me for the first time. Or a new side of me, anyway. "You could return," I say, seizing the opening. "Plant false leads. Tell them you couldn't find—"

"I can't do that."

"You think I'll just wake up one day and think, gee, I want to be property of the pride again, a tool to be used for *breeding*." I cross my arms. "I won't go back."

He stares at me for a long moment. My belly quivers beneath that stare and for an instant I totally get the effect he has on so many girls. On my sister and every other female of the pride. "Very well. You can't like it here. You can't want to stay. You're not bred for this misery. No matter what you say, what you think now, you'll tire of the human world. This heat must be hell on your draki. Really blistering it. I'll wait. Check back in on you in about—" He tilts his head back as though calculating just how long I could make it here. "Five weeks," he announces.

Five weeks, huh. I'm almost surprised he would grant me that much time.

"Oh, my mother will just love you popping in. She'll probably cook a pot roast."

"She doesn't need to know I've found you . . . or that I'll be around." His lips twist. "Don't want her to take you and run again." And she would. He was right about that.

His eyes bore inside me and I feel a surge of the familiar unease. But something else, too. Something I never felt before with Cassian. A strange sense of longing. I tell myself it's just for my pride, my own kind. That makes sense. It's not him specifically. It's what he is. What he represents. I can almost smell the mountains and mists rolling off him. It takes every bit of will not to step forward and inhale, press

169

my nose against his warm, fragrant flesh.

"I can be patient," he adds.

I don't say anything. Simply return his gaze, feeling a little dizzy as I look into the flat pools of purple-black and refrain from stepping closer.

I would never have described him as patient before. He was the kind of guy that took without asking because it was his birthright. The great draki prince. Like any other draki female, I'm supposed to fall at his feet in blissful subjugation. What could have changed him?

I prop a hand on my hip. "Patient? You? Really?"

He sighs and steps closer. I move, back up until I can go no farther, the hard alley wall at my back.

"I'm not going to deny that I hope for something more between us, Jacinda. Something real and lasting." He must see something on my face, for he quickly stresses, "Hope. Never force."

"And if I don't want that? Ever?"

He presses his lips into a firm line, like he's rolling the taste of that around in his mouth. And not liking it.

"Then I would respect your wishes." He spits the words out, like it hurts to keep them inside. His expression of distaste is almost laughable. The notion that I wouldn't ever bond with him, mate, and produce a slew of little fire-breathers doesn't sit well. Whether he sees it or not, he already looks at things like an alpha. King of the pride, looking out for the future of our race. At the expense of any one soul. He claimed he was here for himself. Only he doesn't realize that the pride is part of him. He can never separate the needs and wants of the pride from his own. Therein, lies the danger.

"I need your word. Your promise. You won't interfere while I'm here, you won't force me to go back." Because if he says this, then I'll believe him. He's many things to me, but he's never been a liar.

His gaze locks hard on mine. "I promise."

"Okay," I finally agree, moving past him. "I'll trust you." There's something in his eyes, his face, that makes me believe him. And really, how much of a choice do I have?

"You should," he murmurs. "You can always trust me."

Stepping from the alley, I spot Mom and Tamra leaving Chubby's. A quick glance over my shoulder reveals Cassian gone. A sudden breeze casts my gaze up, to the dark shadow on the air, twisting higher, vanishing into the black night as quickly as fading mist. Only his voice lingers, whispering through me. *You can always trust me.*

I hope he's right.

I jerk as an unexpected bell rings shortly after fifth period begins. Confused, I look around as the entire class vaults from their desks, leaving their belongings behind.

"What's going on?" I ask a girl next to me.

She rolls her eyes. "Where've you been? Haven't you

heard the announcements? Today? All week?"

I shake my head. I'm aware of the principal's voice ring-ing out over the intercom every morning with school news, but even now, one month in, it's not something I pay close attention to.

One month in. I think like a prisoner. An inmate counting down time served.

The memory of Cassian washes over me. I've hardly slept a wink with the image of him as he was in that alley. It's tempting to think he might be close, nearby, ready to take me home should it all become too much. More than I can bear. It feels good to have an exit strategy.

"We have a pep rally," the girl explains.

"Oh." I stare down at my desk, wondering if I could stay in the room.

"Attendance is mandatory," she snaps.

"Oh," I repeat.

She shoots me a disgusted look. "A little school spirit wouldn't hurt. Our baseball team made the playoffs."

I nod, as if I know this. And care that it's a big deal. Already I'm thinking ahead. Bracing myself for the pep rally. Hopefully it will be outdoors.

My skin shivers at the thought of being stuck indoors, crammed into one space with more than six hundred stu-dents. It can't happen. I couldn't handle that. PE inside the gym with sixty students has been bad enough. Standing, I follow the students pouring into the halls.

◆ ◆ ◆

Nothing ever goes my way, I think as the entire school pop-
ulation descends into a gym designed for the smaller student
body of seventy years ago.

The deep beating of a drum vibrates along the old wood
floor and travels up my legs to the center of my chest, an
unwelcome reverberating pulse there.

I clear the double doors and my stomach pitches, twists
at the sight of overstimulated teenagers packed tightly into
bleachers. The band is assembled at the far end of the gym.
Its members wear dark red uniforms with stiff-looking col-
lars. They play their instruments, swaying as if they enjoy it.
Their puffy red faces, shining with perspiration, tell another
story.

Sweat trickles down my spine. It's hotter in here than outside. My pores open wide, grasping, searching for cooler air,
mist, and condensation. But there's only the cloying scent of
too many humans crammed together. Students shove past me.

"Move already," one girl grunts as she bumps me.

I'm swept forward on a sea of bodies, deeper into the gym
than I want to be. Turning, I strain, looking behind me for
the door or something. Someone, *anyone* in the sweaty press
of humans to cling to. Tamra. Catherine or Brendan. Even
Nathan would be okay. Someone to distract me and help me
get through this.

Not Will though. I know better. He's the wrong kind of
distraction.

I lift my face, try to gulp clean air. Impossible. The gym is stale and stinks of sweating, unclean pores. I drag deeper, sucking breath into my shrinking lungs. I get a sniff of blood buried deep in the wood floor and I feel sick, wilted. Cassian's voice rolls over me. *You can't like it here. You can't want to stay. You're not bred for this misery.*

My legs move numbly. Telling myself pep rallies can't last long, I pick a seat. Squeeze into the first spot I find, as low as I can get on the bleachers.

Cheerleaders entertain the crowd, shaking their pom-poms and tossing their bodies in the air. Brooklyn's out there. Those over-glossed lips curve wide as she shouts at the crowd. And up front, dead center, as close as she can get to the action, sits Tamra, an expression of rapture on her face.

"Hey." A girl with braces—green rubber bands stretching like ropes of slime between the metal—nudges me. "Are you a junior?"

I stare at her, at the menacing snap of her teeth as she spits out her words. Words that I can't seem to register.

I'm in sensation overload. The band's pounding drums beat like fists inside my head, determined to split my skull open from the inside.

I shake, jump as screams and shouts break out, even louder than the train wreck of a band.

Bewildered, I look around. From one set of double doors, a dozen guys rush out onto the court wearing red baseball jerseys. The crowd goes wild, surges up on every side of me like a hurling sea.

The principal's voice lifts above it all—a strange, disembodied sound on the microphone. Like God speaking down to the masses.

At a vicious tug on my sleeve, I look to my side. It's the girl again. Slimy Braces. "Hey. This is the *junior* section."

I hear the words, but they don't penetrate. I can't understand.

"What are you? A fish?" she demands.

Oh. "Sophomore," I reply.

She leans closer, thrusts her face into mine, and talks loudly, slowly. As if I'm mentally challenged. "You. Sit. Over. There." She stabs the air with a finger, pointing over my shoulder.

Two girls beside her laugh. Exchange approving looks. Egged on, she shoves at my shoulder. "Go on. Get out of here."

Miserable, I move to go. Not because of Slimy Braces specifically, but because of it all. Because I'm here. Because I've lost everything. The sky, my pride . . . my life.

Because Mom doesn't even care what she's doing to me. Because Tamra is so happy. Because Will, the only one who brings me back to myself, who fills the gnawing ache, is someone I can't be around.

I stand. Several rows above the gym floor, my world spins. The dry heat, the foul smells, the stinging noise, the clammy press of people on every side of me . . .

It's all too much. *Too. Much.* I'm in trouble.

Someone yells for me to sit down. Others pick up the cry. I wince. Tremble. Feel the blood wash out of my face, drain like water from a sieve.

Among the clamor, I recognize Slimy Braces's voice. "Is she going to puke? Gross!"

Puke? I wish . . . wish that I were simply sick. And not dying. Not dead. A *phantom*.

Gray edges my vision. I can't see. I can hardly hold myself up. I lift a foot, try to step down. I see my fate. I'm about to eat wood. Or land on a body. I know this. Feel myself falling. Slipping into deepening gray. The air turns to wind on my face.

Then nothing. It all stops.

A hand closes around my arm. Snaps me back. Catches me. The gray recedes. Light floods my vision and with it a face.

Will.

He leans over me, his face intent and harshly beautiful. His hazel eyes glitter, wild with an emotion I can't identify. He mutters thickly beneath his breath, then clenches his jaw, saying no more.

His hand glides down my arm, folds over my hand. His fingers lace with mine, palms kissing. I can feel the fast thud of his heart through this single touch. This, the steady pulse in the cup of his hand, revives me.

His presence always does this to me. Breathes life back

in. Chases away the phantom like fast-fading mist. My skin tightens, rushes with awareness. My chest vibrates. Swells with relief, gratitude, and something else.

His gaze holds mine. In that moment, it's quiet. Everything fades to a distant hum. We're alone.

18

"Let's get out of here." The sound of his voice breaks the spell. Once again, noise rushes over me. The discordant band. Hundreds of screaming teens. The unpleasant smells. Dizziness returns. I look around at the wild spin of faces. Slimy Braces stares with wide eyes. Her friends watch in similar shock.

I nod. More than ready. Suddenly it no longer matters that I can't be with him. I just need to escape the gym.

He leads me by the hand down the bleachers. His warm fingers twine with mine. It feels good, like I'm once again safe. He moves with confidence, stepping down from the bleachers. Swerving around latecomers. We pass Catherine. She snatches at my wrist.

"Where are you—" Her voice dies when she sees Will. She mouths words I can't make out.

I move on, tugged ahead.

"Hey, Will!"

From high in the bleachers Angus motions Will to sit with him. I don't see Xander. Probably in a bathroom somewhere with another girl.

Will shakes his head up at Angus and tightens his hand around mine.

We pass the center of the gym, right where Tamra sits. I twist my neck, watch as she rises to her feet, frowning darkly. An anxiety I don't understand brims in her amber eyes.

Then her gaze swings to the dancing cheerleaders. And it clicks. I understand why she looks at them right then. I shouldn't look, but I do. I lock my gaze with Brooklyn. Her face burns red and I know it has nothing to do with the exertion of their routine.

Then I can't see anymore, even if I wanted to. Will pushes through the heavy double doors. The noise level drops to a muted roar once we're in the hall. I still feel the beat of the band through the building, rumbling up my body.

"Where are we going?" I ask.

Will keeps walking, eating ground with his long strides. He pulls me after him until we're outside, hurrying beneath the covered walkway. The shade offers little relief from the dry, scalding heat.

"Do you care?" He glances at me over his shoulder, his

eyes glittery warm and intense. My stomach flutters.

And I think, *no*. I don't care. I don't care where we go. Anywhere is better than here. Anywhere with him.

We cross back into the main building and Will leads me to a stairwell on the south end, far from the pep rally.

The slamming door echoes long and deep in the belly of the stairwell, closing us in. It feels like we're in a narrow capsule, sealed within the earth. Kept apart from everyone and everything. The last two people in the world.

Will releases my hand and sits on a step. I follow suit, taking the step below his, too self-conscious to sit directly beside him. The concrete is cold and hard under me. The steel railing at my back digs into my spine.

I usually avoid the tight, airless stairwells in favor of the open ramps in the center of the school that connect the first floor to the second. Even if it takes me longer to reach my class.

But here, with Will, it doesn't bother me so much. I can tolerate the closed-in feeling.

"Thanks for getting me out of there," I murmur, lacing my fingers around my knees, and looking up at him on his step.

"Yeah. You looked a little green."

"I don't handle crowds too well. I've always been that way, I guess."

"You might get in trouble," he warns, staring at me in that strange, hungry way that unravels me. He strokes his bottom lip with a finger. For a flash of a second, his eyes look strange. Different. All glowing irises and thin dark pupils. Almost draki-like. I blink to clear my vision. His eyes are normal again. Just my imagination in overdrive. I'm probably projecting missing home and Az—*everything*— onto him. "Pep rallies are mandatory," he continues. "A lot of people saw you leave. Teachers included."

"They saw you leave, too," I point out.

He leans to the side, propping an elbow on one of the steps behind him. "I'm not worried about that. I've been in trouble before." He smiles a crooked grin and holds up crossed fingers. "The principal and I are like this. The guy loves me. Really."

Laughter spills from me, rusty and hoarse.

His grin makes me feel good. Free. Like I'm not running from anything. Like I could stay here in this world, if only I have him.

The thought unsettles me. Sinks heavily in my chest. Because I can't have him. Not really. All he can ever be for me is a temporary fix.

"But you're worried I'll get in trouble?" I try not to show how much this pleases me. I've managed to ignore him for days now and here I sit. Lapping up his attention like a neglected puppy. My voice takes on an edge. "Why do you care? I've ignored you for days."

His smile fades. He looks serious, mockingly so. "Yeah. You got to stop that."

I swallow back a laugh. "I can't."

"Why?" There's no humor in his eyes now, no mockery. "You like me. You want to be with me."

"I never said—"

"You didn't have to."

I inhale sharply. "Don't do this."

He looks at me so fiercely, so intently. Angry again. "I don't have friends. Do you see me hang with anyone besides my jerk cousins? That's for a reason. I keep people away on purpose," he growls. "But then you came along. . . ."

I frown and shake my head.

His expression softens then, pulls at some part of me. His gaze travels my face, warming the core of me. "Whoever you are, Jacinda, you're someone I have to let in."

He doesn't say anything for a while, just studies me in that intense way. His nostrils flare, and again it's like he's taking in my scent or something. He continues, "Somehow, I think I know you. From the first moment I saw you, I felt that I knew you."

The words run through me, reminding me of when he let me escape in the mountains. He's good. Protective. I have nothing to fear from him, but everything to fear from his family.

I scoot closer, the draw of him too great. My warming core, the vibrations inside my chest feel so natural, so effortless around him. I know I need to be careful, exercise restraint, but it feels too good.

The pulse at his neck skips against his flesh. "Jacinda."

My skin ripples at his hoarse whisper. I stare up at him, waiting. He slides down to land solidly on my step. He brings his face close to mine, angles his head. His breath is hard. Fast. Fills the space, the inch separating us.

I touch his cheek, see my hand shake, and quickly pull it back. He grabs my wrist, places my palm back against his cheek, and closes his eyes like he's in agony. Or bliss. Or maybe both. Like he's never been touched before. My heart squeezes. Like *I've* never touched anyone before.

"Don't stay away from me anymore."

I stop myself, just barely, from telling him I won't. I can't promise that. Can't lie.

He opens his eyes. Stares starkly, bleakly. "I *need* you."

He says this like it doesn't make sense to him. Like it's the worst possible thing. A misery he must endure. I smile, understanding. Because it's the same for me. "I know."

Then he kisses me. I'm too weak to resist.

His lips are cool, dry on mine. They shiver—*or is that me?*

I kiss him tentatively at first, determined to stay in control this time . . . but still have this, enjoy the decadent play of his lips on mine, relish the break in my loneliness. He deepens the kiss, and I respond, thoughts dropping away, like pebbles plopping one by one in water, sinking down, down into dark oblivion.

I'm lost to sensation, to the taste of him, the scent of his clean skin, the mint of his toothpaste. And then there's me. The arousing vibrations in my chest. The invigorating pull of my bones. The dancing tingles in my back . . .

Oh, God. Not again.

I break away, sever myself from him with an agonized gasp, pressing myself against the cold, unforgiving railing, letting the hard metal bruise my back, punish the wings that would dare surface. For now, they're suppressed.

He buries his face in my neck, holding me close, whispering my name.

My face ripples, stretches tight. The bridge of my nose pushes, the ridges thrusting forward. I glance down at my arms. My skin blurs in and out, shimmering faintly. Gold dusted.

With a small cry, I twist around and bury my face into the cold bite of metal railing. Panic coats my mouth. Fear edges in. Like the night in his car. I can't believe I let this happen again. Can't believe that I could have so little control. Be so stupid. Did I learn nothing the first time?

I breathe steadily through my nose, determined to hang on, to recover myself in front of him. I won't be the one to reveal the greatest, most carefully guarded secret of the draki.

Peeking down at my arm, I detect only the barest gold shimmer. I flex my cheeks, test my face and find the skin loose again, normal. *Human.*

Will's hand closes gently over my shoulder, his fingers squeeze hesitantly. "Jacinda—"

After several more moments and I'm certain it's safe, I

turn around, breathing carefully, slowly, calmly. . . .

He watches me, the misery vivid in his changeable eyes. My throat aches. He's the only bright light I've found here. It's not fair. In this case, my draki is working against itself. I touch my lips. They still burn, still taste of him.

His voice rumbles deep and smooth, like that day in the mountains, when emotions flowed as thick as mist. "I'm sorry. I guess I got carried away. I thought . . ." He shakes his head, dragging both hands through his hair, clearly misunderstanding, reading something else on my face. "With you, I just . . . Jacinda, I didn't mean—"

"Stop," I say.

Because I can't stand for him to apologize for kissing me.

Not when I wanted him to. Not when I want him to do it again. I drag a deep breath into my lungs, satisfied that I have regained control of myself and stopped the manifest.

This is good, I remind myself. My draki responds to him. My draki *lives*. Just a little too well. I'll learn better control, I let myself think. Because I need him. He's all I have. Not Cassian. I don't need Cassian to rescue me.

I have Will. Here, he's my way back to the sky.

Will keeps babbling, like he can't help himself. "I don't blame you for thinking I'm a user, a player. I'm trying to get with you in the school stairwell like some—"

I stop his mouth with another kiss. Nothing smooth or deft. Just pull his face to mine and press my lips to his. Partly because I want to, and I can't *stop* wanting to. Partly because

I don't need to be reminded how much I really should avoid him. And partly because I have myself under control and want another try.

My lungs are cool. My skin is relaxed and loose. He doesn't seem to mind my clumsiness. After a moment of shocked stillness, his hands slide around my back. Instantly, the skin there starts to tingle again, the muscles tightening in readiness.

Proving, again, how wrong I am. I *can't* control myself. Can't stop my draki from surging to the surface around him. *Bad, bad, bad, Jacinda.*

His kiss grows crushing, devouring. He seems out of control, too. Before I have time to tear away again, the doors above us swing open, banging against the concrete wall. The heavy sound jars us both. Shoes skid and voices fill the air.

Will jumps away from me.

I press back as far as I can against the steel railing. My fingers curl around a paint-chipped rail.

Two guys and a girl trot down the steps. They look us over as they pass.

"Hey, Rutledge," one of the guys says, a nasty smirk on his face as he surveys us, smug and knowing.

Will nods once, his face grim.

We remain frozen, sitting apart as they descend, their feet loud slaps on the steps. The door below opens and clangs shut, sealing us in again.

"We better go." Will stands.

I push up off the rail, legs wobbly.

"You gonna be okay now?"

"Sure." I try to sound airy and offhand. "It was just a kiss, right?"

His face is expressionless. "I meant about the pep rally. You're not feeling sick anymore?"

"Oh," I say. "No. I feel fine. Thanks."

He looks away and starts down the steps. I follow reluctantly, not sure what comes next for us. The bell rings as we emerge from the stairwell.

"Pep rally's over," he says unnecessarily. The hall is still empty, but it won't be for long.

"I've got English," he adds.

I cross my arms over my chest like I'm cold. And I am shivering, despite the heat.

My draki likes him too much to stay hidden. No matter how I try, I can't control myself around him. I won't kid myself that I can anymore. I can't risk exposing the pride. Not even to keep my draki alive. And I can't risk seeing the contempt in his eyes if he learns what I am. Not to mention what his family will do if they find out. And there's Cassian . . . somewhere out there. Waiting. Watching. He could show at any time. He and Will can never meet.

I nod, my chest tight and aching. "I've got Spanish." On the other side of the building. "I'll see you around."

I say this first, an empty promise.

The hall comes to life. Fills with students slamming

187

lockers. Voices seem louder, bodies faster, scents stronger.

Will still stands in front of me, looking at me like he wants to say something. My eyes tell him no, tell him to not say anything. What would be the point?

I have to end this thing between us for good . . . even if it means leaving this town without Mom and Tamra. I can't keep this up, and I can't bring myself to tell Mom that I've been consorting with the enemy. Both enemies. Will and Cassian.

In my mind, it's settled. When Cassian comes back, I'll be leaving with him.

Will shakes his head, frowning at me. "You can't run from me anymore. I'll see you later." He utters this firmly.

I smile sadly. Because I can keep running forever if I need to. At least I can run where he can never find me. Students flow past us, like fish in a stream. Turning, I disappear into the current.

19

"What," Catherine demands as she slides in beside me in study hall, "was all *that* about?"

I try for an innocent, blank look, but she just drops her notebook and copy of *To Kill a Mockingbird* on the desk with a slam and squares off in front of me. "Spill it. I thought you were over him."

"What are you talking about?" I try to stall, grasping for some explanation. She deserves one. I haven't made too many friends in this town. Just Catherine and Brendan. I realize with a sharp pain that I'll miss them when I'm gone.

"Uh, pep rally?" She bobs her head, choppy bangs bouncing. "You. Will. Whole school watching? Ring a bell?"

"Oh." I glance at the door, hoping he doesn't arrive the exact moment we're talking about him. "That was nothing.

He saw I looked sick and helped . . ." My voice fades. I lift my shoulder in a pathetic shrug.

"Oh." She nods with mock seriousness. "Sure. I see. And the two of you making out in the stairwell was just his way of making sure you were okay?"

I close my eyes in a slow blink. *Great.* Now all the stares I've been getting make sense.

"News travels fast," I murmur.

"Well, news like *that* anyway."

"It was just a kiss."

"Uh-huh. Well, that's more action than any other girl's ever gotten out of him."

It shouldn't, but my heart thrills at this. I duck my head to hide my smile. Catherine nudges me playfully with her elbow. "Huh. You like him! I knew it. Since that first day. Hey, he can't be that bad if he likes you. Got taste, at least. And Brooklyn can just suck it—"

"Shh." I look up, tensing, sensing his approach, waiting for him to enter.

He clears the doorway.

Only he's not alone. His cousins are with him. Perpetual shadows. My heart sinks.

It won't be Will. Not really. Not the Will who talked to me in the stairwell. Kissed me with such desperation—like I'm the oxygen his lungs need. Not with his cousins at his side. He won't be the Will who sets my draki free. And he can't be. I no longer even *want* him to be the boy I can't resist. It's cruel and senseless when I can't control myself enough to be around him.

This way is best. I need to see him with them, remember that he's my enemy. Wedge a wall between us until Cassian comes for me and I leave Chaparral.

I peer down at my hands on the table, hoping to avoid the moment when they pass my table. But looking down, I see Xander's shoes stop at my table. Pause. "Hi, Jacinda."

A dark shiver scrapes my spine. I fold my arms across my chest and lift my face. Don't care that my stare is less than friendly.

With a twisted curve of his lips, Xander glances at Will. "Aren't you going to say hello, Will?"

Angus studies me like I'm suddenly worth his attention. Like I'm a piece of meat that needs inspecting, weighing.

"We said hello earlier," Will says stiffly.

"Yeah." Angus laughs. "I heard about that hello. Didn't realize she was so much fun to hang with. I might have made a play for her myself if I knew just how fun."

Air hisses from Catherine. She surges forward. I grasp her arm, stopping her from doing anything.

"Shut up," Will growls.

I remember what Will said about his family in the car the other night. *Poison,* he called them. I remember that room, the tiny red and black flags scattered across the North American continent—and Xander's face when he caught me in there.

Angus laughs again, his mouth wide in his brutish features.

"Well," I begin, hardly recognizing the strangeness of

my voice, as thick as molasses in my mouth. "It wasn't all that memorable." It hurts to say the lie, something cruel and untrue, but I have to.

Xander looks confused, unconvinced as he glances back and forth between me and Will.

Will's stare burrows into me, probing. For a moment, I imagine a flash of hurt there. Then, it's gone.

"Maybe you should try a different Rutledge." Angus waggles his thick red brows.

"Aren't you all interchangeable?" I ask. "Try one, you know them all."

He frowns. The word *interchangeable* is lost on him.

"Pig," Catherine mutters.

I give her wrist a warning squeeze.

"No one was talking to you, freak," Angus shoots back.

And I don't like that. I don't like the wounded ripple that passes over her face before she's able to look stoic and tough again. The familiar smolder begins at my core.

"Ow." She looks at me with bewilderment, tugging her arm. I forgot that I'm still touching her. Quickly, I release her. She rubs her wrist, and I know that she felt my building heat.

Great. First, I almost reveal myself to Will when he kisses me. Now, this.

Maybe tonight would be a good night to try the golf course again.

"Take your seats," Mr. Henke calls from the front.

Angus moves to the back of the room. Xander studies me

for a moment with those demon-dark eyes before joining him in the back.

Will lingers, watching me like he expects me to do something. Say something. "Guess you're not interested in me sitting with you."

My gaze flicks away. I can't manage another word—can't make myself utter another ugly lie. Without looking, I hear him move away. *Feel* his presence fade from my side.

"Wow," Catherine mutters in an awe-filled voice. "You really just rejected Will Rutledge."

I shrug, fighting the painful lump in my throat where words strangle.

"You okay?" she asks.

"Why wouldn't I be? He's not really my type."

I glance over my shoulder, glimpse him hunched between his cousins. They're talking, but not Will. He stares out the window, his gaze fixed on a spot outside. The expression on his face reminds me of Mom. Tamra. Of how they used to look when we lived with the pride. Trapped. Always looking for a way out.

My chest feels tight, a dense and twisting mass at its center. A punishment he doesn't deserve.

"What were you thinking?" Tamra snaps the moment I join her at the curb. Mom's still several cars back, slowly inching toward us.

"You should know. That gym, that crowd . . ." I shiver,

squinting against the desert sun. An arid wind lifts the hair off my shoulders. The wild mass of it crackles, as dry and withered as straw.

Her eyes spark, and I know she's been waiting for this moment, ever since the pep rally, to light into me.

Anger builds in my veins. Because she, if anyone, should know what sitting through that pep rally would do to me. She may not be a draki directly, but she understands. We share the same history. We descend from dragons. Dragons who ruled the earth and skies millennia ago. How am I to endure confinement? In a gymnasium brimming with harsh sounds and humans?

"I know only that you're out of control. Especially around Will Rutledge. I thought you were going to stay away from him."

I'm trying. Even as it kills me. *I'm trying.* But I don't say that.

Instead, I think of all the time I've spent with him that she doesn't know about and feel a shot of grim satisfaction. "If you're so worried, then tell Mom," I toss out, daring her because I know she won't.

"So she can move us again?"

And that's the crux of the matter for her. I answer with a shrug.

Her lips press into a hard line and she shakes her perfect head of hair. "I don't think so."

I look back to the row of cars. Mom's hatchback edges

closer. The sun beats down on my head, roasting my scalp and I shift impatiently on the balls of my feet.

My fingers flex around the strap of my backpack and I ask before I can help myself, "Do you even care what being here does to me?"

Her head whips as she turns to stare at me. "Like you cared about me all those years with the pride?"

Of course, I cared. I wouldn't have resisted Cassian nearly so hard if I hadn't. Cassian had been my friend. Well, mostly Tamra's, but he's always been there. As permanent and solid as the mountains surrounding me. I could have let myself like him. But I didn't. I refused to do that to Tamra.

"What did you want me to do? The pride was our home," I reminded.

Her nostrils flare, pain burning bright in her eyes. "Your home. Never mine. I was always the intruder, stuck watching Cassian fawn over you. Everyone loved you. Wanted to be your friend, your boyfriend, your everything—"

"I never asked for that. Never asked for Cassian to—"

"No, but you got it. You got *him*. And not because of you. Not because he loved you." She shakes her head. "You know, I could have lived with that, with the two of you together . . . if he *really* loved you."

She utters this like it's the greatest impossibility. A joke. I lift my face as if there's a breeze in the sucking heat that might give me some relief.

No relief. She continues, "But it's not who you are that

lures people in. It's *what*. Firstborn wins the prize. Everything. Everyone. Even Dad. You two had your little members-only club." She inhales deeply through her nose.

"Are you trying to be cruel?" I snap. "I can't change any of that. I couldn't then. I can't now."

She doesn't speak for a long moment. When she finally does, her voice is softer. "Can't you learn to like it just a little, Jacinda?" Some of the spark fades from her amber eyes, and while I see that she resents *me*—she doesn't hate me. At least she doesn't want to.

I shake my head, not to signify no, but rather that I don't know how to answer. I know she doesn't want to hear the truth, that she won't like it. She doesn't want to hear that I *have* been trying. For me, it's not a matter of choosing to like it here or not. It's not something I can control. What does it matter anyway? I won't be here much longer. Of course, I can't tell her *that*.

We climb into the car then. Tamra in the front seat. Me, in the back.

"Hey! How was school?" Mom asks.

Tamra says nothing. Neither do I. The air is thick, strained. Mom looks between us as she works her way out of the parking lot. "That bad."

Tamra grunts.

I wait, holding my breath to see if she will say anything about the pep rally. About me and Will. Moments crawl by and nothing. I sigh softly, relieved. Guess she wants to stay here that badly. Or maybe she regrets her outburst. She's the queen of bottling up her emotions. Knowing her, she's regretting letting it spill out.

I wonder if she would speak up if she knew the truth. Knew who Will really was. Would it matter then? Probably not. For once she's too focused on herself and getting what she wants. And I can't blame her for that. Because she's right. It's never been about Tamra before. And I always felt bad about that. Then and now.

But not bad enough to give up on myself. Not bad enough to embrace the ghost my draki will become if I stay here and do nothing. And it's easy to justify. Because my leaving will set her free. Tamra and Mom. A sad realization. To know the ones you love will be better off without you around.

"Jacinda?" Mom prods.

"Great," I lie. "I had a great day."

Because that's all either one of them wants me to say.

20

We're almost home when Mom makes her big announce-ment.

"I'll be leaving tomorrow."

I'm stunned for a moment, actually thinking she might mean *we* all will be leaving tomorrow. Then I remember. She's going to sell a gem. The glowing amber. Frozen fire.

I lean forward to look at her, straining to see for myself if she's serious.

How can she do it? How can she pretend she's not taking away a piece of me, tearing off a bit of my heart and selling it to someone who thinks it's just a chunk of rock? Valuable, but lifeless. Dead.

"First thing tomorrow morning. You'll have to take the

bus. I plan to be back in time to pick you up Friday afternoon. I've told Mrs. Hennessey already and she'll check in
on both you guys."

A feeling starts in my belly, a twisting dread . . . the same
way I felt years ago when Severin arrived at our door to tell
us Dad was missing.

"Mrs. Hennessey?" Tamra wrinkles her nose. Since she
doesn't ask *why* Mom's leaving, clearly she already knows. And
doesn't care. Only I care. Only *I* feel sick at the thought. . . .

"Where are you going?" I demand, needing to know.
Like it will somehow matter. Like maybe, someday, I can
find the stone and save it from being lost into perpetuity.

Mom is silent.

"Where are you going to sell it?" I press.

"This is so great," Tamra says, digging for something in
her backpack and asking with an idleness that sets my teeth
on edge, "Can we move? But stay in the same school zone,
of course. Oh, and how about cell phones? I think we're the
only two in the entire school who don't—"

"Settle down, Tam. Don't get ahead of yourself." Mom
pats her knee. "This is just to ease some of the strain. We're
not moving yet. This should help buy you girls some new
clothes . . . cheer supplies if you make the squad. And maybe
I can ease up on my shifts. Stay home a couple nights. I
miss my girls. Maybe"—she slides us both a warm look,
her eyes bright, shining with promise—"maybe I'll even
see about getting you two a car."

Tam squeals. Flies across the seat to strangle Mom in a hug as she drives.

A car? A family gem for a car? A hunk of machinery that will last maybe a decade? Hardly a fair trade. I stare out the window, too outraged. Hot emotion thickens my throat, moving me beyond speech.

The car will be for Tamra, of course. Tam wasn't kidding before about me not driving. I can't. The world would be safer with a toddler behind the wheel.

Blinking burning eyes, I watch the yards fly past. All rock and strategically arranged boulders. Cacti, sleeping bougain-villea, and desert sage. Flowing ribbons of heat dance above the sun-bleached asphalt.

"I need you girls to promise to behave, check in with Mrs. Hennessey. Let her know if you need anything. I'll call every day."

"Yes! Anything!" The seat springs protest my sister's bouncing.

"Jacinda?" Mom says my name from the front seat. Like she's waiting. Expecting something from me.

It's no use arguing with her. Her mind is made up. But so is mine. Something has to give. Break loose. And it's going to be me.

They're too happy here, settled, well on their way to making the life they've always wanted. They don't want to leave. And I can't stay.

"Whatever," I choke out—vague enough to satisfy her, I hope. For a moment I feel winded, like the air has been punched from my chest.

Once Dad took us to an amusement park in Oregon. One of those brief getaway vacations from the pride Mom always made a point to plan. Back when Tamra and I were simply sisters whose chief complaint with each other revolved around sharing toys. Before I ever manifested. I plummeted twenty stories on a drop ride. Totally helpless to gravity. Unable to fly, to save myself . . .

I feel that same helpless terror now. Because nothing I say will divert Mom off her present course. Nothing will make her realize what she's doing to me.

I'm falling.

And this time, nothing will save me. No mechanical device will work its wonder and jerk me back at the last minute.

But she does realize, a small voice whispers through me. That's why she's doing it. That's why she brought you here. She *wants* me to hit ground.

Later that night, I find Mom packing in her room. She's dressed for work, planning to leave after her shift ends. The stainless steel box sits on her bed, near her half-packed duffel. Alarm stabs my heart at the sight of it. "You're not selling them all?" I demand.

She looks up, folding a shirt. "No." She resumes packing, her movements measured, slow.

I nod, relieved, inch toward the lockbox. My palms tingle, itching to open it. "Can I see it?"

201

She sighs. "Don't do this to yourself, Jacinda. Just forget about it."

"I can't." I touch the lid, stroke it. My throat aches. "Just show me. One last time."

She shakes her head. "You're determined to make this hard on yourself."

"Show me."

She digs in her pocket, her movements angry, her voice a low mutter as she brandishes the key. Unlocking the box, she flings back the lid.

I suck in a breath at the instant glow of color.

Lilting voices surround me. Whisper-soft, they embrace me, remind me of my true nature, slowly fading from this world. But not as fast as Mom thinks. Not with Will around. He's probably the only reason my draki still lives. In this desert, without gems, without him, I'm doomed. Like Will's kiss, the stones reach my core . . . resuscitate me. My skin snaps. Trembles.

One stone reaches me over the others. I close my eyes, absorbing the thread of fresh energy.

"Which one?" I whisper, opening my eyes, but already suspecting.

She lifts the amber from the cozy nest of its brethren.

Of course. My jaw tightens. I knew. Somehow I knew this was the one leaving me.

I lean in, staring, memorizing, vowing to find it again. Silently, I communicate this, watch the amber pulse with light. Wink and glint as if it hears me and understands.

I will reclaim you. Someday. When I'm no longer a prisoner of my mother's whims. If I haven't faded entirely by then. Wilted to nothing, turned into the phantom she wants me to be. I reach out to stroke its surface. Warm and throbbing. Life infuses me instantly.

Like she knows it's feeding me, Mom pulls back, holding the gem just out of reach.

My skin weeps, contracts. I surge forward, hungry for its feel again.

"You have to stop this. Let go of the old life." Mom's gaze burns into me, and I'm reminded of the way she used to look. Alive, vibrant. Maybe the stones are still singing to some part of her, too. "There's so much waiting for you here, if you'll just open yourself to it."

"Yeah," I growl. "Maybe I'll try out for cheerleading."

She angles her head, looks at me sharply. "There's nothing wrong with that."

Yeah. She would love that. And I wish I could. It would almost be easier if I could do that. If I could be like Tamra.

"I'm not Tamra, Mom! I'm a draki—"

"No, you're—"

"It's who I am. If you want to kill *that* part of me, then what you really want is to kill *me*." I inhale deeply. "Dad understood that."

"And he's dead. It got him killed."

I blink. "What?"

She turns away, slams the amber back into the lockbox, and I think she's decided the conversation is over, but then she faces me again, and her face isn't hers at all. A stranger stares at me, her eyes overly bright, darting wildly like an animal's emerging from the cover of woods. "He thought he might find another pride to take us in. One that wouldn't expect that we sacrifice our daughter—"

"A rival pride?" I demand, hot denial sweeping over me. It's forbidden to consort with other prides. Ever since the days of the Great War when we practically killed one another off. "Dad wouldn't do that!" Did he think he could simply find a pride that wouldn't slaughter him on sight?

"For you? For us?" She laughs a broken sound. "Oh yes. He would. Your father would go to any length to protect you, Jacinda." Her eyes turn bleak. "He did."

I shake my head, fighting her words. Dad did not die because of me. It can't be.

"It's true," she says, like she can read my mind, and I know it's the truth. The terrible, sickening truth. I tremble, hurting so much I can barely breathe. *I'm the reason Dad's dead.*

I suck in air. "And you blame me for that. Why don't you just say it?"

Her eyes flash wide before narrowing. "Never. I blame the pride."

I move my head side to side slowly, as if underwater. "I want to go back." I don't even know anymore if I mean this. I just want to get away from her, from all she's telling me. It's too much. I almost tell her about Cassian right then.

Something stops me though, keeps the words from tumbling out. "You and Tamra can stay here. Maybe I can visit—"

She shakes her head fiercely. "Absolutely not. You're my daughter. You belong with me."

"I belong with the pride. With mountains and sky."

"I'll not have you bonded at sixteen!"

Can't she see? There's only trouble, pain, and death, for anyone who tries to leave the pride? "They won't do that." *Cassian promised.* "I won't let—"

She laughs then. The wild sound frightens me. "Oh, Jacinda. When are you going to get it? Do I need to spell it out for you?"

I shake my head, confused, starting to feel like maybe I shouldn't have believed Cassian so readily. That night outside Chubby's suddenly feels long ago. Why is it I believed him again? "I already know they want me to bond with Cassian . . . sooner than—"

"That's not the half of it." She stalks forward, snatches hold of my arm. "Do you want to know what the pride planned for you?"

Cold dread sweeps over me, deep and awful, but I nod.

"If we hadn't left when we did, they were going to clip your wings."

I jerk my arm free and stumble back, shaking my head . . . just shaking. *No, no, no.* Our pride hasn't performed the barbaric practice in generations. Wing clipping is an ancient form of corporal punishment for draki. To rob a draki of the ability to fly is the ultimate punishment . . . and extremely painful.

"They wouldn't do that to me," my voice rasps.

"You're property, an object to them. A precious commodity for their future. They would do anything to keep you."

I see Cassian's face, remember his earnest expression. He couldn't have been lying, couldn't have known this was in store for me. He couldn't have wanted me to return with him and face that. No way. I don't believe it. "It's not true. You would have told me before—"

"I'm telling you now. They had very specific plans for you, Jacinda. They weren't willing to take any chances with you. Not after that last stunt you pulled."

Now the tears roll down my face, hissing on my steaming cheeks. "You're just saying this so I won't go back." My voice isn't my own. Hot emotion clenches my throat so that I can hardly breathe.

"Grow up, Jacinda. You're not a little girl anymore. It's the truth. Deep in your bones, you know it. Do you want to go back to that?"

"Mom," Tamra says from the doorway. She stares at me in concern. Her smooth brow creases in a way that reminds me of when we were little girls, both so protective of each other. We constantly snuck into each other's bed at night . . . just to assure ourselves that the other one was okay.

With that memory, I don't feel so terribly alone. Just

embarrassed. I dash a hand against my wet cheeks. Tears make me feel weak, small. Two things a draki shouldn't be.

Maybe I'm more human than I thought.

Mom's voice softens and I jerk as she touches my shoulder. "You can't go back, Jacinda. Ever. You understand now?"

Nodding, I lower my head. Let my hair fall into my eyes. So she won't see the tears. The defeat. Because I know she's not lying. Everything she said is the truth. I can't go back to the pride.

I'm trapped if I stay here. I'm trapped if I return to them. Either way, it doesn't matter. I'll never be free.

The truth presses down on me. A brutal, cutting pain driving into my shoulder blades.

I dart past my sister standing in the doorway, nearly tripping in my rush to escape. Numbly, I hear her whispering to Mom. For a second, I wonder if she knows about the wing clipping, too. If she's known all along. Cassian had to know that his dad and the elders intended to cut my wings. How could he stare me in the face and lie with such sincerity? Did he care nothing for me? For the friendship we once shared?

I feel foolish and lost . . . *stupid*. My certainty that they would never force me to bond too young is ridiculous knowing now that they were willing to cripple me in the worst possible way. They're capable of anything.

Hunching over, I clutch my midsection as I shove through the bathroom door. Lunging to the toilet, I empty my stomach, sobbing through the painful shudders, retching over and over again.

Shaking, broken, I finally stop. Collapse back onto the floor. Weak. Listless. Leaning against the cool wall, I grip my quivering face with both hands and accept that everything I ever knew to be true, everything I ever believed in, doesn't exist.

I can never go home. I have no home.

I don't know how long I sit on the floor before a knock sounds at the door. From the painful needles prickling my numb back and bottom, I'm guessing it's been a while.

"Go away," I call.

Exhausted from crying, I listen to the sound of my own breath sawing from my lips for several moments.

Tamra's voice floats through the wood, so soft and low it takes me a moment to process.

"It's not your fault, Jacinda. Don't beat yourself up. Of course, you trusted them."

My head snaps up, stares at the door.

She knows? She *cares*?

I guess I shouldn't feel surprise. She's my sister. As different as we are, I never felt she hated me or blamed me for fitting in with the pride when she couldn't. At her core, she never blamed me for Cassian. For *having* him without trying. Now if I screwed things up for her here, in Chaparral, she would blame me for that.

As if she can read my mind, she continues, "The way they treated you . . . like some kind of monument for the pride. Not real, not anyone they respected or cared about . . . it was wrong. Cassian was wrong." She sighs, and I wonder how it is she knows what I need to hear from her right now. "I just want you to know that." Pause. "I love you, Jacinda."

I know, I almost say.

The shadow of her feet beneath the door disappears. I bite my lip until the coppery tang of blood runs over my teeth. Slowly, I stand and leave the bathroom.

21

That night it rains for the first time since I've been here.
I'd started to think that I might never again see it or
taste it on my skin. That I had moved to some forgotten corner of the world without rain, without lush greens. Where
the earth whispers no song.

But tonight the sky breaks open—weeps copious tears.
On the day Mom reveals the final ugly truth she hid from
me. It's appropriate. Fitting somehow that rain should fall.

With droplets licking at the windows, I think about Will
stuck with his awful family. A prisoner like me. I trace my
chapped lips, feel him there with the brush of my parched
fingertips.

Idly, I wonder what it would have felt like if Cassian had

kissed me. Another draki. Would my draki have responded to him? Would the kiss have held the same magic? Could he have kissed me and still lied to my face? Would he have stood by and watched as they clipped my wings?

I roll onto my side. Listen hard. Listen like I've never heard rain before. My skin savors the thrumming sound. Its gentle beat on the pebbled path outside. Its pinging on the metallic roof of the garden shed.

I smile a little. Feel hope in the soft, steady pattern that fills the silence of night. Exhilaration. Anticipation. The same way I felt when Will's lips touched mine.

Dad wouldn't want me to blame myself for his death, and he wouldn't want me to give up. I love my mother, but she's wrong. My draki is too much a part of who I am. I can't go back to the pride. And I can't stay here, avoiding Will, waiting for Cassian to show up.

There has to be another way.

Dad would want me to fight, to find a way to keep my draki alive. He died trying to find another option for us. He made a choice. And it wasn't to bury us within the mortal world. Even if he didn't succeed, he believed it was possible.

His voice floats through my head, almost as though he sits beside me: *Find a new pride, Jacinda.*

My fingers curl, flex open, and shut against the edge of my comforter. That's it—the answer. What I need to do.

I may not know the exact location of any other prides,

but I know someone who does. I can question Will. And I saw the map with my own eyes. If I could just study it a little longer, I could memorize the precise spots.

It's something. A start.

Whether I can get the information out of Will and get into that room again without raising his suspicions is another matter. Clearly, I'll have to spend more time with him. . . .

A chill rasps the back of my neck as I contemplate how I might do that without making him wonder at my sudden change of heart.

A bird calls outside. The sound is bewildered, desperate. A yippy *ka-kaa-ka-kaa*. And I wonder at the stupid creature. Picture it sitting on its branch as the rain beats down on its frail, slight body. Wonder why it doesn't take shelter. Seek cover. Hide. Why it doesn't know any better. Maybe it's lost, like me—out of its element. Maybe it can't go home. Maybe it has no home.

My contented smile melts away. I shiver at a sudden cold in the room. Pull the bedspread higher, up to my chin, and try to get warm.

Rolling into as tight a ball as possible, I squeeze my eyes shut and try to block out the sound.

I feel Mom kiss my cheek, brush the hair back off my forehead like she used to do when I was little. The room is dark. Not morning yet. The barest light spills in from the kitchen.

She must have come home after her shift to pick up her

things. *The amber.* My heart seizes with the memory.

I inhale, detect the nutty musk of coffee in the air. She'll need it to help her stay awake on the drive. Wherever she's going can't be close and she's been up all night.

"Be good," she whispers just like I'm six again. She would say that every day when Tamra and I walked out the door for school. "I love you." Yeah, she said that, too.

Through slit eyes, I watch her shadow move to Tamra, asleep in her bed. Hear Mom's lips pat her cheek. Another hushed good-bye.

Then she's gone from the room. Gone to sell our family's legacy. A piece of my soul I may never get back.

The light in the kitchen disappears. Snuffs out like a doused match. The front door lock clicks into place behind her. I resist jumping to my feet, running out the door, grabbing her, stopping her, throwing myself in her path and begging her to see me, love that part of me she could never love inside herself.

Tamra rustles in the bed opposite me, settling back to sleep and peaceful oblivion.

Then, quiet. A funereal hush. Only I'm awake. Aware.

My heart bleeding.

22

We hurry out the door and rush along the pebbled path circling the pool. Without Mom here to push and prod us, we're running late. Again.

Last night on the phone, she promised to be home in time to pick us up from school today. I'm glad at least we won't have to take the bus anymore. I hate the smell, the choking exhaust that finds its way inside.

Mrs. Hennessey's television blares from her house and I see the blinds snap apart. A red chipped fingernail holds down a slat. Checking on us while Mom's been gone has failed to significantly alter her normal routine of spying. Now she just has an excuse.

Tamra speed-walks in front of me. She's always eager to

get to school, but today especially. Today, she tries out for the squad.

I'll be there after school. Watching and clapping. Showing my support. Even as I plot to leave it all behind. An unpleasant lump rises in my chest. Maybe even leave *her* behind.

When the time comes, I hope she and Mom will join me with the new pride, but I know it's more likely that I will do it on my own. Regardless, it's a chance I have to take. Just like the chance I'm taking in leaving . . . in locating a pride that will accept me and not cut me down before I have time to explain myself to them.

Walking through the side gate, I sip from a travel mug. Mom doesn't usually let us have coffee, but then, she's not here.

Tamra jerks to a halt in front of me. Her Pop-Tart tumbles to the ground, only one bite missing. I collide into her, hissing as hot coffee dribbles over my fingers.

"What are you—"

"Jacinda." She bites out my name like she does when I do something really annoying. Filch the carefully buttered roll from her plate. Steal the drink off the counter that she just poured for herself. Replace her matched socks for one of my mismatched pairs.

The tiny hairs on my nape prickle. I follow her gaze to the street. A black Land Rover waits at the curb. Motor rumbling. The driver door swings opens and Will steps out.

Approaches slowly, digging his hands deep into his pockets.

I freeze. He's been gone the last few days—another hunt, I'm sure—delaying my plans to pump him for information. He steps onto the sidewalk and rocks on the balls of his feet. He looks beautiful standing there, and a familiar ache starts in my chest as I wonder how I can love and fear the sight of someone with the same intensity.

I don't move. My chest starts to hurt.

"Breathe," Tamra commands quietly beside me.

Right. I inhale through my nostrils. That eases the ache a bit. But there's still the hot vibrations starting at my core, the need to purr welling up inside me.

"What are you . . ." The pathetic whisper of my voice fades.

Tamra drops back beside me. Our shoulders brush. I shoot her a look. She's glaring at me like I have something to do with Will standing on our curb.

In the distance, the bus approaches. The roar of its choking engine growls louder. Any moment it will round the corner of our street.

I shake my head at her. She says my name again. Stretches it out like a long hissing wind. "Jacinda."

"I didn't do anything," I deny.

Will speaks at last. "I thought you might like a ride to school."

We gawk at him.

"Both of you," he quickly adds, lifting one hand out of his

pocket and motioning to each of us. Tamra and I exchange glances.

The bus turns the corner.

"Does this normally work for you?" I try for boredom, diffidence, but my voice is all wrong. Rings with something like anger.

He looks confused. "What?"

"Show up uninvited on a girl's lawn—smile sweet and expect her to jump in the front seat with you?"

"Easy," Tamra whispers, and I wonder if it's because she's afraid I'll lose my temper and manifest in front of him or because she actually wants me to get somewhere with the guy she warned me to stay away from. But why would she want that? So I'll fit in and like it here?

He nods, ducks his head. Looks sweetly—*disgustingly*— humble. Like he can read my mind, he says, "Only once before." His lips curve in a slow, conspiratorial smile. I can't help it. I blush madly and my face tightens in that dangerous way as I recall the night I first hopped in his car.

"Hi," Will says to Tamra, as if just remembering he has never met her. Officially, anyway. He stretches out his hand so very adultlike. "I'm Will—"

"I know." Tamra doesn't shake his hand. Cutting her eyes to me, she announces with a sigh, "C'mon. Get in the car." She moves ahead of me.

Will holds the door open for her. She climbs in the back as the bus rumbles past us.

Will flashes a crooked smile at me. "Missed your bus."

"Yeah." We stare at each other for a long moment before I finally ask what's burning through me. "Why are you here?"

His chest lifts on a deep breath. "I'm done."

"Done with what?"

"Done letting you avoid me."

I cock my head. I hadn't run him off? Could it be so simple? So easy? Poof! He's here whether I like it or not. I didn't even need to convince him that I had changed my mind? "Are you sure that's a good idea?"

Because I'm not. Like the truest coward, when presented with my self-professed goal, doubts assail me. I'm not sure I'm ready for him. Even if being with him gets me the information I need about other prides, I'm still left with the issue of manifesting whenever I'm too close to him. And I want to be close to him. Can I be with him without *being* with him? In my true form?

Am I capable of that kind of control?

"I'm sure," he answers in a firm voice.

"You ever heard of the expression 'be careful what you wish for, you just might get it'?" It's as close as I'll ever come to warning him off.

Tamra calls from the car, "Are we leaving?"

Will's smile returns, warms my already over-warm skin. "Want that ride?" he coaxes.

Like I have a choice. "I missed the bus," I remind him

as I stride past, climbing in the front before he can move to the door.

A moment later, as he pulls away from the curb, I'm assuming the ride to school will be awkward with my sister in the back. It's confirmed when she asks, "So what's the deal with you and my sister?"

He laughs shortly and rubs the back of his neck like something is there, tickling, tapping.

"Tamra." Clutching the dashboard, I turn and glare at her. "There is no *deal*."

She snorts. "Well, we wouldn't be sitting here if that was the case now, would we?"

I open my mouth to demand she end the interrogation when Will's voice stops me.

"I like your sister. A lot."

I look at him dumbly.

He looks at me, lowers his voice to say, "I like you."

I know that, I guess, but heat still crawls over my face. I swing forward in my seat, cross my arms over my chest and stare straight ahead. Can't stop shivering. Can't speak. My throat hurts too much.

"Jacinda," he says.

"I think you've shocked her," Tamra offers, then sighs. "Look, if you like her, you have to make it legit. I don't want everyone at school whispering about her like she's some toy you get your kicks with in a stairwell."

Now I really can't speak. My blood burns. I already have

one mother doing her best to control my life. I don't need my sister stepping in as mother number two.

"I know," he says. "That's what I'm trying to do now—if she'll let me."

I feel his gaze on the side of my face. Anxious. Waiting. I look at him. A breath shudders from me at the intensity in his eyes.

He's serious. But then he would have to be. If he's willing to break free of his self-imposed solitude for me, especially when he suspects there's more to me than I'm telling him . . . he means what he's saying.

His thumbs beat a staccato rhythm on the steering wheel as he drives. "I want to be with you, Jacinda." He shakes his head. "I'm done fighting it."

"Jeez," Tamra mutters.

And I know what she means. It seems too much. The declaration extreme. Fast. After all, we're only sixteen. . . .

I start, jerk a little.

I *think* he's sixteen. I don't even know. I don't know anything about him other than his secret. That sort of eclipses everything else. But he has to be more. More than the secret. More than a hunter. More than a boy who doesn't want to be a force of destruction. More than the boy who saved my life. The boy I've built a fantasy around. I don't know the real him. Xander mentioned Will being sick, and I don't even know what happened to him.

But then I don't feel bad about that for long. Because he

doesn't know the real me either. And yet he still wants to be with me. Maybe it's perfect because I want to be with him, too. And not just because I *need* to get close to him and use him for information. Although there is that. Something I would like to forget but can't let myself. Forgetting is resigning myself to a life here. Forever. As a ghost. A small voice whispers through me, a tempting thought. . . . *Not if you have Will.*

23

As soon as Will parks, Tamra leaves us. I watch her walk quickly through the parking lot. She waves to several people. Drops into step with a girl whose name I don't know. They start chattering like they've known each other all their lives.

Will and I sit in silence. From our spot, far in the back of the parking lot, we watch other cars fly past us for better spots near the doors.

I can think of only one reason he parked so far in the back. So no one can see us together.

Laughter rises, bitter in the back of my throat. I swallow it down. Guess he isn't as ready to face the world with me at his side as he thinks. I hug my books close to my chest, feet bouncing lightly on the floorboard.

"I guess we better go in," he says.

I nod. He turns off the ignition. "So what's your first period?"

"Why?"

He gives me a funny look. "Jacinda," he breathes my name, almost laughs. "Haven't you heard a word I said? Did you think I was kidding?"

Maybe. Yes. It's funny how doubt can make you ignore what's as plain as day in front of you.

"I'm walking you to class," he announces, like it's so obvious.

This is what I want, I remind myself. To let myself get close to him, to explore this thing . . . this connection between us. To be close to him and become his confidante. Learn all I can about other prides. Just some subtle questions should do the trick. Then, when I have my answers, I can make my move. Break and run.

I wither inside a little at the thought of leaving him forever behind. Staring down, I admire Will's broad hand gripping the steering wheel, I wonder whether it's possible to love a guy's hands. To feel such deep longing just looking at them? So strong and tanned, the veins faint ridges in the backs.

"Are you okay with this?"

I pull my gaze back to his face. For a moment I think he's asking about my plans. *Am I okay using him?* A bad taste coats my mouth. Shaking my head, I blink, try to think. If it was just about what I got from being with him, then I guess I would be okay. But it's not. It's not just that he keeps the core of me alive. Well, a large part of it is about that, but it's more. It's that he took one look at me in draki form and saw me as beautiful, as something—*someone*—worth saving. That will forever be there, branded deep, forever imprinted.

That's what draws me to him and always will.

The leather squeaks beneath him as he shifts in his seat. "The way I feel about you, Jacinda . . . I know you feel it, too."

He stares at me so starkly, so hungrily that I can only nod. Agree. Of course, I feel it. "I do," I admit.

But I don't understand him. Don't get why he should feel this way about *me*. Why should *he* want *me* so much? What do I offer him? Why did he save me that day in the mountains? And why does he pursue me now? When no girl spiked his interest before?

"Good," he says. "Then how about a date?"

"A date?" I repeat, like I've never heard the word.

"Yeah. A real date. Something official. You. Me. Tonight. We're long overdue." His smile deepens, revealing the deep grooves on the sides of his cheeks. "Dinner. Movie. Popcorn."

"Yes." The word slips past.

For a moment I forget. Forget that I'm not an ordinary girl. That he's not an ordinary boy.

For the first time, I understand Tamra. And the appeal of normal.

"Yes." It feels good to say it. To pretend. To drink in the sight of him and forget there's an ulterior reason I need to go out with him. A reason that's going to tear us apart forever.

Stupid. *Did you think you might have a future with him?* Mom's right. Time to grow up.

He smiles. Then he's gone. Out the door. For a second, I'm confused. Then he's at my door, opening it, helping me out.

Together we walk through the parking lot. Side by side. We move only a few feet before he slips his hand around mine. As we near the front of the building, I see several kids hanging out around the flagpole. Tamra with her usual crowd. Brooklyn at the head.

I try to tug my hand free. His fingers tighten on mine.

I glance at him, see the resolve in his eyes. His hazel eyes glint brightly in the already too hot morning. "Coward."

"Oh." The single sound escapes me. Outrage. Indignation.

I stop. Turn and face him. Feel something slip, give way, and crumble loose inside me. Set free, it propels me.

Standing on my tiptoes, I circle my hand around his neck and pull his face down to mine. Kiss him. Right there in front of the school. Reckless. Stupid. I stake a claim on him like I've got something to prove, like a draki standing before the pride in a bonding ceremony.

But then I forget our audience. Forget everything but

the dry heat of our lips. My lungs tighten, contract. I feel my skin shimmer, warm as my lungs catch. Crackling heat works its way up my chest.

Not the smartest move I've ever made.

I break away before it's too late. I feel the steam of my breath and compress my lips. My nostrils flare, and heat escapes that way. I brush my fingertips over my face, checking my skin.

"Hey, Will. Jacinda." Xander passes us, his narrow face strangely mild, dark eyes slivered, empty, soulless.

Will tenses. That muscle is back, feathering the flesh of his jaw.

Angus is more obvious. A great burly ape walking beside his brother, gawking with his mouth open.

Will watches them walk away with hard eyes. The first bell rings.

"We're going to be late." I glance at the front doors. Everyone's on the move. Bodies flood through the double doors. Tamra nods once at me before joining the mass exodus.

All except one. Brooklyn stands there, glossed lips pursed to a pinpoint, her glare fixed on me. I look away. Back at Will. He's not looking at her. His eyes are fixed on me. My heart clenches. Nodding like he's answering some silent question of himself, he takes my hand again.

And I forget about Brooklyn.

◆ ◆ ◆

Catherine catches me in the hall before seventh period.

"Where's your boyfriend?" she teases. Again.

She's teased me all day. Ever since Will walked me to our lunch table before heading off to his class.

"I don't know."

I look around the crowded hall. So far, he's been waiting outside my classes when the bell rings. I haven't quite figured out how he gets there so quickly, but I'm not complaining. Struggling through the jammed hall is easier with him by my side. I suppose it's what he does to my draki. Makes me strong. Makes everything else melt away . . . even my skin when I don't want it to.

"Real quick. Let's go to the bathroom before class." I follow Catherine and duck into the bathroom near our study hall.

As I wait, she chats from the stall. "I'm going to a concert with Brendan tonight if you want to come—"

"I have plans."

"Let me guess. Will."

A girl leaves the bathroom and it's just the two of us. The warning bell rings and the drone of students outside reduces to a faint murmur. Catherine emerges and moves to the sink.

"Better hurry," I say.

The bathroom door swings open then, and we're not alone anymore.

Brooklyn enters with four other girls. Her usual crew.

None of them smile. All wear identical expressions on faces that I can't help think look the same. Shiny lips. Smoky eye shadow. Perfect iron-straight hair.

Catherine shuts off the water. Shaking off her hands, she turns, her gaze assessing the group of girls blocking the door.

I sigh, strangely unmoved. I know why they're here . . . guess it was bound to happen sooner or later. I'm only sorry that Catherine has to be involved.

The tardy bell rings.

The hall outside grows quiet, and we're buried in sudden, tomblike silence with a group of girls determined to put me in my place.

24

Moments pass. Maybe minutes. I don't know how long we wait for someone to speak or move. Watching Brooklyn, I'm not even sure *she* knows her next move, what she's going to say or do.

I finally speak, hoping to take advantage of her indecision. "That was the bell. We don't want to get marked absent." I glance at Catherine, signaling her to follow me through the wall of girls.

"Yeah." Brooklyn cocks her head, her tone caustic. "That's just not such a big deal to me right now."

I stop inches from her. She and her followers haven't broken rank. Nothing short of bulldozing them is going to have an effect.

She continues, "But you know what *is* a big deal for me?"

I wait, hold her stare.

"Redheaded skags like you who come into my school and act like you own the place."

Catherine breaks in, her voice the height of tired impatience. "Give it a rest, Brooklyn."

One of Brooklyn's girls gets in Catherine's face. "No one's talking to you, loser."

Brooklyn moves in. We're nose to nose.

I shrug, certain I've stepped into some bad flick about angry cheerleaders vying for a championship. "What do you want me to do about it?"

My calmness seems to fuel her anger. "Go back to whatever rat hole you came from."

"I didn't exactly choose to come here. Maybe you can talk to my mom about it. . . . I'm not having much luck."

The angle of her head deepens as if she's seriously contemplating it. "How about this? You disappear or your sister will pay."

I inhale sharply and scan all five girls. Are they serious?

"Yeah. You want it to suck for both of you here?" a blonde with braided pigtails pipes up—I think I remember her on top of the pyramid at the pep rally.

"I thought you liked Tamra," I say.

Brooklyn shrugs. Crosses her arms. "She's okay. Respects the order of things. We could have tolerated her." Her gaze flicks over me. "But not you."

"Leave Tamra out of this." My hands curl at my sides, nails

sinking into my palms. I welcome the pain. My anger likes it. My lungs squeeze, burn. Smolder deep within. "This is between us."

"Oh," Brooklyn mocks in a pouty voice. "Isn't that sweet? Aren't you the good sister? Maybe if you stop throwing yourself at Will, I can see my way to letting Tamra on the squad."

The girls nod, smile smugly.

I can taste the tension, as acrid as smoke, burning cordite on the air.

"This is such crap. C'mon, Jacinda." Catherine tries to shove past them, working her body and arms to nudge an opening. Wrong move. The action ignites Brooklyn and her crew. The mounting tension splinters free. Springs like a popping coil.

The girls converge on her in a blur. Catherine cries out, the sound sudden and sharp in the charged air. I catch a glimpse of her seawater eyes, wide and panicked before she's gone, pulled beneath the blanket of bodies.

"Catherine!" I dive into the pile. Suddenly, I'm caught in a confusing tangle of writhing bodies.

An elbow in my ribs knocks the air from me. I can't find Catherine. Can't tell who anyone is . . . Pain drums me in the face. I think it's someone's fist.

A buzzing fills my head, swells inside my ears. Deep vibrations break up from my chest. Then it's too late. Somehow, I end up on the floor. A delicious scald purrs at my core, simmers, bursts, flares over me like a rash of wildfire. I'm consumed.

The cold tile hisses against my hot, crawling skin.

A pointy shoe kicks me in the ribs. I grunt, jerk from the force. The pain.

I try to rise, but get shoved back down. My chin cracks against the floor. Blood runs over my teeth, the coppery odor filling my nose. I swallow back the bitter flood, hope it might cool the searing tide inside me. No such luck. I continue to burn, smoke. My lungs froth heat. Steam rises to fill my mouth, chars the inside of my nostrils.

Profanities burn on the air. Along with advice. Encouragement on how to pummel me. Whatever their intention when they first walked into the bathroom, they're lost to a mob mentality now.

"Get her!"

"Hold her!"

"Grab her hair!"

A hand tangles in my hair, grips a fistful. Long strands rip. Tears prick my eyes. I blink, fight to clear them.

Without thinking, I turn my face into the suffocating press of bodies. Find the arm holding me, hurting me . . .

Parting my lips, I inhale, drawing deep from my contracting lungs.

And blow.

The scream ends it all. It's not the type of scream you hear in a movie. It lingers, echoing off the walls, residing in my ears for moments more. It brings everything to a jarring halt. Including my heart, which seizes in the dark burn of my chest.

Everyone looks around wildly, searching for the source.

Except me.

I look at Brooklyn. Her face is pale. Her mouth trembling. Raw pain glazes her eyes. She rocks on the bathroom floor, fingers clasped over her arm, the tips white where they dig into her flesh. I sniff the air. Smell scorched flesh.

Top-of-the-pyramid blonde crouches beside her. "What happened?"

Brooklyn's gaze fastens on me. "She burned me!"

Brooklyn lifts her hand to reveal the burn. Second degree easy. The damaged skin is baby pink, greasy looking, the edges white and peeled back. All eyes swing to me.

I resist correcting her. It's more of a *singe* than a burn. I'd swallowed back the river of flame as quickly as it left my lips. It barely made contact. Could have been much worse, really.

Catherine looks me over, demands in a hush, "Do you have a lighter?"

I don't have a chance to answer.

"Get her!"

They pounce on me. Again. I struggle, try to break free from the pileup. My skin shivers, eager to fade out.

Catherine shouts my name as Brooklyn howls directions.

My lungs open wide, fill with smoke. Pulsing steam eats up my throat, widening my windpipe. I seal my lips tight, determined to keep the fire in this time, but I taste the fear in my mouth. Fear of them. For them. Fear for what my draki will do if I don't escape this bathroom. Fear for what that will mean to so many . . .

All that fear does the trick. I don't stand a chance against instinct a millennia in the making. My wings push, the membranes straining to break free from my back. I whimper, fighting, resisting for as long as I can. Bones pull. My human flesh fades and my true face sharpens, nose giving way, bridge broadening, the ridges pushing forward.

It's no good.

I give in. At least partly. I manage to stave off manifesting completely on the dirty bathroom floor, but not for long.

I exhale through my nose—it's my only choice. Carefully, I turn my neck, roll my head, and fan them all with steaming breath.

They release me, shrieking as they stumble away. Fall back on the floor.

Pushing to my feet, I catch a glimpse of myself in the mirror. The red-gold luster of my skin. The sharpened features and ridged nose. The face that blurs in and out like shimmering firelight.

With a gasp, I dive into a stall, slam the door shut. Gulp air and fight to cool my lungs.

And hope, desperately hope, that none of them saw what I just did in the mirror.

25

I press vibrating palms against the door. Bowing my head, I stare blindly at the scuffed toes of my shoes, dragging air thickly between my teeth as my tingling back arches. I focus. Push back at the wings itching to spring, unfold, and rip through my shirt.

Panting, I fight every instinct, every fiber of my being. My arms tremble, muscles burn. It's so hard with a little bit of myself released. . . . The rest of me wants out, too.

For once, it's the reverse. Me, straining to be human, to bury my draki.

Not. Now. *Not now!* I toss my head, catch hair in my mouth and spit it out.

Voices overlap outside my stall, but I can't process them.

Can only fight down the swamping heat.

Then I hear it.

Him.

The one voice I would hear even in death. A rotting corpse in the ground, I would sit up and take notice. It reaches inside me, stokes the fire.

My fear intensifies.

"Go away!" I beg, my voice already thick, garbled with char and smolder. I work my jaw, my throat, try to stop the altering of my speech, the conversion of my vocal cords.

He can't be here. Can't see me like this.

"Are you all right?" Will beats on the door. "Did they hurt you?"

"Hurt *her*?" Brooklyn snarls. "Look at my arm! She lit me on fire! I barely even looked at her and she attacked me! Come out of there!" A kick shudders the stall door, throwing it against my trembling palms. I jerk back.

My face tightens, cheeks sharpening, stretching—bones dragging into position. I'm losing the fight. I stare down at my arms, moan at the sight of the blurring flesh. Ancient instinct grips me. I need more time.

Why did he have to be here now?

My wings push, just a little, just enough, and I hear my shirt rip.

The cotton tee loosens around my shoulders, slithers down my arms. My wings unfurl, the gossamer membranes stretch behind me, rippling, eager for flight. Not yet fully manifested, my wings are still strong enough to raise me in the air.

The soles of my feet lift up from the tiled floor.

I grasp the slippery sides of the stall, fighting to still the quivering sheets of red-gold. Heat courses through me. Struggling to demanifest, I clench my teeth against a scream. A groan spills through.

"Jacinda! Open the door!"

Then there's another sound. A slam. Shoes squeal on tile. A jarring thump. The stall shakes all around me.

A breathless "Jacinda . . ."

His voice isn't at the front of my stall anymore. I follow it. Heart in my throat, I blink tightly, and look up.

Will stares down at me over the top of the stall, his mouth parted in a small O of shock. His hazel eyes gleam dully, something within dying as he looks at me.

"Will," I manage to get out in a breath of steam, my English barely intelligible. "Please."

I don't know his face. The beauty is the same but not. Different. Terrible.

Then he's gone. I hear the beat of his footsteps, hard smacks striking the floor, fleeing the bathroom. Fleeing me.

According to the clock above the principal's desk, we're still in seventh period.

I'm sure it's a mistake. I didn't betray my kind, lose everything, every hope and chance—*Will*—in so little time.

The principal hangs up the phone and faces me again. His eyes are a harsh blue beneath bushy gray brows. I'm sure it's the type of stare that inflicts fear in most adolescents, but it has little effect on me. Not when right now, somewhere nearby, Will is connecting all the puzzle pieces.

I sit numbly, turning to stare out his office window at the red-brown earth edging the quad, cracked and wrinkly like an old man's skin beneath the baking sun.

I managed to fully demanifest before the staff arrived to investigate the commotion. Despite Catherine's assertion that we didn't start it, that Brooklyn and her friends attacked us, I've been suspended.

Several of the girls showed their burns as evidence against me. Even though they couldn't find a lighter on me, the theory was that I flushed it down the toilet.

"Your mother's on her way."

I nod, knowing she would be home by now. She promised to pick us up this afternoon.

I'm wearing a red Chaparral T-shirt that smells like the cardboard box from which it emerged. My ripped shirt sits at the bottom of a wastebasket. Everyone assumes it got that way during the fight. Another assumption I'm willing to play along with.

"We have a strict no-tolerance policy at this school, Ms. Jones. No violence, no bullying."

I nod, barely processing his words. In my mind, I see only Will's face. Hear the fast beat of his footsteps as he bolted away. Think how he must hate me.

Gradually, it sinks in, the dread settling deeper and deeper with every passing moment. Something else has happened. Even worse than Will hating me—as terrible as that is.

I've done it. Exposed all draki. Revealed our greatest secret. The one thing that has protected us for centuries. The one thing the hunters and enkros don't know. Can never know.

Now they do.

Well, at least one of them knows. All because of me. I close my eyes. My stomach cramps. Cold misery washes over me, prickling my flesh.

Apparently, the principal reads my misery. Mistakes its source. "I see you are contrite. Good. At least you appreciate the gravity of your actions. I expect you'll behave yourself when you return to school. You're new here, Ms. Jones, and you're not starting out on a very good note. Think about that."

I manage a nod.

"Good. You can wait for your mother outside." He motions to the door. "I'll speak to her about your suspension when she arrives."

I rise and leave the room. My body moves slowly, weakly, too tired from the hard fight with itself. I sink into a chair and suffer the secretary's narrow-eyed gaze. No doubt word has traveled that I'm some kind of bullying pyromaniac. Crossing my arms over my chest, I drop my head back on the wall and wait for Mom. Wait and worry.

Worry about what Will will do. Will he tell his dad? His cousins? Or will he simply confront me? How can I convince him that he didn't see what he clearly saw? Especially after he caught me snooping around in his house.

I'm actually glad that I'm suspended. Glad that it will be a while before I have to face him and find out. Assuming he doesn't show up on my doorstep, cavalry in tow, all eager to obliterate me.

School is over by the time Mom finishes talking with the principal. I'm relieved that when we step out of the front office, the building is deserted, the halls stripped bare.

Mom doesn't speak to me as we exit the front door and head into the parking lot. She's ominously silent. I shoot her a few glances, want to ask about her trip, want to know about the amber. Even now, after everything that has happened, I need confirmation that that piece of me is lost.

Tamra is waiting at the car. Red splotches mottle her creamy complexion, and I know it's not because we've left her waiting in the sun. She's been crying. Her red shorts and white T-shirt explain everything. Tryouts were this afternoon. In all the excitement, I almost forgot that today was her big day.

She wastes no time. "How could you?" Her face burns bright. "It didn't matter what I did. I could have been a gold medalist gymnast and they wouldn't have voted me in! Not after you attacked them!"

Air hisses from my lips in a pained breath. Little does she know I was trying to defend her. Nor does she realize just how evil those girls are. One look at her face though and I know she's not in the mood to listen to any of that. "I'm sorry, Tamra, but—"

"Sorry?" She shakes her head, the motion bleak. "No matter where we go, it will always be this way." She waves her arms, groping for words. "Why does everything have to be about *you*?"

I stare at her. Into eyes like mine, and wish I could answer. Wish I could deny the accusation, but I can't.

Mom's voice lashes us both. "This isn't the place. Get in the car. Now." She darts a nervous look around. We're not unnoticed. A few people linger in the parking lot.

I slide into the back. I'm already buckled in when Mom slams her door.

"We don't need you two going at it in public." She looks over her shoulder, keys in hand. "I already talked with the principal. Now do you want to explain what really happened?"

I bite my lip, release it with a gust of breath. There's no good way to say it. "I got jumped in the bathroom." I shrug like that's an everyday occurrence. "So I manifested."

My sister groans.

Mom's shoulders slump. Turning, she starts the car. Warm air pants from the vents. "How bad?"

Because manifesting can only ever be *bad*. And I guess, this time, it was.

"I hid in the bathroom stall. They didn't see. Or didn't know what they saw. But I burned one of them. To get free." I wince. "Maybe more than one of them."

My sister is furious, shaking in her seat. "This is terrific."

"Tamra," Mom says, sighing deeply. Her nostrils flare in and out. "None of this has been easy for Jacinda. She's held up better than we could have hoped."

I start a little, wondering if she means that. I haven't felt like I'm "holding up." I feel like I'm barely hanging on.

Mom puts the car in drive and rolls out of the parking lot. "A week at home might be just what you need."

"A week at home?" Tamra twists around to glare at me. "You were suspended?"

Mom continues, "Maybe I rushed you, Jacinda. Shouldn't have stuck you in school right away. All of this . . . has been a lot."

"I wanted to go to school," Tamra's voice rings out.

"I shouldn't have expected you to change overnight. We're almost through May. If you can just make it until summer, I'm sure by the time school starts again in the fall—"

"Can anyone hear me?" Tamra exclaims. "I lost something I really wanted today!" She beats a fist against her thigh.

Mom looks at her, startled.

Tamra shakes her head side to side, as if she just can't understand. "Why is it always about Jacinda?"

Mom's voice soothes. "Give it time, Tamra. Soon all this will be over—"

"You mean I'll be dead," I insert accusingly. "Why don't you say what you mean? You mean that my draki will soon be dead. Can't you ever stop? Quit acting like killing a part of me . . . killing *me* is this inevitable thing that you're happy about. Why can't you just accept me for me?"

Mom's lips press into a thin line. She stares at the road.

Tamra drops her head against the back of her seat with a disgusted grunt.

And I realize both of them will never do that. They're the only family I have left, but they may as well be strangers for how disconnected I feel from them.

I've lost Will. Exposed my draki. Alienated my family. Even my pride wants to break me.

I have nowhere to go, no escape.

But I can't stay here.

My sister has a date that night. The same night Will was supposed to take me out for our official first date. The irony isn't lost on me. Dinner. Movies. Popcorn. She'll have that. Not me. I don't expect Will to come now. Not after today. And yet when I hear the knock at the front door my heart skips and butterflies dance with hope in my belly.

I recognize her date from school as he stands nervously in our small living room, rubbing sweaty palms on his jeans. His name is Ben. Cute with nice eyes. Blond. Not quite as tall as Tamra and I are.

I try not to think about Will and what I'm going to do now that he knows. I can't expect him to pretend he didn't see me the way he did. Any moment he and his family could storm through the door and snatch me up. It's the memory of the first time we met that keeps me going, that gives me hope. He let me go then. Certainly knowing me as he does now, he couldn't bear to see me hurt, couldn't turn me over to his family. Right? A family he wants no part of. That he hates.

Still, it's a huge leap of faith. I should come clean with Mom so we can leave Chaparral, but I just can't make myself say the words. Words that will take me forever away from him. Not that I have any hold on him. Especially now. *Stupid,* Jacinda. I can't just do *nothing.* Can't risk my family this way . . . can't count on the fact that Will won't become the hunter he was bred to be and expose me to his family.

As I watch Tamra and Ben from the window, I sit in silence, saying nothing.

I feel terrible. Not because Tamra's on a date and I'm not, but because I didn't know she'd even been asked out. I didn't know she liked anyone. I can't say anything to ruin this for her. At least not tonight. Maybe tomorrow . . .

She's right. It's always about me. That realization leads to another. One that makes tears spring to my eyes.

Soon it will only *ever* be about me.

When I leave this place, I have to go alone. *Be alone.* Maybe forever.

26

I'm awake when Tamra leaves for school on Monday morning, but I don't get up. I pretend to be asleep as she dresses. When she and Mom are gone, I rise and make a cheese omelet like Dad used to make and eat it in front of a morning talk show with dull awareness.

In the afternoon, I've had enough of the tomblike stillness of the house. Enough worrying over what Will will or won't do. I take a walk. Within five minutes, I'm plucking at my tank clinging to my sweating body. When I reach the golf course, I pause to feast my eyes on the verdant expanse so out of place in the midst of dry, cracked earth. I park myself on the edge of the green and run my fingers through the grass until I earn curious stares from silver-haired retirees in bad pants. Vowing to try another flight this week, I head for home, plotting my next move—breaking into Will's house and getting another look at that map.

When I arrive, Mrs. Hennessey is outside watering her plants. "So you're the one."

I stop. "Excuse me?"

"Your mother told me one of you got suspended from school."

Great. I've fulfilled her every suspicion that she let a family of miscreants rent her pool house.

"I guessed it was you," she adds with a certain amount of relish.

Nice, I think, slinking toward the pool house.

"I made goulash," she calls out.

I pause. "What's that?"

"Beef, onions, paprika. Little sour cream on top." She shrugs. "In case you're hungry. I made plenty. Never did get used to cooking for one."

I stare at her for a moment, reevaluating my opinion of her. Maybe she's not nosy so much as lonely. Especially stuck all day and night alone in a quiet house. Lonely, I get.

"Sure," I reply. "When?"

"It's hot now." She shuffles inside.

After a moment, I follow.

The next day, I don't wait for an invitation. I head over to Mrs. Hennessey's soon after Mom and Tamra leave.

Mrs. Hennessey doesn't talk much. She cooks. And bakes. A lot. She wasn't kidding about always making too much food. She feeds me like I'm an invalid who needs fattening up. It's kind of nice.

The company helps keep my mind off Will.

Over a breakfast of French toast sprinkled liberally with powdered sugar and dripping syrup, I hear a sound. Knocking. I lower my fork to my plate.

Mrs. Hennessey hears it, too. "That your door?"

I shake my head, rising and moving to her living room window. "I don't know who it could be," I say as I peer through the blinds.

Will stands at the pool house door.

I freeze, weighing my options. Can I drop to the floor and hide without him catching the movement? I'm not ready for this. For him.

"Is that your boyfriend?"

I angle my head. "No . . . yes . . . no."

Mrs. Hennessey laughs, the sound rusty. "Well, he's something to look at, that's for sure. Why don't you go talk to him?"

I swing her a glance.

"What? Bad idea?" she asks. "What're you afraid of?"

I shake my head a little too fiercely. "Nothing."

But it's a lie. Yes, I'm afraid. Afraid of what he'll say. Afraid of the words that he failed to say in the girls' bathroom but were there, in his eyes. And now, he would have them solidified, ready to fling at me like barbed arrows.

I scoot to the side of the window, peering out. Watching him knock again.

He calls my name through the door. "Jacinda?"

Mrs. Hennessey squints through the open blinds. "If you're not afraid, why are you hiding? He's not abusive, is he?"

"No. He wouldn't hurt me." At least I don't think he would. He didn't the first time we met. But now . . . I snort. Bury shaking hands in my shirt.

My skin tightens. I scan the backyard as if I expect to see his cousins hiding in the bushes, waiting to pounce. I glance upward through the blinds. No buzzard-circling choppers.

I remember him in that bathroom. Looking over the stall at me. I haven't been able to shake off the expression on his face. The wide-eyed horror. The shock as he looked down at me—a girl he liked—transformed into the very creature he'd been raised to hunt. Such a contrast from the last time he saw me in draki form. That difference is what makes my stomach twist into knots.

"Well, then what are you waiting for?" Mrs. Hennessey asks.

For it to get easier. For life to stop being so hard.

Since that's not going to happen, I send Mrs. Hennessey a shaky smile and step outside.

"Hi, Will," I say softly.

He spins around. Looks me over like he's checking for

something. What? Does he expect me to stand before him in full manifest? Wings, fiery skin, and all?

His gaze shifts over my shoulder and I know he sees Mrs. Hennessey in the window.

"Let's go inside." I quickly walk past him into the pool house, into the blast of icy air that acts like a salve to my steaming skin. I turned the thermostat lower when Mom and Tamra left, craving the coolness, the frigid air on my skin.

I'm especially glad for it now. With him here.

I hear the door close after me. In the middle of our small living room, I turn and face him. Dig my hands deep into the pockets of my shorts. The waistband rides low. "Shouldn't you be in school?"

He stares at me. His eyes intense. Bright. More gold today than brown or green, and my heart pinches a bit as I'm reminded of the amber Mom sold, a piece of my soul lost. His eyes have always been piercing, but this is different. It's like he's seeing me for the first time.

And I guess, in a way, he is.

It's there in those expressive eyes. The hurt. The betrayal. I did that to him and can't hide from it. Hurting him hurt me. More than I could ever expect. The pain is up there with losing Dad. With leaving the pride, leaving Az and Nidia. With feeling my draki slip away like mist between my fingers. And betraying my kind . . . even if they were planning to clip my wings and betray me.

"I took the day off," he announces. Like I asked.

"Your dad just lets—"

"I don't ask my dad. For pretty much anything. As long as I don't flunk out, he doesn't care." The grooves along his cheeks deepen. "He cares about other things." He nods slowly at me. My stomach cramps. "You can guess what those things are."

The cramping takes a severe twist. Here we go. I might as well say it. Get it out there. He knows I know.

"The family business," I volunteer.

His lips press into a grim line. "Yeah. My family business is hunting *your* family."

I inhale, hate to ask, but have to know. "Did you tell them about—"

His voice bites out, "Do you really think you would still be alive if I had?" His angry eyes claw me.

I sink onto the couch, pluck at the edge of my shorts. "I guess not."

He shakes his head. "You saw that room at my house—"

"Yes," I say quickly, not wanting to discuss his family's trophy room. It haunts me every time I close my eyes. "I know what your family is capable of."

"And you still came to my house?" he snaps. "Do you have a death wish?"

"I didn't have much choice!" I hug myself, squeeze tightly as if I can shield myself from his anger.

Sighing, he lowers himself beside me. Closer than I

expect. Closer than I want him right now. I smell his soap. His skin. Slowly, the smolder builds in my chest until I taste heat in my mouth. Smoke in my nose.

"Guess you're not an enkros," he says. "You're a . . . *dragon.*"

I can tell he has a hard time saying this. I almost smile. "No. I'm not an enkros. And we're not dragons. Not in a long time. We just descend from them. We call ourselves draki."

"Draki." He nods slowly, then leans in close, eyes angry. "You've had a good laugh over all this, huh?" His voice is as soft as a feather dragging across my waking skin.

"No." I tremble. From dread or pleasure, I don't know. Maybe both. He really shouldn't be this close to me. "None of this has been what I'd call amusing."

"I guess not. You know, you could have told me—"

"Could I?" I rub a hand over my forehead, directly at the center where it's starting to throb. "Like you were so open with me." At least my voice is strong, even as my insides quiver.

His expression hardens to stone. "What did you expect me to do? Tell the girl I can't get out of my head that my family hunts mythical creatures? That they're obsessed with the chase? The kill, making money by butchering up—"

"Stop!" I hold up a hand, working my lips, trying to chase down the bad taste from my mouth, stop the churn of my stomach. Because I don't want to know all the details.

Can't bear hearing about what his family does to my kind. What he's witnessed them do . . . maybe even had a hand in it. Standing in that shop of horrors he calls home is a memory I've yet to erase from my head.

"But you knew," he says. "You saw me before." His eyes are fierce, his words a savage rush—each one like the sharp dig of a knife. "You knew me from the mountains. That first day in the hallway, you recognized me." His eyes feast on my face, dropping to my neck, down my body. Again, like he's seeing me as he did in that cave. In the bathroom. Seeing through my human skin to the draki underneath. "You had to know I could never hurt you. I didn't then. How could I now?"

I get up and move into the kitchen, desperate for distance from him just then. But he's not about to grant me that.

He follows close on my heels, announcing, "I knew it was you all this time. Don't kid yourself." His gaze burns feverishly bright. He reaches for my face with both hands, like he's going to pull me close for a kiss.

"What do you mean?" I jerk away, and move around the small island, comforted to have something between us.

Frowning, he stares at me and continues, "Before I could understand it, I . . . remembered you. *Sensed* you."

Somehow, this doesn't surprise me. Standing at my locker with Tamra, there had been something in his eyes, his face.

He lifts a hand again, and this time I let him touch my face. I turn into his hand. My skin sighs against the cup of his palm. I move my mouth, taste the salty musk of his flesh.

His voice stokes the fire within me.

"I remember you. You were like burning firelight in that cave, all shimmery, dancing color." I lean closer over the island, mesmerized by his words, his hand on my face. If he keeps talking this way, he's going to see me like that again. "Tell me you thought about me. That you think about me *now*."

My lips move, but I can't speak.

His hand drops, and I feel suddenly cold. Bereft. The way I've felt for so long now. Even before arriving in Chaparral. Since I manifested at age eleven and lost myself. Became simply the *fire-breather* to everyone who knew me. My parents. My sister. Cassian. They saw me as that first and foremost. I guess even I'm guilty of that. Of seeing myself as nothing beyond the last draki fire-breather.

Only now, here with Will, I realize I'm something more. Someone not bound by the rules of her pride, her race, her family. Someone who can be loved for herself, draki or not.

"I thought about you," I whisper, my voice not my own. It belongs to someone else. Someone brave, someone about to risk everything and follow her heart. "I've never stopped thinking about you." Somehow, I doubt I ever will.

Then, I'm rewarded with his hands on my face again. His lips on my mouth, brushing so softly, so tenderly, but the hunger is there, held in check. I feel it like a storm rising on the air. My breath shudders against his lips and he kisses me harder, his hands on my face tightening. For a moment, I let myself forget the rumbling winds. As his hands angle my head, I grip the hard curve of his biceps and enjoy the press of his body against mine.

His lips start to feel cold, icy moving against mine, and I realize it's not him. It's me, growing hotter. Too hot. With a gasp, I break from him, round the island, and grip the hard edge of the counter in both hands. The storm winds settle. He still doesn't know about my particular *talent*, and I'd rather him not learn this way.

His chest lifts and falls with ragged breaths. He says my name with such need that I take a long blink. When I reopen my eyes, he looks calmer, steadier. I don't feel quite the same need to bolt when he holds out his hand. His eyes promise the refuge I crave. Placing my hand in his, he guides me back into the living room.

"Tell me now," he urges, the glitter in his eyes desperate and hungry for the truth. "I want to know everything about you."

He already knows. At least the biggest secret of all. And while logically I know I should keep as much as I can to myself—for the sake of my pride, my species—I can't. Not anymore.

Not with him. I can hold nothing back. Not with the boy who protected me countless times. In the mountains. In his house. Even that day at school. If he wanted to harm me, he would have done so long ago. If he wanted to hurt me, he would not look at me the way he does. He couldn't fake that. I don't want anything coming between us again. It's time for the truth.

"My mother, Tamra . . . they're not like me. Not . . . draki."

He looks at me, confused as he takes my other hand in his. I plunge in, explain the pride to him, how we live, manifest and demanifest. How our evolution has provided us with the greatest means of protection—allowing us to shift into human form. "You see, it's impossible to maintain human form while we're afraid and threatened. It's a defense mechanism of our species . . . to revert back to our true form where we're stronger and can use our talents. That's why I started to manifest in the bathroom when Brooklyn and her crew jumped me."

We're quiet for a few moments, then Will asks, "You mentioned talents. What's yours?"

I look away. "You might have noticed mine already."

This is the hard part. It shouldn't be. He already knows I'm draki, after all, but this takes it to another level. I'm not just a draki. I'm a draki that's freakish even among my own kind.

Drawing a deep breath, I face him. "I'm a fire-breather."

He looks confused, and I yearn to smooth the wrinkle from his forehead.

"There's no such thing. Not anymore," he says. "There are no reports of any fire-breathing—"

"Guess I pulled some lucky recessive genes."

He doesn't smile. His hand flutters over my face, hovering. But this time he doesn't touch me. Gradually, understanding fills his eyes. "In the stairwell . . . your skin got so hot. Your lips . . . just now . . ."

My face burns even as his words make me feel bitter cold inside. I nod. "Yeah, I kinda . . . heat up when you kiss me."

"So . . . what does that mean? When we kiss I might catch on fire or something?" His eyes widen then. "That's why you've avoided me. Why you ran away when we kissed that night."

I resist pointing out that's why I ran away *every* time, not just that night.

His hands touch his lips as if remembering the warmth of my lips moments ago. I laugh. A miserable sound. Can this be any more mortifying?

"I can only hurt someone if I release fire or steam," I confess. At least I think that's true.

As I speak, his fingers trail down my arm. I'm just so relieved he's willing to touch me after I've told him this. He turns my hand over and traces the fine lines on my palm. "And?" He looks up beneath heavy lids. "What else should I know about you?"

"My skin—" I stop, swallow.

He leans down, presses his lips to my wrist in a feathery kiss. "What about your skin?"

"You know. You've seen it," I rasp. "It changes. The color becomes—"

"Like fire." His gaze lifts from my wrist and he says that word he said so long ago surrounded in cold mists, tucked on a ledge above a whispering pool of water. "Beautiful."

"You said that before. In the mountains."

"I meant it. Still do."

I laugh weakly. "I guess this means you're not mad at me."

"I would be mad, if I could." He frowns. "I should be." He inches closer to me on the couch. We sink deeper into the tired cushions. "This is impossible."

"*This* what?" I clutch the collar of his shirt in my fingers. His face is so close I study the varying color of his eyes.

For a long time, he says nothing. Stares at me in that way that makes me want to squirm. For a moment, it seems that his irises glow and the pupils shrink to slits. Then, he mutters, "A hunter in love with his prey."

My chest squeezes. I suck in a breath. Pretty wonderful, I think, but am too embarrassed to say it. Even after what he just admitted.

He loves me?

Studying him, I let myself consider this and whether he can possibly mean it. But what else could it be? What else could drive him to this moment with me? To turn his back on his family's way of life?

As he looks at me in that desperate, devouring way, I'm reminded of those moments in his car when he tended the cut on my palm and ran his hand over my leg. My belly twists.

I glance around, see how seriously, dangerously alone we are. More alone than in the stairwell. Or even the first time together, on that ledge. I lick my lips. Now we're alone with no school bell ready to rip us apart. Even more alarming, no more secrets stand between us. No barriers. Nothing to stop us at all.

I hold my breath until I feel the first press of his lips, certain I've never been this close to another soul, this vulnerable. We kiss until we're both breathless, warm and flushed, twisting against each other on the couch. His hands brush my bare back beneath my shirt, trace every bump of my spine. My back tingles, wings vibrating just beneath the surface. I drink the cooler air from his lips, drawing it into my fiery lungs.

I don't even mind when he stops and watches my skin change colors, or touches my face as it blurs in and out. He kisses my changing face. Cheeks, nose, the corners of my eyes, sighing my name like a benediction between each caress. His lips slide to my neck and I moan, arch, lost to everything but him. In this, with him . . . I'm as close to the sky as I've ever been.

I make grilled cheeses for lunch, one for me, two for Will. We don't have any chips, but I find a jar of pickles in the pantry.

"This is the best thing I've ever eaten." He pauses for a

drink, staring at me over the rim of his glass of juice.

"It's the provolone," I say, swallowing my last bite.

"It's the chef."

I smile and look away.

We listen to music. Talk. Kiss until my flesh glimmers gold-red. Warms to the touch from the deep scald at my core. He stops to watch. Leans his face close to my neck and smells my skin. Like I'm something he might taste. He sweeps his hands along my arms . . . making me burn hotter.

"Is this what it's like for other fire-breathers?" he asks, winks, holding my hand up in his broad palm. "Or is it just me and my magic hands?"

I shake my head. "I don't know. I'm the only one in my pride."

His gaze snaps to mine, laughter gone. "Seriously?"

I nod. "That's why we left the pride. Mom says it isn't safe for me there anymore."

His hand on my arm tightens. "They would hurt you?"

I shiver, thinking of the wing clipping they planned for me. I close my hand over his, force his fingers to loosen their grip. "No. Not like you think. They just want to plan out my life for me." I think of Cassian and shiver again. "Own me."

His brows dip. "What do you mean?"

"Your information wasn't totally off. Fire-breathers were thought to be extinct, lost. Then I came along. I'm the first fire-breather in my pride in generations." I shrug, trying to make light of my words. "And they want more. More like me. It's simple, really."

I deliberately don't tell him about the wing clipping. Maybe I don't want him to think we're barbaric creatures. Considering his family, I know it shouldn't matter to me, but it does. It shames me that my brethren planned to misuse me so cruelly.

He stares at me for a long moment, his eyes hard, penetrating, processing. Then, he gets it. Understands how my pride plans to get more fire-breathers like me. His hazel eyes deepen to a forest green. He utters a profanity. "Your pride expects you—"

"Not the entire pride," I say quickly. I can't think that Nidia does. That's probably why she let us escape that night. Az and my other friends wouldn't support such abuse of me either. "Our alpha picked his son, Cassian, for me. . . ." I wince at his expression, slide my fingers over the back of his hand. "It's all right." I lean over and kiss the side of his mouth. "I'm here now. With you. They're not going to find me." Well, except Cassian, of course. He already has. But I'll deal with him later. I still have a few weeks until his return.

He turns his hand over to lace his fingers with mine. "Promise me you're not going to leave."

I hold my breath, stare into his eyes, know I must decide now. Not whether I'll return to my pride. That's already decided. I can never go back there. But I need to figure out once and for all if I'm going to stay here in Chaparral and forget about finding another pride.

Will could help me leave. I believe he would, if I asked, if I convinced him I needed to go. Explained to him Cassian would be coming for me soon. He cares enough to do that for me even if he doesn't want to see me go.

He squeezes my hand. "Promise."

"I promise," I whisper. Even if I shouldn't. Even if a small part of me will never feel safe here and never should.

At least I don't need to leave anymore in order to keep my draki alive. With Will around, it will never fade. And together, we can keep what I am hidden from the world. I believe that together we can do anything. And Mom and Tamra get the lives they want. Win-win for everyone.

Somewhere in the distance, I hear a sound. A yippy, broken *ka-kaa-kaa*. It's that bird again. Or one just like it. From the night it rained. The one I thought too stupid for failing to seek shelter.

"What is that?" I ask.

For a moment, he looks confused, then Will hears it, too. "Desert quail. Distinctive, huh? They come into town when it starts getting hot. Looking for food and water. A mate."

For some reason, I shiver once again.

"You cold?" He chafes my arms.

I haven't been cold since I moved here. This is something else. "No, but you can put your arms around me anyway."

◆ ◆ ◆

That afternoon, Catherine comes over after school.

"Miss me?" she asks with her usual wryness, tossing her backpack on the floor and dropping down on the bed beside me like she comes over all the time. "I feel like a rebel just knowing you. Everyone keeps asking me if you really lit Brooklyn on fire."

I arch a brow. "On fire?"

Catherine plumps up a pillow beneath her head. "The actual event has gotten a bit exaggerated." Her lips twitch. "Maybe I had something to do with that."

"Nice. Thanks."

"No problem."

"So I guess I'm pretty much done for at school." For the first time, it matters to me. If I'm to stay here and make a go of it, it wouldn't hurt to have a few friends. To not be a social outcast. Especially since it seems pretty important for Tamra's success at school, too.

"Are you kidding? You're a hero." Her lips twist with a smile. "I think you've got a shot at homecoming queen next fall."

I give a short laugh, and then her words sink. Next fall. Might I be here then? With Will? It's almost too sweet to believe.

"So," Catherine begins, picking at the loose paper edging my spiral. "Rutledge was absent today."

"Yeah?" I try for nonchalance.

"Yeah." She stretches the word, her blue-green eyes

cutting meaningfully into mine. "And his cousins were around, so he's not off somewhere with them. I wonder . . ." She cocks her head, her long, choppy bangs, sliding low across her forehead. "Wherever could he have been?"

I shrug and pick at the flaking tip of my pencil.

She continues, "I know where Xander thinks he was."

My gaze swings back to her face. "Xander talked to you?"

"I know, right? Can my days as a pariah be coming to an end?"

"Where does he think Will was?"

"With you, of course."

"Me?" I moisten my lips. "He said that?"

"Well, practically. He expected me to confirm it when he cornered me in study hall."

I swallow. There's no help for it. Xander still thinks I know too much, and Will's involvement with me isn't going to change that.

"Why's that guy have it out for you?" Catherine asks.

"I don't know." I shrug one shoulder.

"Yeah, well, he definitely creeps me out. He reminds me of my mom's old boyfriend, Chad. He gets that same intense look on his face. We finally had to get a restraining order on him."

"I don't think it will come to that."

Catherine shakes her head with a wisdom beyond her years. "You never know about these things, Jacinda. You never know anyone. Not really."

"True," I murmur, wishing it were anything but . . . wishing I could see the world and everyone in it for what they truly are. No lies, no pretense, no masks. But then I wouldn't live a very long life without my own masks.

Later that night, my skin still hums with warmth, glowing faintly from the day spent with Will.

I have the house to myself. Catherine stayed for dinner, but left just before Mom went to work, and then Tamra left for a study group. I'm reading *To Kill a Mockingbird* on my bed. I like it but haven't turned a page in half an hour. My concentration drifts.

The scratching at my window begins subtly. It takes a moment to penetrate. At first I think it's nothing more than a branch. *Blowing in a nonexistent breeze . . .*

A chill runs through my skin. I slide off the bed, stare hard at the window between my bed and Tamra's. In the low glow of lamplight, I make out a shadowy shape behind the blinds. Immediately, I envision Xander, imagining he knows the truth and is here to claim me. Not because Will told him, of course, but because Xander figured it out on his own.

Then, I think of the pride. Cassian. Severin.

I draw air deeply, expand my lungs. Remember that I'm no victim. "Who's there?" I demand.

The sound at my window grows louder, like someone's

fighting with the screen. I hear a pop, then a vibrating jerk. The screen is off.

"Who's there?" I repeat, smoke filling my mouth, puffing my cheeks, rushing from my lips in a cloudy gust. My back tingles. My wings move, crawl beneath my skin like beasts seeking escape.

The window slides open. The blinds rattle noisily, ripple with movement. My skin ripples, too. Heat rolls over my flesh in a current. I part my lips, ready to blow fire.

The blinds shove upward, and Will's head pops inside. Those bright eyes lock on me. "Hey," he breathes.

"Will!" I rush forward and hold the blinds so he can climb inside the room. "What are you doing? You gave me a heart attack."

"I saw your sister leave, but figured I shouldn't knock on the door. Is your mom here?"

"She's at work."

He grins, moves in, and wraps his arms loosely around me. "So I have you to myself."

I smile, squeeze him back, loving that he misses me like I miss him. Even though we saw each other earlier today, I feel stronger with him here, the world not so scary and overwhelming.

We sit on the floor, our backs against my bed. Hands laced together, we talk. He tells me more about his family. About his cousins. All of them. Even his uncles and other cousins. But it's Xander that worries me.

"Xander hates my guts," Will comments.

"Why?"

Will pauses, and I feel the tension tighten his body. "My dad, my uncles . . . they favor me."

"Why?"

He sighs, and there's pain in the sound. "I don't want to talk about—"

"Tell me," I insist, determined to figure out this thing with Xander.

"I guess I'm better at certain stuff."

"What kind of stuff?" I ask, even as a whisper winds through me, warning me to stop, to end this line of questioning. That I don't really want to know.

"I'm a better hunter, Jacinda."

My hand stills in his. I stare down at it, marveling at my hand nestled so trustingly in his, and I feel a little sick. I try to tug it free. Because it's just too much. How am I supposed to handle that?

He clamps down. "I don't want to lie to you, Jacinda. I'm the best tracker in my family. It's like I'm tuned in to your kind. . . . I can't explain it. It's just a feeling I get whenever I'm close—"

I nod. It makes sense now. The way he reacted that day in the hall; it was like he felt me there before he even saw me. "It's okay," I murmur, and realize that I mean it. If this is part of the reason he's drawn to me, I couldn't hold it against him. Not when I crave him like oxygen for my starved lungs to keep my draki alive. "So that's why your family needs you so much."

"Yeah." He nods, his honey brown hair tossing forward on his forehead. "But it never felt right. I never believed dragons, uh, draki, were dangerous creatures in need of killing. Not like my father wants me to think. Ever since I saw you in the mountains, I haven't led them to any more draki. I can't. I *won't*."

I smile then and start to wonder if my coming here hadn't been for this reason. For Will. For me. For my species everywhere.

Eventually, we get around to the question I hoped it would never occur to him to ask. Another matter I have not let myself think upon too much. Because I can't stand the prospect.

"So what about life span?" His head drops back on the edge of the bed, watching me. "Is it true?" So calm. So easy. So natural. It's always like this with him. Like he's not asking me this. Not asking me for my expiration date. "You can live forever?"

"We're not immortal." I try to cough up a laugh. Fail. "We can't live forever."

He's quiet for a moment. Still watching me with a calmness that doesn't meet the bright gleam in his eyes. Because he knows. He knows that even if we're not immortal, it's not as simple as being mortal. "How long do you live?"

I wet my lips. "It's different for everyone, of course—"

"How long?"

"Nidia, the oldest draki in our pride, is three hundred and eighty-seven." For a flash of a second, he looks stricken. Then it's gone. Cool neutrality back in its place. I quickly add, "That's long. Really old for us. Not the norm. Two hundred . . . three hundred is a closer average."

"Average," he echoes.

I keep talking, like I can stop him from thinking about it . . . about the gulf my words build between us. Not that we don't already have enough obstacles. "We think sheer will alone is keeping Nidia alive. She's special to our pride. We need her too much, so she's hanging on for us." I laugh weakly, hating how quiet he is.

"So you won't start looking old until . . . when?"

I shrug uneasily. "Well, we never really look . . . old." Not "human" old, anyway.

"How old does this Nidia look?"

I bite my lip and lie. "Maybe fifty-five. Sixty."

Not quite the truth. She looks closer to mid-forties, and that's as old as I've seen any draki ever look. We simply don't age the way a human does. My mom is only starting to age because she's suppressed her draki for so long.

"So when I'm a silver-haired sixty-year-old you'll look . . . ?"

"Younger," I say, my throat tight and aching. And not because he'll look older or less beautiful. But because if I'm around, I will be able to *do* nothing. Nothing but watch him

269

decay, weaken, and ultimately die.

"Can we talk about something else?" I tear my hand from his to drag it through the impenetrable mass of my hair, hoping he doesn't notice when I sneak in a rub at my eyes.

Right then, I hear the front door open and shut.

We scramble to our feet in a mad rush. Will's out the window minutes before Tamra enters the room.

Sitting on my bed, I try to look casual, try not to glance at the window he disappeared through. Try not to think about our last words, the look on his face . . . the chill in my heart knowing he will die long before me.

I never let myself think about it before, never mulled over the distant prospect. But knowing what I do now— that *he loves me*, that I'll never leave here, that I want us to be together forever—it's impossible to stop the dread from sinking its teeth into me.

Forever won't last that long for him.

27

I wake to the smell of coffee and bacon. I sniff deeper. No. Sausage. Definitely. And frying eggs.

I glance at Tamra's empty bed across from me and then the clock. Eight fifteen AM. The aroma swims around me. Rubbing the sleep from my eyes, I prop up on my elbows, wondering if Mom forgot to turn the coffee off. My stomach growls. But that didn't explain the food smell.

"Well, I guess that answers my question." The deep velvet voice startles me.

I jump, grab my pillow like I'm going to use it as a weapon.

Will stands in the doorway, sipping from a metallic travel mug. His gray T-shirt stretches across his shoulders and chest in a way that makes my throat close up.

"What question?" I ask, breathless.

"Whether you're as beautiful in the morning as you are during the rest of the day."

"Oh," I say dumbly, pushing the tangle of hair back off my shoulders, certain I don't look good right now, just rolling out of bed. Not that I take pains with my appearance on the average day, but still . . . who looks their best fresh out of bed? "You're here again," I murmur.

"Apparently."

"Can't stay away?"

"Apparently not."

I'm okay with that. Great, in fact.

"I made you breakfast," he adds.

"You can cook?" I'm impressed.

He grins. "I live in a bachelor household, remember? My mom died when I was a kid. I hardly remember her. I kind of had to learn to cook."

"Oh," I murmur, then sit up straighter. "Wait a minute. How'd you get in here?"

"Opened the front door." He takes another sip from his mug and looks at me like I'm in trouble. "Your mom really should lock the door when she leaves."

I arch a brow. "Would that have kept you out?"

He smiles a little. "You know me well."

And I guess I do. I understand the whole not-being-what-your-family-wants thing. Understand what it feels like to be a constant disappointment. Together, in this, we are the same.

His smile fades. "But there are other threats—"

"And a locked door would keep them out, right?"

Instantly, I regret reminding him of that fact. Regret the shadow that falls over his face and darkens his eyes to green.

"Hey," I say, rising from bed, determined to make him forget that sinister forces exist, ready to harm me . . . and tear us apart. That he lives side by side with some of them. Probably the worst of them. The pride doesn't want me dead, after all. Even the enkros aren't an immediate danger. They're faceless, misty-figured demons to me, a hidden boogeyman, a threat only if hunters catch me and turn me over to them.

"Let's not go there," I say, wrapping my arms around his waist.

He squeezes me so hard air gusts from my lips. "I don't want you hurt. Ever."

There's something in his voice, in the way he holds me—a starkness, an intensity that makes my skin tremble and my stomach clench.

And I wonder if he knows something more. If he hasn't told me everything.

What else could there be?

I ignore the feeling and bury my face in his warm chest. The soft cool cotton of his shirt feels pleasant on my skin. "Then you might want to relax your hold 'cause you're crushing me," I tease.

"C'mon," he says, taking my hand and leading me into the kitchen. "I'm starved. Let's eat."

His voice is normal now. Velvet deep. Smoothly even. Whatever I heard is gone. Later, I wonder if I imagined it.

"Will hasn't been at school lately."

I look up from my book at my sister's nonchalant comment. Tamra works on the floor beside her bed. She watches me carefully, pen poised over her paper.

"Oh?" I say, proud at the calmness of my voice, that I don't bite the baited hook. "Maybe he went out of town again."

"No. His cousins are in school." Evidently she's aware of their fishing expeditions, although not their true prey.

I shrug and look back at my book. After a moment, I hear the scratch of her pen resume, and I breathe again . . . hoping I passed her test. Fortunately, Mrs. Hennessey hasn't mentioned Will's visits, and I don't think she will. Somehow we've formed an alliance.

"Have you heard from him?"

Apparently, she's not finished. And this is where it gets hard. Lying to my sister has never been easy, but telling her the truth may lead to other truths that she's not ready to hear . . . and I'm not ready to confess.

"Nope."

"Huh. Guess he's not such a prince after all." She looks at me directly. I resist insisting that Will is everything. A prince and more. "You okay?" she asks.

"Yeah. Never much believed in princes."

"No kidding." She shrugs, and I can't help think about Cassian. She used to believe he was a prince. I'm not sure she still doesn't. "This running into frogs is new for you, that's all."

I grunt. Hoping to redirect her thoughts, I ask, "How's Ben?"

"Fine. I guess."

Meaning that Tamra isn't into him. He's not Cassian, after all. No matter how she had determined to move on, I'm certain Cassian is still there, larger than life in her head. Too bad. A boyfriend would distract her from worrying about me—from worrying over whether or not I'm going to blow it for her here. That is, more than I already have. A boyfriend would also give her that taste of normalcy she wants so badly.

Maybe I should tell her about Will. Explain to her that I want to stay here now, that I want to make it work. That I like Will that much . . . that I *more* than like him. That because of him, I *can* stay here. I sigh. That would be a big conversation. Bigger than I want to have. She'll find out tomorrow night anyway when he shows up for our date.

"I kind of like someone else now," she says before I can say anything.

I look up. "Yeah? You found your prince?"

"Hmm. Maybe." She nods, not elaborating, and I don't push. Tamra won't tell more than she wants to. We're alike in that way, I guess. For too long, we've lived together, but separately, holding the deepest parts of our hearts hidden because the other won't like what's there. Problem is, we know each other well enough that it's hard to hide much of anything.

I watch her for a moment, my lips parted, ready to break that trend. But no words materialize. Some habits are hard to break. I'm not ready to tell her about Will yet. Right now it's a warm little secret hugged close to my heart. A beautiful butterfly I've managed to capture and hold carefully in my cupped hands.

She'll know soon enough. For now, I'll hold my lovely butterfly close and try not to crush it.

The following day, Will doesn't put in his usual appearance.

Not surprising. He told me he would go to school today. . . . I harassed him until he promised. I don't want him to get in trouble or flunk out because of me, and I don't want to draw any more attention to myself with his family.

But since he's promised me that before and always showed up anyway, I can't help feel disappointed when the day wanes with no sight of him. Even with our date tonight, it's a long stretch of hours without him.

I visit Mrs. Hennessey for a while. We watch a little

television together before her nap, then I head home and spread out on my bed to catch up on schoolwork. I breeze through chemistry and start on my geometry—the quadratic formula. I learned it two years ago, so I'm working through the problems in an easy rhythm when I hear it.

A soft click.

A creaky floorboard.

My skin pops, dances, shivers with excitement. *Will.* I lower my pencil and sit up, brushing anxiously at my hair.

"Hello? Mom?" I'm convinced it's not Mom but ask anyway. Just in case.

Nothing. Silence.

"Mrs. Hennessey?"

Rising, I move to my door and stare into the living room. The front door is open. Light streams in and tiny motes of dust dance inside the beams of sunshine. Just beyond, the pool gleams a blue so bright it hurts my eyes.

"Will?" I risk calling. My voice rings hopefully.

I stride forward, shooting a quick glance at the empty kitchen. Just in case he's there, making us a snack. Nothing. At the front door, I peer outside, see nothing.

My lips twist in disappointment. No Will.

I close the door slowly, make sure it shuts solidly this time. My skin still ripples, snapping with energy. The kind of energy I feel around Will. Except Will would answer me.

Staring at the door, I chafe my arms, puckered to goose-flesh despite my body's warmth. For what it's worth, I go ahead and lock the door. The quiet feels thick and oppressive. Far too still.

My skin swims in heat, uncomfortably warm. A dip in the pool might help. With a hand on the hem of my shirt, I turn to get my suit. And scream.

28

I bite back my cry, cut it short before it can wake Mrs. Hennessey and bring her running.

"Hello, Jacinda."

Dread strikes deep in the well of my heart at that voice. I knew this moment would eventually arrive, but that didn't make me ready. He promised five weeks, after all. I swallow hard, knowing that persuading him to leave a second time will be harder.

My lungs smolder. My windpipe widens, swells with heat, ready to defend myself. The fire inside me intensifies when I think about the wing clipping that awaits me . . . that he wants to take me back to endure. "Get out," I rasp.

His eyes flare wide, the pupils thinning to vertical slits.

"Your mother told you," he states flatly.

"Yeah," I snap. "She told me."

"She doesn't know everything. She doesn't know me . . . or how I feel. I would never force you to do anything against your will, and I would never, ever let anyone harm you."

His words enrage me. Lies, I'm convinced. My hand shoots out, ready to slap that earnest look off his face. The same earnest look he'd given me the first time he lied to my face.

He catches my hand, squeezes the wrist tight. "Jacinda—"

"I don't believe you. You gave me your word. Five weeks—"

"Five weeks was too long. I couldn't leave you for that long without checking on you."

"Because you're a liar," I assert.

His expression cracks. Emotion bleeds through. He knows I'm not talking about just the five weeks. With a shake of his head, he sounds almost sorry as he admits, "Maybe I didn't tell you everything, but it doesn't change anything I said. I will never hurt you. I want to try to protect you."

"Try," I repeat.

His jaw clenches. "I can. I can stop them."

After several moments, I twist my hand free. He lets me go. Rubbing my wrist, I glare at him. "I have a life here now." My fingers stretch, curl into talons at my sides, still hungry to fight him. "Make me go, and I'll never forgive you."

He inhales deeply, his broad chest lifting high. "Well. I can't have that."

"Then you'll go? Leave me alone?" Hope stirs.

He shakes his head. "I didn't say that."

"Of course not," I sneer. "What do you mean then?" Panic washes over me at the thought of him staying here and learning about Will and his family. "There's no reason for you to stay."

His dark eyes glint. "There's *you*. I can give you more time. You can't seriously fit in here. You'll come around."

"I won't!"

His voice cracks like thunder on the air. "I won't leave you! Do you know how unbearable it's been without you? You're not like the rest of them." His hand swipes through air almost savagely. I stare at him, my eyes wide and aching. "You're not some well-trained puppy content to go along with what you're told. You have fire." He laughs brokenly. "I don't mean literally, although there is that. There's something in you, Jacinda. You're the only thing real for me there, the only thing remotely interesting." He stares at me starkly and I don't breathe. He looks ready to reach out and fold me into his arms.

I jump hastily back. Unbelievably, he looks hurt. Dropping his immense hands, he speaks again, evenly, calmly. "I'll give you more space. Time for you to realize that this"—he motions to the living room—"isn't for you. You need mists and mountains and sky. *Flight.* How can you stay here where you have none of that? How can you hope to survive? If you haven't figured that out yet, you will."

In my mind, I see Will. Think how he has become the mist, the sky, *everything*, to me. I do more than survive here. I love. But Cassian can never know that.

"What I have here beats what waits for me back home. The wing clipping you so conveniently failed to mention—"

"Is *not* going to happen, Jacinda." He steps closer. His head dips to look into my eyes. "You have my word. If you return with me, you won't be harmed. I'd die first."

His words flow through me like a chill wind. "But your father—"

"My father won't be our alpha forever. Someday, I'll lead. Everyone knows it. The pride will listen to me. I promise you'll be safe."

Can I trust him again? Even after all he said? If I do and I'm wrong, the cost is too high. My life. "You'll wait for me to *agree* to go back with you?" I want to be clear on this point. "You won't force me in any way? Or reveal yourself to anyone, no matter what?"

"I'll wait," he promises. "However long you need."

He'll wait. But he'll be lurking about. Nearby. Watching. And I won't always know it.

Funny how things change. In the beginning, I thought I could never stay here. Now I don't want to leave. Mostly because of Will, but also because I've decided to give Mom and Tamra what they want. A chance. It can't be all about me. If I'm strong enough, smart enough, my draki can make it. And of course, Will can help with that. A few kisses. A smile. A brush of his hand and my draki is revived. And I no longer have to hide it from him.

I can last through high school. For Mom, for Tamra. After graduation, I can go with Will when he cuts free from his family. Just two more years. We'll figure out the specifics. The how and where. For the first time since coming here, I feel the stirrings of hope. I won't let Cassian ruin that.

"You're going to wait forever," I vow. "I won't change my mind."

Cassian's mouth curves enigmatically. Like he knows something I don't. He's eighteen, but in that moment I can believe he has several more years than that on me. "Things change all the time. People change. I'll take my chances."

I shake my head. "You'll see. I won't change my mind."

And then he'll go. Because he can't wait forever. No matter what he says. He's got a pride to lead. He's not going to hang around here for two years. No matter how *interesting* I am to him.

"We'll see."

I glance at the blinking clock on top of the TV. "You better go before my mom gets home."

"Right." He moves to the door. "Bye, Jacinda."

I don't return the farewell. Don't want to pretend we've reached a level where niceties exist between us.

We're not friends. Not even close. And we never will be.

29

At five o'clock, Mom sticks her head in the bedroom. "What do you want to do for dinner tonight,
Jacinda?"

She switched shifts with someone so she could stay home
with us one Friday night for a change. I feel a flicker of guilt.
For all her trouble, she's going to be alone.

Tamra has plans, too—no surprise. And I haven't told
either one of them about my date with Will yet. Right now,
looking at me, Mom thinks she's going to have a fun night
with at least one of her girls.

Tamra is trying on clothes. She didn't volunteer anything
more than that she's going out with friends. And I don't ask.
Don't expect to know these friends if she did tell me. Given

recent events, I'm pretty sure they're not cheerleaders.

I spot a pretty eyelet blouse she's tossed—eliminated as an option—on the bed, and think it's perfect for my date with Will.

Inhaling, I confess, "Um, I'm actually going out, too."

Tamra swings around.

"Really?" Mom asks, crossing her arms and stepping into the room. "With who?" A small note of hope rings her voice. That the difficult daughter might actually be coming along. Fitting in. Making friends.

"With Will." I avoid calling it a date. No need to alarm her.

"Will?" Tamra's voice cuts in. "Isn't that kind of . . . *stupid*?"

Mom's brow scrunches like she's concentrating. "He's the reason those girls harassed you in the bathroom, right?" Apparently, Tamra has been talking to Mom. "The boy who makes you . . ."

Manifest. Like it's something dirty, she can't even say it anymore.

"I can control it around him now," I lie. Better than telling her I don't need to.

Mom's eyes harden. "I don't want you going out with him," she says this quickly, flatly.

"Yeah. Me too," Tamra chimes in, like she has some kind of authority over me.

"You don't get a say," I snap at her.

Tamra's livid now, and I'm sure it's because I lied to her when she asked me about Will. Guess I should have told her the truth then instead of wanting to keep it a cozy little secret just between me and Will. "He's caused us nothing but trouble—"

I stab a finger through the air. "He's the only reason I even want to stay here! The only reason I haven't run away yet! You should be thankful I met him." Not totally true. Mom and Tamra play a part, too . . . but I'm too mad to admit that.

Mom jerks, blinks. Color bleeds from her face.

"Jacinda." She exhales my name in a hushed breath. Like I've said something horrible. Done something even worse.

"What? You think I haven't thought about running away?" I demand. "I was miserable until Will! I don't think I could stand a day here without him!"

Tamra grunts in disgust and turns back to the closet.

Mom's quiet. Looks pale and afraid. I can see her thinking, processing. I stare at her, try to feed her my hope. Make her understand that everything's better, everything will be all right as long as I have Will.

She shakes her head sadly, regretfully. "It's too dangerous for you to be with him."

If only she knew how dangerous.

"Fine," I say tightly, tossing my hands up. "Keep me in a bubble, why don't you? Or homeschool me! Don't you think any boy that I like . . . that I'm attracted to might make

286

my draki come to life?" I don't think this is true, but I say so anyway. It's strictly Will. There's something about *him*. Something in him reaches inside me. No other boy could affect me the way he does.

Mom shakes her head. "Jacinda—"

"Should I try going out with a guy that grosses me out just to play it safe?"

"Of course not," she quickly says. "But maybe you shouldn't date anyone until your draki—"

"Is *dead*?" I finish, biting out. "I know." I fan my hands in the air. "It's that great event you've been waiting for. The day you can call me human."

And this hurts. Like a wound that just won't heal, but pulses open and bloody. The knowledge that I'm not what she wants, that I have to be someone I don't want to be in order to have her approval. . . .

Tears burn in my eyes at the unfairness of it all. I pull in a deep breath. "Has it occurred to you it may not die? That my draki is not a part of me you can just kill off? That it *is* me. Forever. All of me. Who. I. Am." I splay my hand over my heart. "I know you think it will eventually wither away here, but I'm a fire-breather, remember? That makes me different from everything we've ever known about our kind."

She shakes her head. Looks tired. Old and a little scared. "You're not going out with him."

I clench my hands until the bones ache. "You can't do this—"

"What? Be your mother?" she snaps, her amber eyes lively again. "That's never going to stop, Jacinda. Get used to it."

I know she's right, of course. She loves me and will always do what she thinks is right to protect me. Even if she makes me miserable in the process. She'll do whatever she has to do.

I cross my arms, settle my lips in a grim line. And so will I.

Two minutes before Will is scheduled to arrive, I sneak out the window, sliding it shut quietly.

Mom's in the kitchen, getting a drink and snack ready for the movie I agreed to watch with her. The buttery aroma of popcorn fills the air, the frenzied staccato of popping covering up any sounds I make.

Tamra left half an hour ago, still angry at me. She didn't even say good night.

As I run around the pool, I spot Mrs. Hennessey looking out the window, the blue light of her television pulsing behind her. I wave, hoping I don't resemble a prison escapee too much. Air crashes from my lips as I hurry.

Will's at the curb, just stepping out from his Land Rover. His face relaxes when he sees me. A loose smile forms on his lips. "Hey. I was coming in—"

"That's okay. Let's go." I open the passenger door before he can reach it and hop inside. Breathless.

He gets back in, moving slowly, sending me curious looks.

My hands tap an impatient rhythm on my thighs.

"You sure you're all right? I wanted to meet your mom—"

"Not such a good idea right now." I glance at the house. No sign of Mom, thankfully. "Let's just get out of here."

He nods with slow uncertainty. "All right."

I can tell he's not happy—he wants to be the proper boyfriend and everything. I wish I could let him. But I know it won't work with my mother. Not yet.

"I missed you," I say, hoping that's enough to make him feel better. "It's been a long day."

He laughs. "I missed you, too. I could have cut school, you know. You're the one—"

"I know. I know." I shake my head. "I just don't want you doing that for me anymore."

"Well, I won't have to. You'll be back on Monday."

He starts the ignition and drives. I sigh with relief as we pull away. Finally on our date.

I stare into the deepening night, the flashing lights of oncoming traffic mesmerize me in the clinging silence. My thoughts swing from Mom to someone else. Someone who's in all likelihood nearby. Hopefully, not too near.

I tell myself he'll keep his word. Hang back. Even if he sees me with another boy. But I'm not a hundred percent convinced.

I glance over my shoulder, at the car following close

behind us. It's impossible to see the driver. To tell if it's Cassian. After a moment, it pulls around and passes us. I sigh.

"Why do I get the feeling that I'm abducting you? Should I be on alert for sirens in the rearview mirror?"

"I left willingly." I force a grin and tease, "I don't think you'll get arrested."

"Great. You don't 'think.' That's encouraging." He gives me a wincing smile. "But maybe not. I am eighteen, after all—"

"You're eighteen? But you're a sophomore."

An uneasy look passes over his face. "I missed a lot of school a few years back. Half of seventh grade and all of eighth, in fact. I was sick."

"Sick?" I echo. The reminder of his mortality crashes down on me. It'll always be there, smoke rising between us. Xander had mentioned Will being ill, but I never imagined it as anything serious.

"How? I mean, what . . ."

He shrugs like it's nothing, but he won't glance at me. He stares at the road. "Leukemia. But I'm better now. Completely cured."

"Were you *very* . . . bad off?"

"For about a year. The prognosis wasn't—" He stops suddenly, like he's said too much, and I get that sense again. The feeling that he's not telling me something. That he's holding back. A muscle in his jaw ripples with tension. "Look, don't worry about it. Aren't I a perfect male specimen now?" He sends me a wink. "Don't I look healthy?"

He does. Everything about him screams virile young male. But then not everything is what it appears. I know that better than anyone.

"It's amazing what doctors can do these days." He's staring intently at the road again, and I'm convinced there's something he's not telling me. Maybe something he never will. But then why would he hide anything from me? After everything we know now about each other? What would be the point?

I nod. Feel a little cold inside. I don't like thinking he's keeping something from me. Almost as much as I don't like thinking I could have lost him. That we may never have met. That I would have died in that cave when his family found me.

And then there's the fact that he could still die. That he *will*. Sure, not now, but someday. Long before me. A dull throbbing gnaws at my temples. I dig my fingertips into the pain.

But this is our first real date. I don't want to ruin it, so I change the subject. "So. Where are we going?"

"You like Greek food? It's a bit of a drive, but it's worth it. Great hummus. Our first date should be special." He grins, slides me a glance. "Finally, huh?"

I smile, but my lips feel brittle, trembly. I manage to hold it in place. For a little while at least, I can pretend everything's okay. That Cassian's not somewhere out there . . . and farther away, beyond this desert, the pride isn't waiting for me.

Lights tattoo our rearview mirror. I twist in the seat and squint against the glare. The vehicle sticks close. Directly behind us. This time it's no car eager to pass us.

My heart thuds, the sound fast in my ears. I can't help it—I think of Cassian. Or worse, the pride. Severin. I don't imagine Cassian would be so obvious. He already confronted me. He might be following me, watching from the shadows, but he wouldn't reveal himself like this. He promised.

I twist my fingers in my lap and glance at Will. He lifts one of my hands from my lap, laces our fingers together and squeezes. The touch makes me feel strong. Safe.

Strange that I should feel so safe with a draki hunter. But there it is. I can't deny it. Don't even try anymore. Nor can I deny the hopeful stirrings in me that make me believe I can stay here. Forever. In this desert. If maybe I couldn't survive and flourish with him at my side.

The vehicle behind us honks its horn. My skin contracts, snaps sharply.

"Are they tailgating us?" I ask, hoping I'm overreacting, that I'm just paranoid because of Cassian's visit, still so fresh.

Will sets his mouth grimly. "Yeah."

"Who are they? What do they want?"

"It's Xander."

My heart chills above my surging lungs. "Oh." Cassian would have been better in my mind. At least I know what to expect with him.

He glances at me. "We don't have to pull over. He'll go away. I don't want you around him anymore. It's too risky."

"No." I shake my head. "We should pull over. Why wouldn't we? It will make him more suspicious if you make a big deal about keeping me away from him—"

"It's our date—"

"Let's just get it over with. Then, we can have our night." I flutter a hand. "Give him what he wants—"

Will's harsh laughter fills the car. It's an uneasy sound.

"What's so funny?"

"You don't get it at all, do you?"

I stare at him, at his strong profile. "I guess I don't. Why don't you explain?"

He drives, glaring straight ahead. Finally, he says in a growl, "He wants *you.*"

I jerk. "Me?" Feel his words like I've been slapped. "Why?"

"Well, there's that he thinks there's more to you. He still suspects you know too much. That I've told you everything. And then there's the constant competition between us." His long fingers flex over the steering wheel. "We were born three months apart, you know."

I didn't.

Will continues, "He's a grade behind because he hunts. Whenever he can. He's so messed up that he even goes out alone, even leaves Angus."

I arch a brow at that.

"Crazy, I know. But he hasn't been all that balanced since . . ." He stops.

"Since?"

"Since I got so good at tracking and became important to the family. More important than Xander."

I stiffen at the reminder that he's a tracker, the best in his family. How many draki have been killed or captured because of him? Yet I also feel empathy. Because I know what it feels like to be used, valued only for what you can do . . . not who you are, not who you want to be.

"Since birth, we've been pitted against each other. Our fathers did it to us. Their father to them." He nods. "Natural, I guess. To make us stronger. Back when hunting draki was more dangerous, we didn't have technology on our side. A lot who left on the hunt never returned."

This, I know. At least I know that the draki have never been more vulnerable than now. Hunters have become wiser, deadlier adversaries against our dwindling numbers. In this day and age of net launchers and all-terrain vehicles and communication devices that make surrounding and capturing us easier. In a time when draki are losing the dragon traits that have defended them through the generations. All except me.

Now Will and his people hold the advantage—

I shudder, hating this. This thinking of us as separate. Me versus him. A part of me turns cold with dread that it will always be this way.

"Xander hates me." He shrugs like it's natural.

This is beyond my understanding. Despite everything Mom has done, despite the tension between me and Tamra, my family would never deliberately hurt me. Our bond runs too deep.

Will looks at me as he eases his foot off the gas. "Sure you want me to pull over? He'll steal you away at the first chance if for no reason than to bug me."

I cross my arms. Lift my chin. "He can't *steal* me. I'm not a toy for two boys to fight over. Pull over."

And yet unease slides into the pit of my belly, rests there like a coiled snake.

Because the creepy feeling I get around Xander is now justified. Has become more than a vague feeling. Sick dread curls around my heart as we slow down. If Xander ever finds out, he'll do his best to destroy me, not just because of what I am but also to hurt Will. This certainty sinks slowly, deeply into my chest.

We pull over into a diner parking lot. The smell of greasy bacon hangs in the air. We idle at the back of the lot, far from the few cars parked near the doors.

A big four-by-four truck pulls up alongside us. Windows roll down and I look across Will. Xander and Angus sit in the front, smiling artificially. Easy and friendly in a way that makes my flesh shiver.

"Hey, we went by your house," Xander calls out. "Your dad said you left for the night."

"Yeah." Will's hand squeezes mine. "I have plans."

"I see that." Xander nods, his gaze fixed on me. "We're headed up to Big Rock. Want to come?"

"We have other plans."

Angus's fleshy lips curl. "Ah, whipped already, I see."

I really hate him.

"Shut up," Will tosses out, already moving to put the gear in drive, but then I catch a motion behind Will's cousins. A hand emerges from the backseat and closes over the headrest behind Xander.

"Wait—stop," I hiss.

Tamra's head pops up from the backseat.

"Tamra?" I call, practically in Will's lap now.

She's hanging out with Xander? This is the guy she was talking about . . . the new guy she likes? No wonder she didn't want me going out with Will tonight. She must have known there was a chance she'd run into us. My stomach churns with the knowledge that I might have put a stop to this development if I had been around and not suspended—if I had demanded more information about her life. Maybe if I had paid closer attention to my sister. If I had just told her the truth, she'd understand the danger. My fingers clench around Will's hand.

Tamra grins at me, an impish light glinting her eyes. She's enjoying this. Knows that I won't like her hanging out with these guys. "Hey, Jacinda. See you made it out tonight after all."

I slide my gaze to Will, hoping he can read the message

in my eyes: *I can't leave Tamra with them.*

"You sure?" he whispers, leaning his head close.

I nod, mouth the word, "Yes."

He sighs in understanding. "All right," Will calls grimly, turning back to his cousins again. "We'll come for a little while."

Xander smiles smugly, and I know this isn't by accident. He knows exactly what he's doing. He set my sister up as bait. For whatever reason, he wants me and Will on Big Rock.

30

S everal other vehicles converge at the bottom of Big Rock at the same time we do.

Bodies climb out of cars. Shadowy figures against a smoky night. Doors slam. I search for Tamra as we start out, hoping to pull her aside and tell her everything. Anything to get her to leave with Will and me.

Electric lanterns swing from hands, lighting the way as we ascend Big Rock. I spot her flaming hair. Even in the darkness, it holds light. She avoids me, moving neatly amid the group as we climb, never looking at me.

"Hey, you okay?" Will says close to my ear.

"What is this place?" I mumble.

"Just a place people like to party."

I shake my head, glance into the pressing blackness,

where the light does not reach. "What's she doing here?" I mutter.

"Looking for some fun. Same as everyone else here."

Yes, being a normal kid, I think. Stirring up trouble. Except she couldn't have chosen worse company.

Again, I wonder what she's been up to this week. Has she been studying with Xander those nights she went out? I feel sick at the thought of her in his house, no doubt near a room of horrors like the one in Will's house.

I glance around the group of people climbing to the top with us, recognizing a few as older cousins of Will. Others I don't know. Their faces are hard-edged. The eyes dissolute, flat, and dark in the night. Dark and motionless as black space. When we reach the top, Will nods and greets several of them in a quiet, muted way, keeping me close to his side, almost behind him.

My skin crawls, muscles tense, and my back tingles prickly hot and itchy, readying for flight. Escape.

Will's gaze darts. Uneasy, watchful—full predator mode.

I tug my hand free to face him. My heart slows, stills in my too-tight chest as I search his face. "Is this a . . ." I glance around, notice a few of the guys look in their twenties or early thirties. Xander, one arm draped around Tamra, greets them jovially, slapping their backs. I drop my voice and lean in to Will. "Is this some kind of gathering for hunters?"

His gaze is overly bright, apologetic. He nods only once, but I have my answer.

So many wolves. And I've walked right into their den.

We mill around the top of Big Rock, a smooth stretch of hilltop that crouches above one end of Chaparral. I stare down at the town sitting deep inside the desert basin. The view is beautiful.

An hour passes, but it feels like forever. I'm supposed to be on a date right now, in a restaurant somewhere down in that glowing city. Instead, I'm here with a crowd consisting of mostly hunters. The lanterns form a small jagged circle. A stereo sits in the middle, throbbing music into the night.

I'm glad for the dark. Glad that no one can see my skin glimmer, flash and dim with amber light, my body's warning for me to flee. And I would if I could . . . but not without Tamra.

"We can leave whenever you want," Will says beside me. He holds my arm, his thumb tracing over my erratic skin, and I know he's aware of its constant shifting.

I follow the smooth fall of Tamra's red hair as she steps up to the keg. In the back of my mind, I wonder how they lugged a keg all the way up here. "Just give me a minute."

Walking away from Will, I approach her, determination tightening my shoulders. Closing my hand around her arm, I drag her away from the rowdy group and out of the circle of light.

Xander starts to follow, but Will stops him. The two loom nearby, exchanging heated words as I pull her deeper into shadow.

Tamra clutches an empty cup. I glare from the cup to her. "You don't even *like* the taste of beer."

In the near dark, I make out her smile. Her eyes gleam brightly in the night. "Just assimilating. One of us has to."

I ignore the jibe and shake my head. "This isn't you."

"Careful, Jacinda," she warns in mocking tones. "You're glowing a bit. But then, I guess you could just tell your date you're into body glitter."

"What are you doing here?" I demand.

"What are *you* doing here?"

"I'm here because of you. Xander Rutledge? C'mon, Tamra. You have to know his reputation. The girls who go out with him—"

"Ah, big sister. Really making those eleven minutes count, huh?" She leans in. "I'll let you in on a little secret. I already have a mother. Hey," she says with a laugh, "same mother as yours actually."

Is she drunk? "I know you're mad at me, but you shouldn't be here with these—"

"And you should?" Tamra flings a hand toward the group, toward Will standing at the edge, waiting for me. "You're supposed to be home. Mom said you couldn't go out with him. What are you doing here?"

I glance pointedly at the empty plastic cup in her hand. "It's safe to say Mom wouldn't be happy with either one of us right now."

Tamra shrugs, scuffs her shoe. Pebbles pop, roll down the slope into the black night. "Yeah, well. What are you going to do about it, Jace? Call her?"

"Tamra, please. Come with me—"

"And what? Crash your date?" She laughs shortly. "I don't think so."

"Will won't mind."

"No." She cocks her head and makes an ugly sound in her throat. "But *I* mind. I've lived in your shadow long enough. Xander's into me. And I'm into him." Her voice cracks here a bit, and I don't believe it. Not for one moment. She's not into Xander. She's into doing whatever it takes to fit in, and if it happens to piss me off in the process that's just an added bonus. "Just go away and leave me alone." Turning, she walks back to the party.

"Jacinda?" Will approaches me in the dark.

Shaking, I turn into his arms. He smooths a hand over the side of my face, brushes the hair behind my ear, holds me close. "Are you all right? Do you want to go?"

Leave? Yes. Leave Tamra? A chill chases over my skin.

I suck in a breath, say against his chest, "I hate to leave her with . . ."

"Xander," he supplies grimly.

I nod. After everything Will's told me of his cousin, I'm convinced he'll use Tamra. Hurt her. He can't get to me or Will, but he can get to her. If he thinks there's more to me, that I might be an enkros, he must assume Tamra's hiding something, too. In her state, she'll make an easy target for him. Because she's that mad at me—that fed up with the life forced on her.

"You can't get her to come with us?" he asks.

"She's so mad at me," I whisper, choke a little.

"Ah, Jacinda." He pulls my face from his chest and rests his forehead to mine, kisses me with dry, cool lips. "You can't beat yourself up about this. You can't help what you are."

I nod, but I'm not too sure about that.

I haven't exactly tried to be what Mom and Tamra want. I've fought it—*them*—every step of the way. I've clung to my draki when it would have been safer for all of us if I just let it go. Even stayed here when Cassian tracked me down. Maybe that does make me selfish.

And now, no matter what I try to tell myself, the only reason I've decided to stay, the only reason I'm even here, is because of Will. He's an addictive drug to me that I can't quit. Again, selfish.

He kisses me a second time and I let it distract me. Let the kiss grow hotter between us. Happy to forget where I am.

Crazy as it sounds, Will's my refuge. Someone who knows everything about me. And likes me anyway. *Loves me.* Understands me. Isn't out to change me. He's the only one I can say that about.

I pull back to gaze at him, sliding my hands over his hard shoulders, palms down. Our breaths merge, mingle. Grow fast and hard. His eyes glitter, tiny gold torches in the dark. My fingers tighten. Clutch his shirt. Our mouths brush again. Once. Twice. Savoring the taste of each other.

Abruptly, his lips change. Feel cold. Icy. With dull dread,

I know it's me. He's not cold. My temperature has changed. My skin snaps. Too hot, it hisses like the drop of water on a hot stove.

The pounding beat of music fades. Voices and laughter disappear as the burn builds, twists up through my center in a writhing lick of flame.

I sigh. Feel the release of steam from my lips. It escapes before I can catch it.

He winces against my lips, pulls back sharply. "Jacinda . . ."

Before I can lean away and force coldness back in so that I don't singe my boyfriend—a voice rings out and does it for me. The smolder dies in my lungs. Dropping my hands from Will, I slowly turn.

"So *this* is why you want to stay here."

My gaze finds Cassian immediately, a large, dark shape rising out of the night. His hair swings, brushing his broad shoulders as he walks. "So much for your promise," I spit out.

Will tenses, pulls me close to his side, the stance protective.

Cassian. My every pore vibrates with fury, pulses wide.

He doesn't even look my way. It's like he's not even aware of me. He glares at Will, lips pulled back in a snarl. "Don't touch her."

"Cassian, don't." I stop, cringing, blinking tight, wishing I had not just spoken his name.

Now Will knows.

His gaze swerves to me. The flesh ticks near his eye. "Cassian?" he demands.

I don't answer. Don't breathe. Don't risk freeing the steam that's risen to my throat. The steam that I want to release full blast on Cassian. I turn and stare unblinking at him. Warning him with my eyes to behave himself.

"This is *Cassian*?" Will repeats, really hung up on that point, and how can I blame him?

"Will, let me handle this."

"You knew he was here?" Will demands, his lips pulling tight. "And didn't tell me?"

I wince, admitting, "He promised to keep his distance."

"But I didn't promise," Cassian interjects, "to sit by in silence while you make out with some—"

"Shut up!" I spin around. Steam wafts from my nose.

Cassian's gaze follows the tendrils of smoke. He smiles in satisfaction. Laughs low and deep, menacing. His voice falls on the air, a sneaking whisper. "Look at you, Jacinda. You can't stop what you are." He glances at Will and his smile slips, remembering we have an audience . . . and assuming Will knows nothing of my true self. "Now come with me before you do something we'll both regret."

And I do look. Glance down at my arms to see my flesh wink back at me, glistening fire gold in the shadows.

"You're like me," he adds. "You don't belong here, not with him."

Beside me, Will growls low in his throat. His hand tightens on my arm.

Cassian's flesh flashes in and out, blurs a glimmering charcoal. He lifts his hand toward me. "End this game. Come with me now."

I part my lips to speak. To refuse. A dry little croak escapes. I swallow, wet my lips to try again. But never get the chance.

Will flies past me in a blur. In a diving arc, he takes Cassian down. They strike the ground with a heavy crack. A cloud of red dust rises, consuming them both. I stare, shaking, my eyes wide and aching in my face. *What have I done?*

31

Instantly, they're lost in a tangle—a great mess of flailing limbs. Grunts. Curses. Tearing flesh. The smack of skin on skin fills the air.

"Stop! Stop it!" I dance out of the way.

They roll, writhing across the ground. Pebbles and rocks shake loose and tumble down the slope into the greedy, grasping dark.

"Jacinda!" Tamra's at my side. Xander beside her. Gratefully, the rest of the group are lost in their own little world of drunken revelry in the distance, unaware of the fight. "Is that *Cassian*?"

I nod anxiously.

"Who's Cassian?" Xander asks.

Will twists, surges up on top of Cassian. Swings back his fist and connects it with Cassian's face. I jerk at the crunch of bone on bone. The coppery tang of blood sweeps over my teeth, and I realize I've bitten my lip.

Cassian laughs coldly, touching the blood sweeping from his nose. And something niggles through my mind. *Will shouldn't be stronger than Cassian.* Cassian's the strongest draki I know. A powerhouse onyx.

Tamra wraps her arms around me, everything between us forgotten.

"Tamra," I whisper, clinging to her.

"It's okay. I'm right here."

And I feel awful, hot regret sweeps over me. I should have told her. Told her everything.

Using his feet, Cassian launches Will off him with all the force of his body. With all the force of a draki. Will lands on his side, his face contorting. Cassian leaps through the air after him. Again they're locked in struggle. Together they roll, spin down the angled rock.

I scream as they keep rolling, gaining momentum, all the while still throwing punches.

Then Will must realize what's happening. He stops punching, claws the ground, his fingers grasping. Red dirt flies loose. His hands come up empty, clutching air. It all happens so quickly. I see Will's face. The wild eyes. His mouth frozen on a cry. The sound of fast-sliding rock.

I break from Tamra and run toward him, stopping just

before the incline becomes too steep. With my heart in my throat, I watch as Will and Cassian disappear from sight, a skidding blur down the rocky slope.

"Will!"

I risk it and run even closer, jerking to a stop at the sudden drop-off. Where he vanished. Right off the rock and into the waiting dark. For a split second, there's no sound except the pumping music behind me.

In the far well of the desert below, I hear a few sickening thwacks, each one making me cringe, wither, and die inside. Will reaching bottom.

I know it's not Cassian. Cassian wouldn't fall.

My hands curl, clench into tight, bloodless fists. I whirl around. Feel my heart seize in my chest. Pain. Agony. So much that I can't even breathe. Tears chase silently down my cheeks.

Tamra shakes her head in denial, her eyes fierce, almost as wild as Will's in that last glimpse.

I find my breath. Air saws from my lips—hot thick smoke.

In an instant, I take it all in: Tamra's shocked expression. Xander's pale face, his eyes as dark as the surrounding night. Black ink. Fathomless pools. He watches me. Sees the steam spilling from my mouth.

And I don't care.

Stupid, maybe. But I can't stop it. And Tamra knows it. She lunges forward, hand outstretched like if she can only reach me, touch me, she can stop it. Stop me.

"Jacinda, no!"

It happens instantly. Before I know it, my limbs drag into position, loosening and lengthening for flight. Ridges break out on my nose, quivering and contracting. The small sleeves of my blouse slip from my arms. Fall to earth with a broken whisper. My wings unfurl, snapping wide behind me. Lifting my razor-sharpened face, I brace my legs. Stretch my arms. My skin flickers firelight in the night as I spring into the air.

Then, I'm descending, soaring through the dark toward Will with a beat of outstretched wings.

Instinct kicks in and my vision adjusts to the dark.

Warm air glides over me as I move through the night. Swim through wind with no thought to its thinness. To air so warm and dry it crackles around my body like electricity.

Fear coats my mouth, sour and metallic. But not for myself. I don't even think about what I have done. Only one word ricochets through my head. One name. *Will.*

Later I'll think about the consequences of manifesting in front of Xander. Not now. Not yet. Later. When I find Will. *Alive.* Then, together, we'll work it out.

At the base, I touch down, see nothing. No sign of Will. I push off the ground. Far above, at the top of Big Rock, music echoes distantly. Slowly, I survey the sage and cacti, my wings churning warm, dry air around me. Will has to be close.

He didn't fly away. Unlike Cassian. I glance over my

shoulder. He's close, too. Lurking. Treading air. Watching. He won't be happy that I revealed myself in front of someone. Especially to save a human. A boy he caught me kissing, no less.

"Jacinda!" Will's voice rings out.

My heart lifts. I follow the sound of my name and find him clinging to an outcropping, his biceps flexed, quivering from the strain.

Blood covers half his face. A thick, oozing cut slashes his right eyebrow. Drips into one eye—swollen shut. From Cassian or his fall, I don't know.

I draw closer, reach him, and that's when I notice something's wrong.

His good eye widens, sees me as I am. "Jacinda?" he hisses. *Furious. With me?* "What the hell are you doing?"

My gaze focuses on the blood covering his face. The blood dripping from his eyebrow. *Purple-hued blood.*

A sob scalds the back of my throat. "You have draki blood!" I cry out, then remember he can't understand my growling speech. I swipe a hand over his face and pull back gleaming red-gold fingers stained with his blood. Hold it up to him.

Clinging for life on the side of the rock, he stares at my hand, then utters a curse. "Jacinda, I'm sorry! I wanted to tell you." In his agitation, he slips, loses his grip, and falls.

I drop, dive, and catch him with a grunt.

He's heavy, solid. I pant to keep us from both plunging

to earth. Burning air wheezes between my teeth from the effort.

My wings work hard, snap and strain to ease us down. The burn goes deep, penetrating the muscles of my back. And all the while, I can only think, *He has draki blood.*

Once we're both on the ground, I inspect his body, run my hands over him, checking for serious injuries even as I want to inflict damage on him myself.

His gaze devours me. Smiling wanly, he lifts a hand to my cheek. "You're exactly as I remember you."

I snarl at him, beyond furious. How can he have draki blood? I thought we had no more secrets. I just jumped off a cliff for him. Exposed myself to Xander.

It all makes horrible sense now. Our connection, why he's such a great tracker, why he's so drawn to me. That sense of *knowing* each other. Suddenly nothing seems real anymore. Not what we have . . . *had.*

He shakes his head, wincing as though the motion hurts. "Please don't be mad. I can explain. It happened when I was sick. The cancer . . . I was dying. My father gave me draki blood. He didn't give me a choice. He lost my mom and refused to lose me, too. . . ."

I bow my head, try to leash my anger, the conflicting emotions. His words run together like the distant buzz of an engine.

A breeze stirs, lifts my hair off my shoulders. On a windless night.

I whirl, heat licking up the center of my chest. I hiss a

smoldering breath as the sleek, black shape sets down, the giant iridescent wings winking with purple light. *Cassian.*

Then I notice that he's not alone. He holds Tamra so close to him that I don't notice her at first. Not until he releases her. She stumbles from the dark press of his body as if she can't get far enough, fast enough. Her amber eyes spit angry fire, but I'm glad he went back for her . . . relieved he didn't leave her on top of Big Rock with Xander and the other hunters.

Cassian's not looking at Tamra though. His purply black eyes glow menacingly in the night . . . first at me, then at Will.

Fear bites me deep, takes hold with sharp teeth, but I ignore it and stand before Will, trying to hide the sight of him.

32

I've seen Cassian many times in full manifest. But here, now, with none of the pride around, it's a terrifying sight. He's taller, bigger than when in human form. Muscles and tendons ripple beneath an endless stretch of gleaming black flesh. His large wings look almost leathery. Not cobweb sheets of gossamer like my wings.

I crouch on the balls of my feet and draw a deep breath, let the smolder build, readying to defend myself and Will.

I sense Will rise unsteadily to his feet behind me, and wish he would stay down. Cassian's purple-black gaze whips to him—a hungry predator ready to pounce. His wings flash behind him. Air hisses through his teeth.

"Back off," I bark.

He cocks his head like he hears something far off and

speaks thickly, "They're coming."

I pay attention then, and hear them, too. Xander's voice, and the others descending the rock, looking for us.

On another breath, Cassian commands, "We must go. Now, Jacinda."

Tamra watches, strangely quiet.

Understanding that I'm about to leave—probably for good—Will seizes my hand, forces me around, his expression fierce. "No, Jacinda. Don't do it. Don't *think* it. Don't leave with him."

His grip on my hand tightens with each word.

His image blurs, and I blink tears, fight against the thick sob rising up in my chest.

"I won't let you—"

Words rise on my lips, words I keep in. *I can't stay, Will. Not now. I'm sorry, so sorry.* I wish I could say them. Wish he could understand.

Still, it's as though he heard me. "No, Jacinda!" His gaze swings to where Cassian stands just beyond me. His lip curls. "You're going with him. Back to the pride." He says this like I'm heading into my death. And in some ways, I realize, leaving with Cassian is just that.

"No!" Tamra shouts from off to the side, as if she's waking from a dream, beginning to grasp the situation.

I shake my head, stroking Will's face with fire gold fingers, trying to reassure him.

"I won't let him have you."

Cassian takes a menacing step toward us, growling in

draki speech, even though Will can't understand, "You haven't a say in this, human." His gaze shifts then, his dark eyes bleeding into me, and despite his promise to not force me into anything against my will, unease trickles through me at the dark possession glowing there.

Will sees it, too. He breaks from me and surges toward Cassian in a crippled stagger.

"You don't own her," Will mutters darkly.

Cassian sees then what I've already marked. The purple blood dripping down Will's face, dribbling like ink from a pen. He sees. He understands, knows Will is no ordinary human. I hold my breath, hoping he won't react—

With a roar, Cassian charges Will. I jump between them just before they collide, press a hand on each of their chests, feel their hearts jump wildly against my palms.

"Stop it! Both of you! Cassian, no!"

Will clutches my hand, presses it hard over his heart as he looks at me intently from his bloodied face. I blink and look away, unable to stare at all that purple blood . . . evidence of the life his father stole for him.

A throbbing growl swells from Cassian. I hold up a finger in warning, as if that will be enough to discourage him from ripping Will apart. Then I hear my name being called. And Will's. Closer.

Will looks in the direction of the voices, clearly alarmed. "Did they see you like this?" His good eye fixes on me, glassy bright. "Did Xander see you?"

"Of course!" Tamra hisses, her face unnaturally pale. "She did it to save you!"

Will still looks to me, seeking confirmation from me. I nod once, the motion jerky and pained.

His whole body sags then, the fight gone. He drops his head and drags his hands through his hair. "Jacinda." He says my name so softly, sad and broken as he finally understands.

I'm dead if I stay. We both know there is no choice now. I have to go.

Footsteps grow nearer. A stampede of them. I withdraw from Will and edge toward Cassian.

"Jacinda." Will's voice is strangled now, thick with emotion. He looks prepared to snatch me back against him, and a part of me wants that, craves that despite everything.

I stare starkly into his eyes, conveying what I don't dare say in front of Cassian. He totters too close to the brink already. *I love you. Even if I shouldn't. Even if stolen draki blood feeds your life.*

Will understands. I see it in his eyes. And his pain. The same pain I feel.

Staring hard into his eyes, I shake my head, sorry for the chance we lost. The chance we maybe never had. But not for saving him. I would do that again, no matter the cost.

I leave Cassian's side then and rush to Will. Don't care that Cassian watches me. Quickly, I speak close to his lips in my language, "I love you." I yearn to kiss him, to press my fiery lips to his but dare not try it.

He stiffens against me, pain written all over the mess of a face. He grabs my face in his hands. Holds me. "It's not over. We're not through, Jacinda." His eyes blister, glitter darkly. "I'll find you. I will. We'll be together again."

"Let's go!" Tamra shouts.

My eyes ache, burn. Impossible as it seems, I want it to be true. And I shouldn't. Because it can't be. He can't come after me. He'll die if he does.

I shake my head no, but the gesture lacks conviction.

His fingers press deeper into my sharpened cheeks. "Never doubt it. I'll find you."

"Jacinda!" Cassian snarls. "They're coming!"

I pull away, the pain in my chest so deep, such a coiling, twisting mass that my lungs can't squeeze out a breath. Will's hands slide from my face.

Cassian's already lifted off, rising on the air above me with Tamra in his arms.

I watch Will as long as I can, holding his stare as I work my wings and push off the ground, ascend into brittle-thin air. Still, I look down, watch him until he's barely distinguishable. Until he's gone from sight completely.

We fly a few miles until Cassian motions downward and we descend to the car he left parked along a forgotten road.

In a blink, he demanifests.

I struggle to do the same, resting a hand on the car for

support. It takes me longer because I'm too upset. Shaken. I close my eyes and concentrate. See myself human. Finally, I feel my wings fold back inside me. I gasp at the intense pressure.

Heat fades from my core, and I open my eyes to find Tamra glaring at me.

"How could you?" She trembles, so pale, and I worry that she might collapse. I've never seen her this way, and guilt stabs my heart. For all I've put her through . . .

"Get in. Both of you," Cassian growls, pulling open the driver's door and taking the keys from where he tucked them in the visor.

Tamra gets in the backseat.

I don't budge. Remain standing near the driver's door, shivering in the desert night, my clothes lost, lying ripped somewhere on the desert floor.

He jams the keys into the ignition with his big hand. Stares up at me. "Jacinda." Like he's talking to a child. And I hate him. Truly hate him. "Get in the car. Let's go."

"You did this!"

He rolls his eyes. "Not on purpose. But am I glad I ruined your little romance with that *murderer*? Hell yeah. You bet." I shake my head even as he nods roughly, his face harsh in the flat dark. "What is he? A hunter?" His voice lashes me in a clawing swipe. "How does he have the blood of our kind, Jacinda? *How?*"

"Will's not a murderer." This I know deep in my soul.

Because I know Will. "He's . . . *not*." That's all I can say, all I can defend. Because I can't deny the truth. Will *is* a hunter. And more. So much more.

"Murderer?" Tamra calls from the backseat, her voice shrill. "What are you talking about?"

"He's a butcher," Cassian announces.

I want to hit him. Hurt him. The way I hurt. A surge of burn fuels my lungs. Scared that I might do just that, I take a step back from the car. "You don't understand."

His eyes glitter purple, the pupils shrinking to slits. "Get in the car. You can't stay here. Not after tonight."

I swallow down the burn from my lungs. Nod. The choice has been made for me. "I know that." Moving around the front of the car, I mutter, "Hurry. We have to get to Mom."

"Why?"

I stop for a moment, glare at his shadow through the grimy windshield before hurrying around. "They could kill her for her connection to me."

"Who? Xander?" Tamra demands from the back. "Why would he kill Mom? Just because he saw Jacinda manifest? He can't know what he saw, can't understand it."

Cassian ignores my sister's confusion. I'm grateful. Now's not the time to explain Will and his family to her.

"My only concern is you," Cassian replies in an even voice. "Bringing you back home. Tam is welcome—"

"Gee, thanks," she mutters.

"But your mother is the one who took you away. They won't welcome her back."

"Either you get my mother or I'm not going anywhere," I threaten, my hands knotting to fists at my sides.

"Fine. But they won't welcome her . . . and she doesn't even want to be part of the pride any longer," he reminds me in succinct tones. Like I ever forgot that fact.

"Neither do I." Tamra punches a fist against the back of Cassian's seat.

Cassian flicks his attention back to her for a moment, his expression flat, unreadable. In that moment he looks nothing like the guy who stood in the pool house with me. The softer, caring side I glimpsed of him is nowhere to be seen. This Cassian doesn't look like he possesses a heart.

I open my mouth, ready to flay him with words. Ready to insist that my mother and sister would *choose* to come with me. It's my mom. My sister. We stick together.

But I say nothing. Because I simply don't know. Because the truth, hard as it is, drums me in the face. I've been functioning without thought or concern for them for some time now. Maybe I don't deserve them.

They have to know what happened. Everything from the beginning. Finally everything. I look back at Tamra. "Whether you and Mom want to come with me or not, you can't stay here anymore. Not after I've exposed myself."

She stares at me, her pasty pallor starting to seriously concern me. "Well, isn't this perfect for you. You got what you wanted from the start."

Leaving Will? Not really.

"Let's not do this right now, Tamra. The fact is, you have to run, too." Because of me. What I've done makes certain of that. Only the question remains: Will they hate me for it later? Will they leave me to Cassian and the pride and start fresh someplace else among humans?

Or will Mom sacrifice her life all over again? And Tamra's? For me? I don't expect it of them. Don't blame them if they run in the opposite direction without me.

I've lost my freedom tonight. I've lost Will. Will I lose Mom and Tamra, too?

As Cassian turns the car around and heads back into town, I stare out the window into the night, remembering the awful car ride I took over a month ago when we left the pride. I was so afraid, so unwilling.

Now it's the same. I'm sitting in the front seat of a car and heading into an unwanted future all over again. Hating that I must go with Cassian, I wonder if I'll ever find a way back to Will. I don't expect him to find me despite what he said.

"There will be a reckoning for your actions tonight," Cassian declares as we race headlong into the dark.

No surprise there. *A reckoning.* For revealing the greatest secret of my species. For running away in the first place. For Will. Yeah, for Will.

I slide a slow glance at Cassian. An oncoming car casts his

face in harsh light. There's no missing the grim press of his lips. I swallow past the tightness in my throat.

"I'll try to protect you. . . ." His voice swirls through the air, thick as smoke.

"Don't let them clip my wings," I plead.

His dark gaze brushes over my face, softens for a moment. "I'll try, Jacinda. I'll try."

Not much for reassurance. I draw a ragged breath and stare out into the night again. I glance over my shoulder. Big Rock rises behind me, a great slumbering shape.

I hear a sound above the low rumble of the car's engine. My skin shivers at the bird's broken call, desperate and unremitting. *Lost.* Desert quail, Will called it. Searching for its mate. For family. For home.

I can relate. At the pitiable sound, I close my eyes and lean back against the seat. We'll be there soon.

ACKNOWLEDGMENTS

I would never have started down the path to creating the world of *Firelight* without the support and enthusiasm of my agent, Maura Kye-Casella, who never doubted me for a moment when I said I would like to write young adult fiction. For everyone at HarperTeen, your enthusiasm for this project has been humbling. Farrin Jacobs and Kari Sutherland, you're both marvels. Through your insights, I've learned so much about myself as a writer. Jacinda's life wouldn't be nearly so tough or complicated without the two of you.

I'm blessed to be surrounded by family and friends who get what I'm trying to accomplish each and every day. You understand the journey, appreciate the struggles, and celebrate the successes with me. No one does this more than Jared. Thanks for getting on this roller coaster with me, honey. To the princess and prince of my castle . . . these pages wouldn't be what they are without you. You two make everything worthwhile.

Love and thanks go to my incredible parents, Eugene and Marilyn Michels, for always seeing the best in me. A shout-out goes to my fabulous friend and talented writer, Tera Lynn Childs—you seemed to know I was headed in this direction before I did. Thank you for the countless hours spent talking books, life, and everything in between. Carlye, Lindsay, Jane, Lark, and Ginny—what would I do without all of you? My life wouldn't be nearly as sweet without the support, love, and laughter you've given me.

Can't wait to find out what happens next?
Read on for a sneak peek at

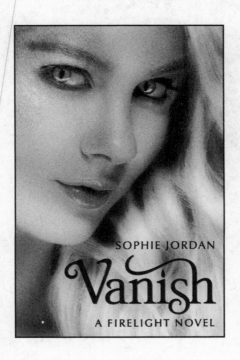

Sometimes I dream of falling.

Of course, I start out flying in these dreams. Because that's what I do. What I am. What I love.

A few weeks ago, I would have said it's what I love most in the world, but a lot has changed since then. Everything, really.

In these dreams, I'm racing through the sky, free as I'm supposed to be. And then something happens because suddenly I'm descending in a tailspin. I clutch air, my screams eaten up by angry wind. I plummet. A human without wings. Just a girl, not a draki at all. Powerless. Lost.

I feel that way now: I'm falling, and I can do nothing. I can stop none of it. I'm caught up in the old nightmare.

I always wake before I hit ground. That's been my salvation. Only tonight I'm not dreaming. Tonight I hit the ground. And it's every bit as painful as I expected.

I rest my cheek against the cool glass of the window and watch the night rush past me. As Cassian drives, my eyes strain through the motionless dark, skimming over rock yards and stucco houses, searching for an answer, a reason for everything that's happened.

The world seems to hold its breath as we slow for a stop sign. My gaze drifts to the dark sky above us. A deep, starless sea beckoning, promising sanctuary.

Mom's voice drifts forward from the backseat, low and crooning as she talks to Tamra, trying to coax a response from her. I peel my cheek from the glass and glance over my shoulder. Tamra shivers in Mom's arms. Her eyes stare vacantly ahead; her skin corpse pale.

"Is she okay?" I ask again, because I have to say something. I have to know. Did I do this to her? Is this, too, my fault? "What's wrong with her?"

Mom frowns and shakes her head at me like I shouldn't speak. I've let them both down. I broke the unbreakable rule. I revealed my true form to humans—worse, hunters—and we will all pay for the mistake. The knowledge presses on me, a crushing weight that sinks me deep into my seat. I face forward again, trembling uncontrollably. I cross my arms, pinning my hands at my sides as though that might still them.

Cassian warned me there would be a reckoning for this night's work, and I wonder whether it's already begun. I've lost Will. Tamra is sick or in shock or maybe something worse. Mom can hardly look at me. My every breath is misery, the events of the night burning inside my eyelids. Me, shedding my human skin and manifesting in front of Will's family. My desperate flight through crackling dry air to reach him. But if I hadn't manifested—hadn't flown to Will's side—he'd be dead, and I couldn't bear that thought. I'll never see Will again, no matter his promise to find me, but at least he's alive.

Cassian says nothing beside me. He did all the talking he needed to do to get Mom in the car with us, to make her understand returning with him to the home we fled is the only viable option. His fingers hold tight to the steering wheel, his knuckles white. I doubt he'll relax his grip until we're free and clear of Chaparral. Probably not until we're safely back in the pride. *Safe.* I strangle on a laugh—or it could be a sob. Will I ever feel *safe* again?

The town flies past, houses thinning out as we near the edge of town. We'll be gone soon. Free of this desert and the hunters. Free of Will. This last thought claws fresh the already bleeding wound in my heart, but there's nothing to be done about it. Could there ever have been a future for us? A draki and a draki hunter? *A draki hunter with the blood of my kind running through his veins.*

That part of it all still stumbles through my head, refusing to penetrate. I can't close my eyes without seeing the flash of his shimmering purple blood in the night. Like my own. My head aches, struggling to accept this terrible truth. No matter how valid Will's explanation, no matter that I still love him, it doesn't change the fact that the stolen blood of my kind pumps through his veins.

Cassian exhales slowly as we leave the city limits.

"Well, that's that," Mom murmurs as the distance grows between us and Chaparral.

I turn to find her looking back through the rear window. She's leaving all her hopes for a better future in Chaparral. It's where we were making a fresh start, away from the pride. And now we're headed back into their midst.

"I'm sorry, Mom," I say, not just because I should, but because I mean it.

Mom shakes her head, opening her mouth to speak, but gets nothing out.

"We've got trouble," Cassian announces. Straight ahead, several cars block the road, forcing us to slow.

"It's them," I manage to utter past numb lips as Cassian pulls closer.

"Them?" Mom demands. "Hunters?"

I give a hard nod. Hunters. *Will's family.*

Glaring headlights pierce the dark and illuminate Cassian's face. His gaze flicks to the rearview mirror and I can tell he's contemplating turning back around, running for it in the other direction. But it's too late for that—one car moves to block our escape and several figures step in front of our car. Cassian slams on the brakes, his hands flexing on the steering wheel, and I know he's fighting the impulse to mow them down. I strain for a glimpse of Will, sensing him, knowing he's there, among them somewhere.

Hard, biting voices shout at us to get out of the car. I hold still, my fingers a hot singe on my bare legs, pressing so deeply—as though I were trying to reach my draki buried underneath.

A fist bangs down on our hood, and then I see it—the outline of a gun in the gloom.

Cassian's gaze locks with mine, communicating what I already know. We have to survive. Even if it means doing only what our kind *can* do. That very thing I already did, that got us in this jam tonight in the first place. And why not? It's not like we can reveal our secret *more*.

Nodding, I move, climbing out of the car to face our enemies.

Will's cousin Xander steps ahead of the others thrusting his smug face toward me. "Did you really think you could get away?"

Crushing pain fills my chest, anger at what these monsters have cost me tonight. Ash gathers at the back of my throat, and I let the acrid burn build, preparing myself for whatever may come.

A hunter beats a fist on the back window, shouting at Mom and Tamra. "Get out of the car!"

Mom steps out with as much dignity as she can muster, pulling Tamra with her. My sister's grown even paler since Big Rock; her wheezy breath scrapes the air. Her amber brown eyes, the same as mine, look cloudy, almost filmy as she stares into space. Her lips part, but no words escape. I step close and lend a hand, helping Mom support her. Tam's icy to the touch, her skin not skin at all. Chilled marble.

Cassian faces Xander, regal as the prince he essentially is. Light glints off the purple and black strands of his hair.

I moisten my lips, wondering how I can convince Xander he didn't see me manifest. "What do you want?"

Will's cousin stabs a finger at me. "We'll start with you—whatever the hell you are."

"Get away from her," Cassian commands.

Xander's attention swings to Cassian. "And then we'll move to you, big guy . . . and how it is you fell off that cliff with Will and don't have a scratch."

"Where's Will?" I blurt. I have to know.

Xander jerks a thumb to one of the nearby cars. "Passed out in the back." I squint through the gloom and notice a figure slumped in the back of a car. *Will.* So close, but he might as well be an ocean away. When last I saw him, he was promising to find me again. He was hurt, but conscious. I shudder to think what his own family may have done to change that.

"He needs a doctor," I say.

"Later. After I deal with you two."

"Look," Cassian begins, stepping in front of me. "I don't know what you think—"

"I *think* you need to shut up. I'm doing the talking here!" Xander grabs his shoulder. Big mistake.

Cassian growls, his skin flashing a glimmering charcoal. There's a flurry of movement and then Xander's on his back on the ground, his expression as stunned as the half dozen others gathered around us.

"Get him!" Xander shouts.

The others converge on Cassian. I scream, glimpsing Cassian's face amid the hunters. I cringe at the smacking sounds of fists and move toward them, determined to help him, but hands restrain me.

An animal growl rumbles on the air. It's Cassian. Several hunters hold him down. Angus grins as he plants a boot on his back. With his cheek pressed flat into asphalt, Cassian's gaze locks on me. His dark eyes shudder, the pupils thinning to vertical slits.

Steaming air rushes past my lips, but I suppress it and shake my head, conveying for him to hold off, to wait, still believing, hoping we can talk our way out of this. That he doesn't need to reveal himself as a draki, too. Maybe I can still protect him. Maybe he can make it out of here with Mom and Tamra.

The cold kiss of a gun digs into my ribs and I freeze. Mom cries out and I raise a hand, stopping her from doing anything foolish to help me. "Stay with Tamra, Mom. She needs you!"

Xander's dark gaze roves over me contemptuously. "I know what the hell I saw. A freak with wings."

It's a battle not to let the fear swallow me in a fiery wash—a shock that I don't shift into my draki skin right now.

"Jacinda," Cassian shouts my name, renewing his struggles.

Xander keeps talking. "Don't worry. I'm not going to kill you. It's just a tranq gun. We'll keep you alive and figure out what the hell you are."

They're beating Cassian now as he fights to get free.

"Stop!" I shove past Xander, but Angus blocks me. I watch in anguish as they keep kicking him. "Stop! Please, stop!" My heart twists. It's them or us.

Fire erupts in my contracting lungs and climbs up my windpipe.

I can't let them take us.

Before I can release the blazing breath, a sudden gust of cold swirls around me. An unnatural chill. I shiver against the swift change in temperature.

As I whirl around, my throat constricts at the sight of Tamra. She stands alone, Mom watching with wide eyes several feet behind her.

My sister's face is dead pale, her eyes not her own anymore. Not like mine. The ice-gray chills my heart. A vapor rolls off her like steam. Except it's cold. The frigid mist grows, swelling in an ever-expanding cloud around us.

She arches her body in a sinuous ripple, tearing at her blouse, ripping it in a fierce move with her hands. Hands that suddenly wink and glimmer with a lustrous pearly sheen.

I've only seen such color on one other soul. Another draki. Nidia: the shader of our pride. I watch as the roots of Tamra's hair turn a silvery white that bleeds through the rest of her hair.

The vapor intensifies, a chilling mist that reminds me of home, of the fog that covers the township in a cool blanket. Shielding us from intruders, from any who would hunt and destroy us; obscuring the minds of those who stumble into our sanctuary.

"Tamra!" I reach for her, but Cassian's there, free from his attackers, his strong arm pulling me back.

"Let her," he says.

I glance at his face, recognize the deep, primal satisfaction gleaming in his eyes. He's . . . *glad*. Happy at what's happening. What *can't* be happening. Tamra's never manifested before. How can this happen now?

In the moment I look away, it's done. By the time I look back to Tamra, she has risen several feet off the ground. Her gossamer wings snap behind her, the jagged tips peeking above her silvery shoulders.

"Tamra." I breathe, absorbing the sight of her, grappling with this new reality. My sister's a draki. After so long. After thinking we would never have this in common. More than that—she's a shader.

Her eerily calm gaze sweeps over all of us on the road. Like she knows precisely what to do. And I guess she does. It's instinct.

I can't move as I watch her, both beautiful and terrifying with her shimmery skin, her hair leached of all pigment. She lifts her slim arms. Mist rushes over us like fast-burning smoke. So thick I can scarcely see my own hand before my face. The hunters are completely hidden, but I hear them as they holler and shout, bumping into one another, coughing, dropping onto the road like so many dominoes. First one, then another and another. Then nothing.

I strain for a sound in the sudden tomblike silence as Tamra's fog does what it's supposed to do and shades, shades, shades . . . everything in its path, every human nearby. *Will.*

I break away from Cassian and fight desperately through the cooling vapor that clouds both air and mind. Hunters sprawl at my feet, lowered by Tamra's handiwork. I see nothing through the all-reaching mist; my arms swing wildly through the cold kiss of fog, groping, searching for the car where Will lies.

Then I see him slumped in the backseat of the car. The driver's door yawns open, letting in the fog. The smoky haze curls around his sleeping form almost tenderly. For a moment I can't move. Only stare, strangling on my own breath. Even bruised and battered, he's beautiful.

Then action fires my limbs. I pull open the back door and reach for him. My shaking fingers brush his face and smooth back the honey strands of hair from his forehead. Like silk against my hand.

I jerk as Cassian roars my name. "Jacinda! We have to go! Now!"

And then he's found me, drags me away toward our car. His other hand grips Tamra. He thrusts her at Mom. Her sparkly new body lights the desert night, cutting us a path through the great billowing mist.

Soon it will fade, evaporate. When Tamra's gone. When we've escaped. *The mist will fade. And with it, so will the hunters' memories.*

I'd once suggested to Tamra that her talent just hadn't manifested yet. That she was simply a late bloomer. Even though I didn't believe it, I'd said it. To give her hope. Even though, deep down, like the rest of the pride, I thought she was a defunct draki. Instead she's one of the most rare and prized of our kind. Just like me.

Behind the wheel, Cassian guns the engine and then we're shooting down the highway. I look behind us through the rear window at the great cloud of white. Will's in there. My fingers dig against the seat cushion until I feel the worn fabric give and tear beneath the pressure. No, I can't think about him now—it hurts too much.

My gaze drifts, brushes over the pale version of my sister, and I have to look away. Alarmed at the sight of my own twin, now as foreign to me as this desert.

I inhale a deep, shuddery breath. We're going home, to mountains and mists and everything familiar. The one place it's safe to be me. I'm going back to the pride.

Country Park Potraits

SOPHIE JORDAN grew up on a pecan farm in the Texas hill country, where she wove fantasies of dragons, warriors, and princesses. A former high school English teacher, she's also the *New York Times* bestselling author of Avon historical romances. She now lives in Houston with her family. When she's not writing, she spends her time overloading on caffeine (lattes and Diet cherry Coke preferred), talking plot-lines with anyone who will listen (including her kids), and cramming her DVR with true-crime and reality-TV shows. Sophie also writes paranormal romances under the name Sharie Kohler. You can visit her online at www.sophiejordan.net.

For exclusive information
on your favorite authors and artists,
visit www.authortracker.com.

The Fiery Romance Continues!

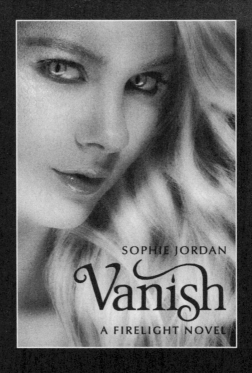

SOPHIE JORDAN

Vanish

A FIRELIGHT NOVEL

Forbidden love comes with deadly consequences in
VANISH, the pulse-pounding sequel to FIRELIGHT. To
save the life of the boy she loves, Jacinda exposed an
ancient secret. Now that she's back within the protection
of her kind, she is seen as a traitor—and knows she can
never see Will again. But when, against all odds, she has
the chance to be reunited with him, is the cost too high?
Or will she risk everything for love?